I0778385

TOKO TUKI

TOKO TUKI

BOOK 2 OF

WRITTEN BY EFREN STAT

Chapters

Prologue: Quest

3.5 years after the burning of Oil Derrick Harmony

A large box waited for Ki La'dori when he got out of prison. For four years he was condemned for arson on Oil Derrick Harmony. Lucky for him, he was given one year off for helping the town's Mayor, Patricia Force, catch a concealed mob syndicate for multiple counts of murder, money laundering, fraud, and extortion. During his time behind bars, he received another six months off his sentence based on his ample behavior and ability to work with others, a characteristic originally unknown to Ki.

After his fight with Sokuru, the Yakuza gangster, the Orthopedic Surgeon went to work on him, but could only bring back movement in one of his hands. His right hand was now unable to close because his tendons were too severely severed. Making his offhand, the left, his new good hand.

Resting his elbows on his knees above a gifted departure box, Ki stared at his left palm, recently tattooed with a skull and crossbones emblem. The scar where Sokuru slid his tanto knife through both of Ki's hands as bladed manacles that represented one of the crossed bones on the skull.

He exhaled a long breath, relieved he was only a few minutes away from being released and free to be amongst his natural divinity.

His left hand opened the box and pulled out a backpack, clothes, nice cargo pants, an earth-toned buttoned-up shirt, a dark blue jacket, a basic hat, socks, and sneakers. He slid a phone and a wallet stacked with $3500.00 cash into his pockets, and there were two more last items at the bottom of the box that made him itch at his temple, an envelope and a worm-engraved staff with a polished triangular stone on top. The stone was smooth and had multiple quartz veins running around it.

The envelope clinked as he picked it up and delicately studied the concealed bulge. Using his limp hand as a base, he stuck his left hand into the envelope and came out with three rings around the first nubs of his fingers. One ring was charred and burnt black, another had an eastern mold resembling wind circlets, and the last ring was just a wooden knot. His elemental rings.

Ki was almost positive this care package had been from his mother, Leia La'dori, but this solidified it. He pulled out a letter with his mother's writing and read with his one good eye.

Ki,

Sorry I wasn't there to visit you, Ki. I'm dropping off your package and heading straight to Ise-Shima's National Forest. When you are released, come find me. To help you find my secret location, Suga Duka will be waiting for you. She will face an enshrined leap towards a rocky reunion of Sun, Moon, and Sea. I can't wait to see you. I love you!

Here is some light to shine upon you because you likely reside in the dark. The E.E.A. has been 'terminated' due to its increased association with corporate development sabotage in the community. This is mostly your fault, but don't worry! The Earth Enforcers Association is just a name. All your friends are still active Environmentalists and are now 'covertly' working together.

Colin Richardson took over the reins of the Ellipsis Waste Industry. Pines and Vander are regulars at the shooting range, but other than that, they stay home with Zoo Za'mara and keep a low profile. After I sold our house, I moved all your stuff into Pines' garage, so maybe you'll need to visit them briefly before coming to Japan. Brock was released from all criminal charges binding him with his father's Mafia syndicate, and there's a rumor going around that he left with Mokes to the Big Island.

Baggans… after Tawa and Fish's funerals, Baggans figured he would start working a graveyard shift at the cemetery. He might even live there now as the night attendant. Pines told me he wanted to keep busy and be left alone. Maybe he feels closer to Fish there, or perhaps the graves are helping him grieve.

Ki, please don't get in any more trouble. When you get out, just come straight to Ise-Shima and straight to me. We will work everything out from here.

Safe journeys my boy.

Love, Mum

Ki got dressed, packed away his mother's gifts, and finally wrapped his good hand around the worm-engraved staff. The lights in the private meeting room slowly fluttered, blinking dimmer and dimmer, and then, within a second, the electric energy brightened so vibrantly it caused Ki to close his eye. Ki could only wait in shock for the pulsating energy to disperse throughout his body.

That feeling would have had Gandolf himself passing the pipe to study the magic within it. Still, the heavy stone bolted to the top made it feel more like a sturdy walking stick than a legendary wizard staff.

Ki's first step out in fresh air and away from the block would have been great in itself, but with the Toko Tuki's worm-engraved staff now working as Ki's new cane, he felt another tremor of electric frequency run through him. He gurgled with suffocating power and swiped his nose with his thumb. This feeling was definitely something new that he'd have to get used to.

It's been three and a half years since he's felt anything other than the cold cement floor and prison walls. He's mostly been alone and, yes, in the dark, as his mother said. The contrast of this natural environment overwhelmed him so much that he keeled over and puked in the dead grass twenty yards outside the prison, out in the middle of nowhere.

These waves of euphoria were so unknown to him. Blinding him with so much light, so much renewed power, the air he inhaled enlarged his heart with every gulp. A colorful tickle of love and happiness floated over his right shoulder, and there he was, just as his dreams depicted, his long-lost spirit of goodness and brotherhood. Toko Tuki, at the forefront of a far-off treeline, grimacing a slight smile and looking cheeky as ever by staring straight ahead and not at Ki.

Ideas were interweaving themselves with the clean air circulating through his entirety. He pondered, resting his weight on his power cane. *A couple of stops before the Airport won't stir up too much trouble… Not with an eyepatch-wearing, cripple-limping, tiki-shouldering ex-convict. Right?*

Uka Buka was gone, and Toko Tuki was with him. Love, and only love, was with him now.

BoneZ

Ellipsis Cemetery was a full-day journey from the prison. Ki caught a cab to the fringe of his hometown, but wanted to walk the last stretch of the long coastal backroad up to the cliffside graves.

When he passed one of Colin's city compost-influenced gardens, he remembered Mr. Zendolini authorized the zone development four years ago. Not such a greedy guy after all, especially since that zone is worth millions. Yet now that Mr. Zendolini had passed away, finished off by the Illuminati hitmen, and Zen Industries had been relieved of their contract with the city, Colin Richardson could permit any significant change regarding the environment's wellbeing in the area.

Ki full-heartedly felt the setting sun hug his skin with compassionate warmth. His town was in great hands, and the sun knew it. Its shining rays thanked Ki for his sacrifice.

His eye drifted across the frontier of this coastal garden, overlooking the remanence of tall wrapping tomato vines and an old veggie fortress combination of corn, bean, and squash, grown as a mutually beneficial system. He wondered what other symbiotic plant propagation was grown over the summer. The garden looked lush even in its dominant gray winter phase. *The town was in good hands,* he thought to himself again.

Brushing off his nose, Ki's nostrils flared with the fresh, twangy decomposition of organic material mixed with the salt of the nearby sea. That scent pushed him the rest of the way up the steep incline to Ellipsis Cemetery.

Finally, at the top of the hill, Ki sat on a bench across the street from the backside of the cemetery. There was a lengthy and very tall spiked fence, heavy mist drooping just above the tombstones, and one flickering streetlight at the corner of the block. The venture really fatigued Ki and seemed to tighten up his whole body.

His staff hand, the right one that couldn't clench because of Sokuru's stab wound, throbbed in pain. It was almost as bad as his right leg, which was also inoperable. Ki's sciatic nerve was severed after Sokuru's partner, Alisano, stabbed him in the back of the thigh multiple times. The docs gave him an ankle brace that was strapped to his calf with a panel for the bottom that kept his foot at a 90-degree angle. This prop kept Ki's foot from dragging after him everywhere he went. All in all, the pain he felt in his limbs was nothing compared to the agonizing headache he had behind his sunken eye.

The left side of Ki's face was… messed up. His entire cheek was now a flat sheet of scar tissue after being ripped off by the Ghost Ninja Alisano. It was her that so erotically caused him pain, but Sokuru had been the one to push his eye into his skull. The doctors scooped it out, so nothing was there now but the occasional pain and a dark green eye patch to mask the skeletal hole. Ki didn't mind too much about his faulty depth perception; it was the nightmarish memory of that entire night that haunted him. Nowadays, Ki's memories frightened him the most. Ghosts and spirits were a breeze compared to himself, the Illuminati, and the Yakuza.

Alas, those were Uka Buka days, and now Toko Tuki ran the show, or at least bobbed up and down in it, floating as he does. The look of Toko Tuki was ancient, almost as if its face was made from a broken gangplank on a pirate ship. Its seven colorful bird feathers seemed to be attached with ancient mossy twine wrapped multiple times around its long, cracked plank face. The spirit hung patiently over Ki's shoulder, holding a stoic and proud tiki expression that peered into the cemetery as its companion did.

Ki was comfortable being around cemeteries and gothic energy. His entire life he had never feared the dead, and now he felt there was something more, almost like a welcoming friendship with the spirits.

Another great realization was that Toki Toku was alive. His color, vigor, and restlessness were all proof of that. So many spirits had an essence of life. Even the dead held onto life in a way, even if it only existed as an essence. Dead had an all-new meaning to Ki, as if the definition of life and death was how the essence of energy prioritized its time.

While Ki was away in prison, his cellmate was an anciently old witch doctor. He drew symbols and did repetitive chants during most of their practices together, but the overall lesson Ki gathered from the witch doctor was the intrinsic nature of spirits. The immaterial characteristic of a being. The undefinable circulation of a soul. Spirits were nature's most incredible creation, and a holistic form could be manipulated by specific offerings, sacrifices, or rituals. Spirits could be used as unseen, undetectable energy sources. Spirits were Ki's new allies.

Like a good, obedient spirit, Toko Tuki became very close to Ki and was mostly visible at all times, at least since he got out of prison. Ki noticed that Uka Buka and Toko Tuki never appeared when he was in jail or prison. The Witch Doctor, named Irking, told him that was because spirits flourished in the creations made by their Sky Sisters and Mother Earth. They obviously didn't want to be imprisoned by a man-made hole made for troubled beings.

Living spirits of Mother Earth are the offspring energy of her immense power. A creation of Mother Earth's characteristics leaked out into inanimate natural things. When absorbed with enough of Earth's energy, a spirit splits from its parent essence and natural being, becoming supernatural. The so-called Sky Sisters, whom Ki had never heard of before Irking spoke of them, were six daughters of Mother Earth who helped transcend natural things into deeper consciousness. Beautiful angelic guardians of our world that Irking most likely made up to aid with his incarceration.

Ki rubbed at his leg and watched the mist with Tuki. He hoped he'd see Baggans walking around the graves; that way, maybe he'd be able to gauge his depression from a distance before getting up close. Yet, there was no sign of Bags, and he couldn't sit on the concrete bench all night, so he got up, slapped his cane into his broken palm, and meandered toward the streetlight, which vibrantly lit up amongst the fading sun. He couldn't wait to have some time to sit down and try casting some spells with Toko Tuki and this imbued worm-engraved staff.

***

"Get outta here, Ik," Baggans growled the name given by only one other, Pena Mokalua, or Mokes for short.

"You are no longer my friend. In fact, you are my enemy… Tawa and Fish are… Get the hell out of here…"

The floorboards creaked in Ki's advance to console Bags.

Baggans slid him up the wall with his forearm to his throat and fiercely tried to stare down Ki's one good eye, making Ki feel like a dagger was centimeters away from his iris.

"I just want to be left in the dark!" Baggans pushed his bear forearm harder into Ki's throat, and his arms twitched, causing him to clink his cane against the wall.

All the light in the room vanished, and then suddenly, the cane lit up with all of the room's light concentrated into its wood, majestically beaming out of the worm engravings.

Baggans released Ki and watched the light shine. A slight twinkle of sorrow in his eyes.

"How did that happen?" Baggans said dumbly.

Rubbing out his throat, Ki shook out the uncomfortableness of Baggans' stranglehold and began to muse with his old friend.

"Pretty epic, huh? I found her up the Mountain five years ago, and now… well."

Baggans didn't want to give Ki any credit for having something this cool, so he kept his eyes low and turned around to shuffle through some paperwork on his desk.

"You have a name for that..? Wizard Cane?" Baggans' mocking tone insinuated that it was something you could easily buy on Amazon.

"Ahh, yeah, I don't know. I may have to get high and choose a name, or maybe Toko Tuki has one already."

"Toko Tuki?" Baggans weirdly asked.

"Yeah, Toko Tuki." Ki tossed the cane over to his left hand and raised it up to where Tuki was floating, causing Baggans to let out a bamboozled yell.

Because the room was already so dark and ominous, the light from the staff gave Toko Tuki an even greater eeriness. Contrasting thoroughly with the dark, Tuki's vibrance and liveliness cheered Baggans up considerably.

Ki set the cane down and slid closer to Baggans' stunned expression.

"Wow, you can actually see him too, huh?.. Well, Bags, this is Toko Tuki, a brother spirit of love and companionship. Tuki helped me defeat another spirit called Uka Buka, a spirit of rage, chaos, and destruction… Many things are hard to explain, bro. Things are a little more complicated than you think, and… and I'm sorry about what happened to Tawa and Fish…"

Baggans gritted his teeth and pushed his knuckles deeper into the desk he was now lackadaisically sitting on. As his eyes forced themselves away from Ki's, Toko Tuki floated behind Ki's head to trick Baggans into looking at his friend.

"I just need some space. I like being alone."

Ki enjoyed the low, almost incomprehensible mumbles of his buddy Bags. He swayed as he watched him sulk for a moment and then started to make his way to the door. Tuki, however, had something else in mind.

The colorful tiki head flew rotations around the shadowy room and finally dashed into the far wall. The boys shared an emotion of bewilderment, and finally, Baggans and Ki looked at each other with something more than anger and sorrow. It wasn't long before Tuki returned with a bone in its mouth.

"Ah, oh," Ki said, looking back at Baggans to see if he was pissed or not. Baggans kept his befuddled stare. Nevertheless, he was still soaking in the floating spirit of spunk and childish energy.

"Ah, Tuki," Ki breathed in a calming voice. He didn't want Tuki to go wild in a cemetery, especially Baggans' cemetery. And then, simply by thinking of what he feared, Tuki dropped the bone and dashed back into the wall, coming out with two more bones.

Baggans' eyes widened.

Tuki floated low off the ground and pretended to hobble around like Ki, bone notched under a wooden knot at the side of his plank head.

"Tuki, do you want to call the cane Bone?"

Tuki spun up and up in his elation, eventually disappearing through the ceiling. Baggans clapped his hands to the sides of his big head and looked back at Ki anxiously. "Dude…"

Tuki flew right back into the room, thankfully for Baggans and Ki, with no additional bones, and started methodically clattering the three bones into some kind of symbol. When Tuki was finished, the bones made up the letter Z.

"You want to call it Z?" Ki asked with a hint of prideful mockery.

Baggans let out a long overdue chuckle.

Tuki shook its head wildly, almost creating gusts of wind with its tasmanian way of saying no.

"He wants to call the staff, Bones… with a z… Z." Baggans

humorously noted.

A bit of relief washed over Ki, and he smiled as well. Baggans going from calling Ki, Ik to Z made a world of difference. Ki was happy to be slowly gaining back his old friend. Toko Tuki bobbed up and down, eagerly nodding its approval.

"Wow. Well then. Bonez it is, Tuki."

"Yeah, that's a cool name… Could… Tuki put those boneZ back where he found them? And how do we turn the lights back on? I'm a little creeped out."

Spirit Night

Feeling good about his interaction with Baggans and Tuki, Ki wanted to continue having fun with his friends. Later that same night, Ki caught a taxi a short distance out of town and crept under the stars and up to the outside window of a home. This took more time than he was used to because of his actual crip walk, but he really wanted to spook the boys.

He didn't want to half-ass this, not today, not after being locked up in the hole for three point five years, mostly spending his time dreaming about seeing his friends every single night.

He smiled. The air in his lungs was held at a certain elevation, making his chest tingle.

Another factor he wasn't used to was sneaking up on Zoo Za'mara, his old doggy. She was attentive to encroaching sounds as well as encroaching energy. Ki slowed his silent waddles even more and turtled his cane softly forward.

Now hidden at the side of their kitchen window, he peered around the frame and peaked into their home. Adam Vander, a short-haired, blue-eyed adrenaline devil, was hanging from a pullup bar at the flow point between the living room and kitchen, and spiky-haired Kavika Pinederosa was making sushi rolls, a dozen already sitting on bamboo sheets in organized arrangements. Zoo Za'mara patiently looking up at the primo fish being prepared.

Outside in the cold and watching with excitement, Ki flexed the upper left side of his body, and his left arm began to shake with intensity. His good hand, now his left, white-knuckled Bonez the Cane, and his neck ballooned out with popping veins. The feeling of light flooded through him, a sense of power on the brink of losing control, vibrating with an allowance of ecstasy.

Ki had to keep testing his newfound power. The possibilities twisted over him, causing his mind to buzz with the sensation of learning the unknown. It would take time to discover what Toko Tuki had given him because he first had to master this overwhelming feeling of bliss.

It was hard to think through the haze of light, happiness, and love. He guessed he could intuitively live with those emotions without problems, but he wanted control. Or *perhaps control was the antonym of light, happiness, and love,* he thought. He'd have to slowly flow into managing his bliss.

Did that mean I could maneuver happiness and love in an extorior plane, the Astral plane?

The thought didn't seem too outlandish since light was a form of life, and life at its best was love and happiness. Based on the law of attraction, his loving energy could easily bleed into another's life. It would be difficult to stop in fact. We all have some kind of desire for nurtured well-being and connection with others. Even without magical abilities, regular people trade emotional energy like this all the time.

Ki's thoughts spiraled around and around till again all he could think about was the euphoric feeling tingling in his mind as light danced from one source to another.

Inside, the light in the kitchen bounced over to the living room, then to the outside patio, and then suddenly cut into flat darkness.

Kavika Pines drawled, "Adammm…"

"Hey, wasn't me!"

Ki relaxed his grip on Bonez the Cane and stretched his fingers on the worm engravings. The stretch also produced a flux of exuding power, like stripping back layers to reveal a nexus of tender energy. A lighter feeling of ecstasy that gave subtle residing flickers to the house lights before fully wha-whapping back on.

This was Ki's time to say hello. Inside, ZooZa started her excited barks as Ki clicked his way to the front door. The light overhead dimmed as he squared up to their door and knocked.

***

After eating a delightful late sushi dinner and catching up on the past four years, the guys sat on the living room couches and smoked a large blunt between them. Somewhere halfway through their session, Ki stood up, gathered all the candles around the house, and dispersed them in a staggered orderliness of seven candles, all different in girth, height, and color.

Pines readjusted his position on the couch, "I knew something like this was going to happen. I felt it back when we fought Sokuru at the park, and I felt it again a few minutes before you knocked on our door."

Adam blew out a cloud of smoke and flicked a lighter over to Ki.

"Not to mention our lights turning off and on before Ki arrived. I mean, you look like an old pirate wizard, so you might as well be one, right? Was the prison you went to called Azkaban?" Adam jokingly fantasized, easily falling into House Hufflepuff by the looks of him.

Adam passed the blunt over to Ki, and Ki took it and leaned back with his cane angled between his legs, nice and cozy-like.

"You know what, Adam? You're not too far off." Adam visibly shook, a shock of shivers running down his spine.

"My cell mate's name was Irking Caldor, and he was as witch doctory as a guy could get behind bars… We didn't have candles or fire in the cell, but we had other things to practice with, like blood and light…" Pines gulped, his hand covering his mouth just in case Ki was thinking of stealing his teeth.

Ki told his friends his story while soothing the secured stone on top of Bonez the Cane.

"Early on in that fateful year of Scott Pruitt's death and fall of the Zendolini stronghold, I kicked three bums off a seacliff… actually, it was the day after Lexi broke up with me, and we all partied our asses off…

"Adam, you're spilling your beer."

Adam tilted his beer bottle back up and jogged into the kitchen for a rag.

"Maybe if you hadn't killed three bums, I wouldn't have spilled my beer, Ki," Adam said incredulously.

"I didn't kill them, just… hurt them. You know how it goes."

Adam and Pines looked at each other to see if they did.

Ki continued, unfazed and smiling.

"So, after being so spun up about my altercations with the bums, I went deep into the mountains with Zoo Za'mara. While we were there, I came across a worm engraved stick… and next to this stick was… a spirit."

Ki blew out a puff of smoke, and it coalesced into a broken

skull. Wispy and deformed as it was, the guys still witnessed the grim creation and shuddered in recognition.

"This weed is really good." Whispered Adam, and Pines glammed, "So you're a Witch Doctor too then?"

Ki even amazed himself. "I… didn't mean to do that. Adam's right, this weed is wicked good."

They all looked around at each other and began laughing. Adam threw a couple of pillows at Ki, and Ki dropped the blunt down a crack in the couch. The sudden panic of extinguishing the ember heightened their applauding laughter, and Pines kept calling out. "Let it burn, let it burn!"

Finally, Ki pulled the smoking blunt from between the couch cushions and successfully lit it back up, still choking with laughter at the look of his two friends' faces.

"Anyways, this spirit Uka Buka. It was with me that entire year up until July 4th, the night Pines fought Sokuru and my dear mother Leia destroyed… Uka Buka." The lights in the living room dimmed lower and lower, flickering ever so often. Again, Ki wondered about death and if a spirit like Uka could ever be destroyed.

"Uka.. Buka…" The boys said simultaneously.

"Yes," Ki started lighting all the candles with the final embers of the blunt.

"I believe this spirit, Uka Buka, was an ancient spirit of the mountain, forest, and Earth." All seven candles were lit, and a chill ran across the room as Ki clenched his cane. The lights snapped out suddenly, leaving only the fire from the seven wicks to reflect orange glows dancing with shadows amongst everybody's faces.

"Ahhh Ki, what the hell is going on…"

"Don't worry guys, you'll see," Ki said with a slight smirk, catching the tooth gap in his smile with his scarred upper lip. Adam ran his hand down his face. Ki's scarred zombie cheek and eye patch really added a foreboding intensity to the story.

"Uka Buka only brought destruction and hate into my life. A trait I found not only humans possess but also our planet Earth possesses as well. And for a good reason. I mean, we are all descendants of Earth, are we not?" The boys were still anxious about Ki's mystical powers of shutting off the lights. They waved off the question and showed more eagerness for Ki to get on.

Ki paused, seeming to have forgotten where he left off.

"Yeah, so… Oh, yeah. Obviously, Earth has the characteristic of anger and rage, not only shown through the creation of the Uka Buka spirit, but also in her storms and quakes that wreak havoc.

"I'm getting their Pines, just relax bud… So just as an earthquake can rumble with anger, it can also open up waterways of love and growth." Ki turned his eye from the candles to Pines, who twisted his tan fili-islander face in confusion at him.

"That night when we fought with Yakuza member Sokuru, Uka Buka attached itself to him, imbuing him with its strength, destruction, and hatred. An easy possession because Sokuru was already filled with this negative energy. Yet, there was another spirit there that helped us survive through the night… That spirit, Pines, attached itself to you, brother."

Pines kept his steady gaze on Ki's eye, and Adam unhinged his jaw while watching Pines in pure amazement.

Ki puffed up his chest, took a long inhale, and clenched his whole body in a powerful flex. As Bonez the Cane rose from its slouch, so did Ki, and he stood like a wizard summoning a storm while holding the worm-engraved staff overhead, filled with mystical light. He pushed the staff close to the candle's fire, and above the flames, a face appeared. Wooden, stoic, and colorful.

"Hail Toko Tuki, the Earth spirit of Love, Companionship, and Kindness."

Ruggers

Kavika Pines, Adam Vander, and Ki La'dori had an all-night slumber party Shabanza. Most of their night was bumping music while Toko Tuki manipulated the fire on the seven candles to dance, flames mimicking Tuki's spins, bobs, and jives. Wax drooled over itself as the fire burned with its exotic vitality. Other parts of the night were spent casually playing with fire and light. Tuki even puked up a baby flame into Ki's hand, and Ki hopped it across his knuckles until he reunited the baby flame back to one of the candles.

That early morning, Ki rode back into Ellipsis with Adam Vander. After spending time behind bars, the mind cleans itself up in many ways, and right now, Ki was confident in his mind's ability to decipher reality and to constitute an agenda. Sometimes, during a journey to get to the dragon egg, you had to brush up on your constellations first, and Ki's next constellation was sex with a Scorpio.

Prison had ways of hardening the mind based on basic forms of depression. At the start of Ki's second year in prison, he felt like he was going to explode, like he *needed* to touch a woman or he would die if he went another day without it. Six months later, after surviving the *need* for a woman, his *need* turned to a simple *want,* a longing desire, an empty cylinder that wanted filling.

Now out… and free. The air, the sky, the water, the candle wax melting down, the freedom… the magical power felt coursing through his veins. This desire for a woman turned to patient blissness. He had other things to keep his mind busy. However, he was so close now that the possible feeling of a soft touch was overwhelming.

In the tradition of Ellipsis rugby, every Saturday before Christmas was their annual Rugby Day. This Saturday, December 17th, all the surrounding clubs, all the Mermaids, all the youth rugby Stingrays, and all the Grunion gathered for a fun and friendly tournament. It was a nice way to warm up their bones before the start of the January season. A great way to socialize with old friends.

Adam pulled the e-brake of his Yota Tacoma and drifted to a stop in the dirt of the upper parking lot. Their Rugby club's pitch was on a hill and over the sea, sitting humbly amongst the Saturday sun.

Ki hugged ZooZa goodbye and slapped Adam's farewell high-five.

Right after he would cuddle up with Dr. Kate Neilsly, he'd book his flight to Japan. And even though he so desperately longed for a woman's touch, he also longed for more of his friends' faces.

After Adam left Ki in the dust of the parking lot, he took a moment to organize his thoughts and plan his appearance. He had to remind himself that he was a felon, a cripple, and a one-eyed, scarred face looking monster. During his prison sentence, he spent a lot of time working out. Ki was now twenty pounds heavier than he had ever been and full of ripped muscle. The difference was easily seen in his neck, shoulders, and forearms.

So Ki wanted to ease onto the pitch. He liked his greetings one at a time, and if he walked out where everyone could see him, he wouldn't get the compassionate, heartfelt meetings he'd been dreaming of.

Was he considered a menace to society by his closest friends, or was he a hero? Ki pondered either and let the dust settle around him while listening to the far-off whistle of the referees calling the games.

Because he handed in Pruitt's datachip, the Sheriff was able to put a stop to the Zendolinis, an Italian Criminal Syndicate. With the Zendolinis gone, Colin Richardson and the dispersed Earth Enforcers Association members could take over the waste management industry for their little town, Ellipsis. Pines had told him the compost pickups and garden builds were working better than any of them dreamed. Because of their influence on the waste management system, plastic bags were now banned from every grocery store in town as well.

He also felt like he helped reveal a whole secret society of evil manipulators, the Illuminati. Even though the two Illuminati he saw at the Zendolini warehouse that July 4th, had vanished without a trace, there was still proof on the datachip that a higher society was pulling criminal syndicate strings.

Burning down the Oil Derrick Harmony and fighting Yakuza

Gangsters could go either way, Zero the Hero, Zero the Idiot, or Zero the Murderer. Because the Yakuza showed up at his house, two major people in the rugby and environmental community died, Tawa and Fish, who were enormous figureheads for ecological wellbeing. Now their blood was on his hands, and based on Baggans' reaction after seeing him, others would have definitely put the blame on him as well.

Whatever might have happened between his old friends, Toko Tuki gave him enough loving spirit to confidently limp down the meandering grade and come out behind the fans and rugsters, enjoying the current game out on the pitch.

Of course, Sheriff Worden was there as an overseer and spotted Ki first.

Sheriff Worden, AKA Fentawhap, was in his gray sweats, royal blue Grunion T-shirt, and a straw sombrero to block the sun from his Irish skin. His hair was freshly cut in his short red mohawk fashion.

There were no words as they locked eyes and slowly came together for a hug. "I love you, Conner." Ki smiled, relieved the Sheriff didn't turn his back on him. A tear inched out of his eye duct, but Ki quickly brushed it away.

The Sheriff put one hand on Ki's shoulder and the other on his missing cheek and sunken eye. As he took in Ki's new look, his shoulders began to quiver with laughter.

"You're a bloody masterpiece, Z."

They quickly went over how they'd been doing the last three point five years, and then the Sheriff looked over his shoulder to see if anyone was nearby and inched closer to Ki's ear.

Sheriff Worden whispered in his most curious and empathetic voice, "What the hell happened that night with the…" Worden bobbed around like an inquisitive monkey. He has been under his own extensive investigation on the Yakuza and why they had attacked the La'dori's. Leia's only response to him was that Ki's father, Asagaio was a big shot in one of the Yakuza sister gangs, Kiza. But that was barely any help. He still wondered why they had come the same night as the Illuminati? Were they working together? What secrets did Ki hold?

Behind Worden, Toko Tuki was watching the current rugby game with glee. Being the whimsical spirit Tuki was, he turned his colorful feathered headdress inward to form a replica of Sheriff Worden's Mohawk. Tuki usually played around with people who held love and comradery in their hearts.

Before, Ki knew he could trust Worden, but now he was positive. Tuki positive.

Sheriff Worden had saved him from being charged with Scott Pruitt's murder and helped him save his mother, Leia, by allowing him to take his patrol truck off a swat scene and crash it into his own house. Worden deserved to know more...

"Okay Conner, I'll tell you... My father was like me and focused his entire life on disrupting environmental wickedness and unethical behaviors. Along his journey, he met his Sensi, Hattori Honzo. A great man perched in a sanctuary in the depths of a Japanese National Forest, ready to delegate tasks only an Earthling Vigilanti would do without question. So they worked together to fight back against the sins of their countrymen. Later, Sokuru, the Yakuza guy who came to my house, found out what my father was up to and finished him. Possibly tortured him for more information..."

Sheriff Worden gave him an appreciative yet quizzical look. "What information Ki?"

"Hattori Honzo gave my Father Asagaio the land rights to his 'sanctuary.' Sokuru and the Yakuza wanted these land rights to form a massive operation to turn the sanctuary into a money pit... While locked up I did some homework and discovered what Sokuru was scheming. If they received the rights to this land, they would sell it to a US-based company called Cargill, a company responsible for massive deforestation all over the world, mainly based on immorally harvesting palm oil.

"And what makes Palm Oil so damn important is their rich corporate customers, Mcdonalds, Burger King, Walmart, and so on."

The Sheriff dubiously interrupted. "All this for a small deforestation contract? That can't be."

Ki gave him a penetrating eye, "Right, that's not it. The Yakuza also want to build new Onsens once the forest is mostly removed. These Onsen Hot Spring hotels will not only stack up international cash flow but will slowly change the Japanese culture. Onsens are a holy retreat and masked from marketing and propaganda. However, the Yakuza's plan is to advertise their Onsens to the world and eradicate the disrespect of having historically blood-drunk tattoos in

Japanese mystical waters.

"They've been waiting 30 years to soak their tattoo skin in this affluent environment, and the only thing that stands in their way is my mother, Leia." Looking down, Ki slowly wagged his head from side to side.

"You're right though Conner. How did the Yakuza find me the night the Illuminati were in town? It makes me think there must be a bigger reason why they want this land."

"Oh, shit."

"Yeah, shit is right." Ki was very calm as he told stories of some horrible corporations partnered with Yakuza. He never gritted his teeth, his hands stayed relaxed, and he was just Ki, passing along information. It felt right not to be fuming mad at something he could not control. He smiled and slapped Sheriff Worden on the shoulder as the rugby game finished, and people began to notice Ki was back on the pitch.

"It'll be alright, Sheriff. It's Rugby Day, one of the best days of the year mate." Ki nodded behind Sheriff Worden, and they both opened themselves up to the players and friends who wanted to say hi.

After a time, everyone relaxed, grabbed fresh pints from the Club House keg, and prepared themselves to watch the next rugby game. The Mermaids were playing when he arrived, and now they all lounged under their two pop-up tents like a group of lionesses in the shade. Laughing hysterically, rubbing out each other's joints and achy muscles, stripping off tape and sweaty jerseys, and doing their routine after-match powwow of chugging beers and spitting rhymes.

As Ki meandered over to sit in the first row of the three-tiered bleachers, Kate Neilsly sat at the corner of one of their pop-up posts, slowly taking off her clothes and covertly glancing over at Ki. Hopefully stalking out her prey. Eagerly, Ki wished this was the case.

Because he no longer had his right eye, it was challenging to do periodic, sly glance-overs her way. He had to see her though, so he picked up a conversation with the person to his right, Lindsey Scott, the Captain of the Grunions' wife.

Now, facing Lindsey and chatting about whether there were literally prison Blues singalongs, he simultaneously watched Kate slip off her shorts and throw them at a younger girl next to her, then lay on her stomach so the younger girl could massage out her upper hamstring. Kate's purple thong left him speechless, which was no matter for Lindsey because the next rugby game had started, and she had to cheer on her man.

One of everyone's favorite games during Rugby Day was the newer, younger players of the Grunion rising against the older, mostly retired players, who incorporated a relevant team name for their age, The Fossils.

"The Grunion versus the Old Boys. Can't wait to watch my Stank lay some Fossilized wood!" Lindsey barked out, clapping her hands together for the Fossils. "Get it you old wrinkly balled bastards!"

Jacklyn Poxer, A.K.A Pinky Boxer, was in the middle of the Mermaids yelling mockery at one of the older players, Forrest Galante, a good looking bearded mately man who was the head of his department for Biodiverse Documentation and movie production.

"Forrest you are so old, when you were young, rainbows- *Bop! Wee'u* -were black and white!"

Forrest was 35, the star of the rugby community, and so successful and happy that nothing bugged him, especially anything coming from Poxer. Everybody loved Forrest. He did whatever he wanted, which included letting his four-year-old son paint a big rainbow from one cheek to the other, arching over the bridge of his nose.

After the first kickoff, Forrest caught the highball and quickly caught speed running the ball forward. A tall, beastly fellow that Ki somehow recognized was lined up to take Forrest down. As the young guy adjusted his body right before the tackle, Ki noticed Mohawk Toko Tuki riding on his far shoulder, like a kid dressing up like their favorite uncle, bashing headlong as the tackler's shoulder slammed into contact.

"Who is that Linds? I know him from somewhere."

"Ohhh, that's our new Grunion Z. You remember little 13 year-old Tommy Perez? He is 17 now, but as you can see, he can hit!"

Popping up out of the dog pile next to the stands and fans, Forrest smiled into the crowd. His nose was freshly slashed and blood speckled amongst the rainbow across his face. Safa Scott, also an old boy, ran over to Forrest, rubbed a handful of grass and dirt over his nose, and slapped him on the ass to get over to the next play.

Ki laughed harder than he had for four years. He chatted over his shoulder with loud and rumbling Lunch Lady Jason Su and always smiling Stretch A.K.A Josh Malof. At the same time, other old teammates of Ki's came by and gave him the old mer-kiss, a secret handshake in their Grunion Rugby world. Joy pumped enough spirit into him to want to get up and brave over to the hot thong lady, Dr. Kate Neilsly.

"It's good to see nothings changed. I'll see you later Linds, I'm going to continue my rounds."

As Ki drifted off towards Dr. Neilsly, Jacklyn Poxer intercepted him. She had always been infatuated with Ki. She felt like the environmental push was now, and the zero-waste movement was of top priority. She was even trying to open her own Zero-Waste Refill Shop in town.

She pulled back her curly blonde hair out of her eyes.

"Wowwie, Mr. Zero, you look like- *fuck, fuck, fuck you* -sorry… You're straight out of an Apocalyptic Comic book. Damn man, you took a beating- *Wee'u*." She ended with a tic and a cute bird whistle.

Jacklyn Poxer had Tourette's syndrome and the rare Coporlalia effect that made derogatory remarks, and words burst out during her Tourette tics. It was easy to tell when she was simply speaking versus having a tic because her neck and face would tense up in one way or the other, or her eyes would squeeze shut, or her mouth would work itself around in funny mannerisms.

Ki smiled, "Hey Pinky! Did you end up opening the Refill Shop?" Jacklyn's nickname was Pinky because she was one of the smallest of the Mermaids, but she was still a critical piece of the team. She played the role of the Scrum Half on the pitch, the mediator between forwards and backs, the opponent's antagonizer, the rambunctious one, the one who was at every ruck and play to toss the ball out, the one digging for balls in between girls legs. She was a leader through and through, and the best thing about her playing was that her tourettes mostly went away when she was out on the pitch.

Ki knew she wanted to peek under his eye patch by the way she stared at it, "Ahh, yeah it's going pretty well actually- *Way'oww* -Lots of clients, especially after the Zendolinis fell-" She ticked and whistled.

"People have been very curious about- *screw off* -groups pushing for environmental wellbeing after all that nasty- *Bop* -business." Poxer popped her lips, making a loud bop sound.

"Our planet was put in the spotlight for a while after what you-

Weeh'u - did. Of course, as time goes by, they all forget… We need another event!"

There was a pause, and they both stood there watching the Grunion push for a try on the five-meter line. Like Rams amongst Penguins, Tommy and Thomas the Golden Rooster were blowing up the Fossils.

Ki couldn't help but feel heaviness in his chest, like the blood in his heart wanted to escape and give Jack a hug. She was probably the cutest person he had ever seen. Her *Weeh'u's* and *Bops* came out sounding like a tiny cartoon character, and the way she moaned in a breathy *hmphed* or whistled during a tic was intoxicating.

"Zero, I thought you should know, Brock Zendolini bought your house." Jacklyn Poxer held steady with an indifferent face.

"What? How do you know this?" Ki swiped his nose, tough-like.

She ticked and popped her lips. "When I run down to the beach, you know, I get to run by your old pad. So- *Way'ooh* -" Her cheeks made three different clicking sounds.

"One day guess who I see?" She paused momentarily to see if he'd guess within a two-second break. "Brock- *Fuck You* -Zendolini… Anyways, I contacted this realtor I'm seeing right now," Poxer closed her eyes and bird whistled with a tense curve to her neck. "The gal makes a bomb apple pie… and she was telling me that Brock Zendolini was- *Wa'uw* -buying *your* house." Poxer turned back toward the game and let a moment go by. To her, her tics were an annoyance, and breaks in a conservation were restorative.

"I'm guessing it's because you- *Whaph Wah'oo* -instigated that raid. Killing his father."

Ki felt it again, like he was standing on knives. Guilt sunk into his soul for being responsible for his friends' deaths. Even Mr. Zendolini. People he wanted alive but were now gone, never to return. It's the guilt that kept Ki from his poems. He felt like a shadow had covered that part of his life.

"Maybe… Has anyone spoken with Mokes?"

"That's the other thing-" Her cheek clicked twice, "Rumor has it Mokes left with Brock to Hawaii on some crazy business plan… yet… He was at your house with Brock! He has long, dreaded hair now." They both continued watching the epic rugby game unfold as they talked about Mokes.

"I'm sorry about Fish and Tawa, Z. It didn't- *fuck you* -sound like it was your fault." She whistled like a loony toon, but he was the loony one.

"You're just an unlucky bastard is all."

"Thanks Jack." Ki studied Jacklyn Poxer for a moment. She had a humorous sternness to her. Ki also felt like a brother to her. The way she consistently looked up to him and was consistently a Pinky Boxer, his lesbian badass little sister. And for the most part, little sisters are great sidekicks…

Ki decided he needed an insider while he was gone, and he needed eyes on Brock and Mokes. Poxer had to be his connection back home.

"Jack, I'm going to Japan soon for a family reunion. Could I keep in contact with you while I'm away? I'm curious what Brock is planning."

"Hell Yeah, I'm your girl. My email is Pinky- *shitbag* - No… My email is PinkyBoxer@gmail-Wee'o -.com."

Poxer rolled her eyes, "You get it. We can talk over the phone too, but I don't think you have one of those yet, right?"

"Right. I do, but I still have to set it up. Thanks Pinky, we will keep in touch… New girlfriend, eh? What's she like other than the scrumptious apple pies?" Ki loved leaning on his cane; he felt comfortable anywhere with it in hand. Bonez the Cane, the fallen branch of power and light. He chuckled at the name.

"Oh she is fire, super sexy,- *you stupid bitch* -smart, and super real with me… and you know how I like that dirty talk…" Poxer laughed with her head up in the clouds. Blonde curls falling back down into her eyes.

"Hopefully, you can meet her sometime." Poxer whirled a little from side to side, spinning her wrists around one another and clasping her hands, obviously thinking about her new sweaty pie.

Ki tried to imagine her girlfriend and kept running back to the characteristics of cute, sexy, and hot.

"Good for you Jack. Glad you found a little lady love. I'm going to try for some of that as well and go talk with Kate." Ki said with a lump in his throat. His eye rolled back in love as it glanced over at her. She was standing now, watching the game, but had a certain shuffle that made it seem like she was waiting for Ki to go over and talk with her, still in her purple thong.

Ki strutted over to Dr. Kate Neilsly. Her loose white T-shirt blew slightly in the wind, revealing a strip of purple.

"Hi Doc, you look surgical as ever."

"You have no idea, Lord Zero of the Zombies, because I'm about to rip your heart out." She would definitely enjoy doing so. An innocent little grandma could see in her eyes that she wanted to see others hurt, especially emotionally. She was cutthroat, and Ki loved it. A cutthroat and an undead zombie lord seemed like a good match to Ki. He'd be her monster warden, no problem.

She studied Ki up and down and took a step closer. Ki stood up a hair taller and tried not to use his cane as a crutch.

"You look like an old wardog and you smell of cum." She looked down at his groin and then right back up into his golden hazel eye, her lips close to his.

"I… have a new girlfriend." She finished with a dollish giggle, and Ki couldn't help but smile at her cuteness, even though the news was devastating.

Ki flushed with the image of Doc and another girl together. Toko Tuki always brought him loving thoughts and feelings, but now jealousy and misery ate at his heart. She was right, his heart was ripping in agony. *Good,* he thought. *I'm already on the path to becoming a Buddhist monk.*

Air Travelers

Rugby Night was a blur of colorful lights and profuse amounts of liquid down the gullet. No one seemed to outwardly blame Ki for Fish and Tawa's death. His meeting with Baggans already proved there was some animosity on the team, but no one was as openly truthful as Dave Baggans, so the crew cozily tucked in by his side all night and seemed to genuinely comfort Ki and look after him.

After three point five years of sobriety, the buzz he caught was intoxicating. Wino gave him a microdose of magic mushrooms, and Ki felt like he was floating right there with Toko Tuki. Tuki bobbed around, blabbering to the other tiki masks around the bar, sometimes posing as his inanimate others on the wall, closing his eyes in satisfaction. The extra special feelings of being amonst his own obviously generating over Tuki.

Now, facing the rays of the sun, Ki basked in the glory of last night's merriment. He loved the warm embrace he received from his rugby companions. However, the strangers who caught a glimpse of Ki were a stark contrast to his team. It was entertaining to watch the puzzled looks of others, but it saddened him because they also incorporated looks of fear and pity.

Prisoners and guards treated Ki like Ki, and Mermaids and Grunion treated Ki like Ki, maybe astonished by his crazy exploits and scars, but they knew him to be one of them. Being treated with kindness really tickled him. Happiness wove around his spirit after being around people like that. He was free and had a solid group of friends, and best of all, he was on his way to see his mother in Japan. He was freaking alive. Alive, proud, and ready for an adventure.

Ki smiled, and felt that was a nice touch to his image.

Toko Tuki danced around all the TSA and air travelers like the airport was the most interesting place he had ever seen. Ki wondered if Toko Tuki saw what he saw through a normal human lens or if he saw something different. Because Tuki was a spirit, did he also see others' spirits or things Ki could not?

As Ki's carry-on duffle bag and Bonez the Cane went through TSA's x-ray machine, Toko Tuki did a weird wobbly vibration in front of the security machine operator's face. Ki had never seen Tuki do that before, and it looked like it hypnotized the security guard long enough to let Bonez the Cane and his bag through the machine without alarm. Then after Tuki's wobble, he dashed behind one really obese TSA security lady and smelled her butt, causing the feathers on his headdress stand straight up. Electrified, he shook his head, flabbergasted by the smell.

"Tuki Tuki Tuki."

Ki laughed and quickly swabbed at his nose to focus up. He didn't want attention, and he didn't want to seem crazy laughing at an invisible friend.

Mom, here I come.

***

14 hours later, Ki and Toko Tuki got off the plane in Narita, which was close to the heart of Tokyo City. To get there, the international airport led down to a web of underground subways. With the help of a couple Japanese words he learned on the flight over, Ki finally found the route into the center of Tokyo.

With no knowledge of his new environment and culture, Ki was exhilarated. He was on an epic journey wielding a magical staff and accompanied by a lovely spirit guide. It was his first time in his home country, where he was conceived and where his father grew up. A man who paved the road of lineage for Environmental Radical Juggernauts.

Ki was thrilled and felt like he blended in more because of his one slanted eye. Tuki did a tasmanian spin and morphed his features into a more Samurai-style tiki face. The ancient Kanji, Japanese characters, ran down one side of his wooden face, and cherry blossoms grew beautifully out of his headdress. "Toko. Tuki." Tuki's bulgy eyes narrowed and widened, and then he continued his float by Ki's side.

Ki wanted his first night in Japan to be in the nightlife district, desperately wanting to soak up every aspect of their culture. Lucky enough for him, a delightfully respectful young man, who seemed much too qualified for the information desk he was working at, not only led him to the correct subway train but also suggested a hotel in the nexus of neon lights and nightlife bustle. The young man looked him up and down so many times Ki wondered if he was gay, but then he lifted his hand in a quick salute, and Ki saw a sexy Japanese woman in a skirt run from his pinky down his forearm. So maybe he wasn't gay, just extremely nice, leaving Ki amazed at how respectful and kind everyone had been to him thus far.

After riding the subway train, he clinked along the midnight streets. The more he staggered toward the bustling sound and array of neon lights, the more life he found. Just by the walk of the Japanese people, he found they were respectful to one another and super satisfied with the security of the streets even as the night grew on. Tourists, and anyone that wasn't Japanese, halted in the middle of the sidewalk and were stuck in awe at how many levels of bars and places of weird entertainment rooms stacked latitudinally together.

The neon signs made him feel like he was in the movie *Blade Runner* or some futuristic dark and rainy underworld film. Still clinking through with Bonez on one side and Tuki on the other, Ki tried to observe as much as he could. The market areas had canopies overhead, creating their own little world out of an alley. Robots waved people to come into their establishments. Women pulled men off the street to show them a good time. Trains rumbled underground and zipped overhead. The only difference between a science fiction futuristic underworld and Tokyo was the color, not only in the neon signs but the fashion. Everyone was fearless yet kind, and Ki believed a combination like that showed massive strength in the people. They wore whatever they wanted and loved each other for their individualism. The streets here were even… cute, and Ki wondered where he fit in amongst such an adorable crowd.

The airport information desk guy suggested a hotel called the Knot, next to a blue-lit dive bar. Ki didn't have to stay there, but its placement was impeccably ideal. He went in, got a room for little to no money, put his bag down, and went out to explore.

Ki's normal walk in the United States of America was sulky and scary at best. Here, he straightened up to look smart and more respectable. The grin that creased his cheeks wasn't a hard addition to making himself seem like a sweetheart.

In front of him, a guy and a girl passed a bottle of sake between them, and they walked along happily. The bottle of sake amused Ki, and he decided he'd explore in a different way. Already walking from the subway station to the hotel was breaking down his body. He was damaged goods. *Just an old bag of bones*, he thought, and he wanted to find a remedy to get rid of another one of his headaches.

Not too far from the hotel, stairs surrounded by stone walls lead down to a darkened doorway, pulling Ki to venture down. Immediately after his desire to descend, Tuki floated down and through the door. A moment later, Tuki came back out and nodded vigorously. Another brilliant addition to having a spirit head on your side and able to bond with your thoughts. Feeling blessed, he clinked down the stone steps and entered the astonishingly expansive underground bar.

On the street level the blue neon sign with Kanji lettering flickered on and off.

Inside, Ki ordered an O Cha, diluted green tea, and a small bottle of sake. The place was basically a jungle tea house, bar, slash open Karaoke with a small stage across from the main bar top. A nicely dressed weird guy with a scar that cut his face in two stared at him for a long while before Ki happily went over to him, headache fading.

"Kanpai," and Ki lifted his drink for an air cheers. Ki noticed the man's wrists had tattoos scrolling upwards, probably sleeving both forearms. The grutch grunted and then snarled at Ki. It wasn't what Ki was expecting from the kind people of Japan, but he reminded himself that one bad seed was in every bunch, and maybe he was just having a bad day. He told the bartender to get the scarred man another Asahi, put enough Yen on the counter to cover it, and then left.

He would have stayed there all night, but he supposed the grunting man was meant to give Ki an excuse to get some sleep. Tomorrow night, he will be ready for anything.

Xillian

Ki awoke in his little room and looked out the window to Tokyo City. The sun gave the surrounding rectangular giants a warm, embracing hug as its red orb arose. Ki wanted to stuff the little ball of fire in his front pocket for the day, but Bonez the Cane would suffice for magical luminescent objects for now. He held his cane up to the window and closed his eye, absorbing ultraviolet rays through his skin as Bonez absorbed as well through its wood. Through meditation, he adjusted his future. The plan was to check out the major historical sites around the city and pop into a thrift store before venturing back into the blue neon lit Karaoke bar.

After adequately harassing the sun's love, Ki took the subway and got an underground egg sandwich, which opened his eye to underground Japan being better than any junction food above ground in California. He then continued walking through Imperial Park, the National Museum, a massive Buddhist Temple accompanied with a festival-style atmosphere around its perimeter, and finally, to a nearby thrift store.

It's been three days of wearing the same clothes his mother gave him after he got out of prison, so he grabbed a dark green shirt with Hiragana lettering on the back, and copied at an angle on the small area of the left chest. He tried on a few pairs of Tobi pants, which were tight around the ankles and puffed out around the calves like a steady breeze orbited inside them, keeping them loosely inflated.

As well as assimilating with their culture and their style, Ki's life had changed from wearing practical clothes to fit a warrior to comfortable casual clothes fit for a more muscular wizard.

Wearing his new get up, Ki traveled through the underworld into the next Tokyo ward, Chiyoda-Ku. Because the subway routes made the city so accessible, Ki had a load of extra time in his day than he thought he'd have. The trains were a supremely viable web into all the major parts of the city. Great efficiency was a grand theme here.

During his underworld travels Ki read more about Japan's environmental history. He wanted to know exactly how the country became so efficient in its methodical, sustainable productivity.

For two centuries, Japan has been a completely self-sustainable country. Their isolation and way of life threatened American capitalism and their glutenous desire for trade and wealth, again imposing their Christian Religions on cultures they saw as backward or late...

In 1853, America brought a fleet of ships to Japan's Capital, Edo, to push Japan to join American trade treaties. Japan's stubbornness to stay as a self-sustainable, isolated country caused President Fillmore to threaten them with 100 warships setting fire to Edo. Focused on their cultural development, Japan was unprepared for war, and this American threat was too much for their capital defenses. So this concluded with the signing of trade treaties with Western Civilization, an event that slipped Japan into industrialization.

Uneasy about being bullied out of their culture and way of life, Japan prepared for future military action and began their industrial revolution to catch up with the West. From 1870 to 1920, Japan turned themselves into a major military and industrial force. Because of their rapid industrial growth, Japan's pollution and deforestation rates were unprecedented. However, this all changed after two World Wars and nuclear devastation, dropped by American mass murders. So Japan shifted their focus again to extensive *global* environmental issues, implementing environmental protection laws and creating alternatives to mass pollution.

Suddenly, Ki looked up and realized that his stop was next. He exited the station and looked to the sky. To the East was a little peak of an epic rooftop. The magnificent architecture pulled him over to the temple, and he eventually sat on an open grassy plateau a small distance away from a Shinto shrine. The Torii Shrine gate stood between him and the Shinto shrine, a transition gateway from the normal realms of man, to the sacred realms of Mother Earth. Ki opened up his phone and continued reading.

Japan eventually became a global leader in environmental policy and awareness. Having more than 14,000 companies with environmental programs and creating a focus on less wasteful products while using less raw material for construction. Opening out of their shell, they began exporting their creation of sustainable green products to other countries to influence green business. They increased the production of low-pollution cars and energy-efficient appliances.

Respectfully continuing their environmental leadership, they began hosting United Nations Conferences for Climate Change in Kyoto, created an Overseas Development Agency as an overseer for foreign environmental policy and aid, and conducted several international conferences regarding ozone depletion, climate change, and future pollution control. Japan turned from isolated sustainable living to global sustainability and productivity within a century.

Ki rubbed his forehead and looked up at the Torii. He had spent so much of his time infatuated by American environmental destruction, he missed this magnificent environmental benefactor. Not all nations were as ignorant, greedy and murderous as America was.

He felt a chill of sadness down his spine. Dropping a fucking nuclear bomb on such a disciplined country. Killing so many in an instant, for what?. It was cowardice, it was wrong, and it pissed Ki off.

Toko Tuki floated around his head and ruffled his feathers and cherry blossoms on Ki's nose. Old anger washed over Ki. It was good Uka Buka wasn't around to inflame his rage, just Tuki to try and pillow Ki with peace.

He decided to move through the Torii and bring Tuki closer to his kindred Kami spirits. Showing his respects with tranquility, he bowed through the Torii and clinked Bonez the Cane to a bench next to the Yasukuni Shrine. Toko Tuki flew off like a child at play and danced around the shrine layered with dragon sculptures.

Taking in the moment, curiosity arose in Ki again, and he wanted to know what kind of issues Japan was facing. They were located in a high natural disaster zone, there was industrialized air pollution, waste management to categorize, and climate change patterns to contemplate.

He scrolled down on his phone… Whaling.

Of course, this system was the number one reason his father, Asagaio, fought. Ki glanced over the Google links and read, *The Cove Documentary, Oceanic Preservation Society.*

Yes, Ki remembered this film of Tanji fishermen capturing and slaughtering dolphins in a hidden cove. His cheeks grew red, and he clicked on the link to read more.

Back when this was filmed in 2009, there was an estimated 20,000 dolphins killed each year in Japan. Now in 2024, because of a grander population of awareness, only 415 were killed this year. Even with the decline in numbers, Ki was angry it was still happening. He saw the word Mercury and remembered the film uncovering the Japanese government and Chisso Corporation dumping chemical waste into the ocean, creating extremely dangerous levels of mercury, especially in Dolphins. Then, the local fishermen, either ignorant or evil, would compile onto these ecological atrocities and label the actual dolphin meat as other, more desirable meat. Literally poisoning their people with lies and Minamata Disease, which pretty much paralyzed someone's mind, body and soul because of too much mercury.

When the International Whaling Committee was founded and began putting restrictions and quotes on Cetaceans, Japan responded with loopholes and more lies. After a whaling ban in 1986, Japan responded by killing three times the amount of dolphins to compensate. Japanese diplomats began saying they needed a higher quota of whales in the name of science and experimentation, while it was really still just for their meat.

Unlike the ignorant fisherman, the well-aware government strongly backed their fisheries by adopting the idea that Cetaceans were the pests of the sea and the main reason for the decline of fish stocks and food security, conveniently not factoring in the increase in human population. Scientists in 2006 even predicted that in 40 years, the world's fish stocks would collapse based on the current rate of fishing.

Ki kept scrolling, wanting to know what was happening now in 2024, wanting, deep inside of himself, to be like his father and break these murdering idiots, but also available to be content with a productive legal change. The Wakayama district deemed the Tanji concealment of dolphin slaughter illegal, and fishery quotas drastically dropped. The Japanese public also seemed to take a bigger role in watching what their local fisheries were up to and regulated where this dolphin meat was sold.

It all made sense why Hattori Honzo, Ise-Shima National Forest, and Whalers were all connected. A flood of understanding flushed over his brain like a star illuminating the inside of a blackhole. Light shining in crevices as water flowed into Earth's wrinkled depths.

He felt how he thought his father felt long ago, understanding the genealogy of the blood in his veins like Earth understanding mycelium running through her soil. The Sun is his father, Asagaio is his father, and Ki will not let his father's undertaking fall into the void. For all could be lost without light. Ignorance, close-mindedness, selfishness, and torpidity are all qualities of darkness.

Darkness isn't evil, nor does it have to be wrongness, but if darkness was left unchecked, it could spread into endlessness while the brightest light can only reach so far. The science of our universe has proven this. So, be it in space and time, it is also in the characteristics of one's soul.

Wakayama and Tanji neighbor Ise-Shima. This was his father's battleground, where it all started and where it all came to an end. Ki could picture a Yakuza rebel easily overpowering these local fishermen. He could see now how the Yakuza higher-ups wouldn't like the de-escalation of illegal Cetacean slaughter, because they probably had a hand in the money pit of it all. He could see where the tides had turned.

Ki wanted to take up where his father left off, even with Toko Tuki streamlining compassion into his heart. Ki felt if just a handful of fishermen were whipped out, hundreds of thousands of dolphins and whales would be saved. This thought reminded him why he wasn't a good man. Good men fought against evil the hard way. The humane, respectful way like *The Cove's* Documentarians. His family's way was brutal with quick results, but badness clung to its core. What was embedded in a good person's blood was that everything had to be done ethically.

It was so righteous it made Ki feel queasy. He anxiously looked up to see if Toko Tuku was still with him. He didn't want to lose his spirit of goodness based on his destructive thoughts. After a few moments of panic, Toko Tuki finally popped out of the main shrine building and flew over to him.

The droopiness of Tuki's bluish-purple feathers popped up, and his face vibrated in intervals like a puddle rippling from a T-rex approaching. Only passing by, Tuki sped off through the dormant cherry blossom grove, leaving Ki gazing at where his energetic spirit tiki turned the corner. He was happy Tuki was still his spirit ward, and his thoughts retracted back to the future of the sea. What could he do? The opposition to hurting someone for doing wrongness was having a go at teaching someone to do rightness. However, he doubted he could teach old salty dogs a new ideology in preserving many forms of life, not just their own.

From high above, a great breeze slammed into the ground in front of him, and Tuki shook off a cloud of dust and resumed himself with bulging cheeks and a squat look. Tuki must have shortened the length of his planked face because the tiki spirit looked awfully like a Sumo Wrestler.

Tuki started nodding to Ki's slow acknowledgment and understanding of what was around the corner. In need of a heavy distraction, Ki stood up and clinked himself over to the corner of the building where Tuki had disappeared before. A couple proud badass men with mawashi loincloths walked by with purpose and stoicism. Tuki had found an actual Sumo Tournament. Ki moved on, excited to see these men in action, and passed a bronze statue of two bond sumo wrestlers looming next to the entry stairs, descending down to a grand circular area indented into the earth with thousands of calm fans watching the haughty entertainment of wrestlers in the ring.

Ki could tell these men were putting on a show for their fans, but they were nothing of a joke. Based on their look and the reaction of their people, these sumo wrestlers were the heroes of Japan and renowned for their athletics.

Spending a good hour watching the matches, Ki left the tournament with an uplifting smile and decided to return to his hotel. A whole day walking around the sites wore at his leg, and he found if he closed his one eye, his headache slipped away from the hole of where his other eye used to be. Like darkness was the only remedy to relieve his pain.

Light coursed through his veins with Tuki and Bonez the Cane, but darkness, at least the perception of nothingness or everythingness, was what settled him.

Was his newfound power escaping through his one good eye? Did closing the window to his soul enable his light to ruminate inside of him and cure ailments? Or was darkness simply a restorative practice because the retina was punctured, a light-sensitive tissue directly attached to his brain? *That would make more sense, he* thought. *Even though I have magical abilities now, it doesn't mean practicality doesn't exist.*

He looked West before descending down into the subway and

watched the sunset sky surrounded by tall multidimensional buildings and a 3D dragon scrolling across cyber-animated windows. The sun seemed so powerful here, so beautiful and ancient. No wonder the Japanese carried the sun and its shining rays as their banner. Something Ki dreamt of a long time ago. He didn't know why he had never connected his dream of having a banner of the sun with Japan's banner of the sun. American supremacism, he concluded quickly, swiping his nose and not wanting to think of his past narrow mindedness.

Looking up over his shoulder, Toko Tuki was also staring at the sun. Even as beautiful as this country was, they were still in a concrete jungle with consumerism and plastic beverages every ten feet. Ki could tell Tuki was becoming drained from seeing it all. The ancient forests were calling to them.

Every rigidity step he took in Japan felt like a shock wave linking him to the land. He couldn't wait to get out into nature and press his light into the truly authentic green growth. He couldn't wait to see Tuki dance with the Kami spirits in the mystic mountains, untouched by plagued feet.

"Tomorrow Tuki, we head into the woods. I promise." The love of the land filled him up. He daydreamed of what it would be like. Already, the city gave pulses of gratitude and peace. *What would natural Japan bring?*

***

Ki woke up from his nap and integrated into his body with some stretches. Again, the darkness acquired from sleep helped relieve his light sensitivity and migraines. He was happy for another city excursion and refreshed there wasn't overwhelming pain in his head.

Before his celebratory drinking and bar hopping, he stopped off at a convenience store for candles and ritual stuff. Ki believed a spell-cast was in order to help him find his mom. He brought the candles, prayer beads, and herbs to a semi-level rock overlooking a pond with a beautiful shrine at its center. He laid the string of beads down like a snack, propped the upper ends of the candles on the beads, and lit their wicks.

The PennyRoyal herb, for a negative energy cleansing and discovery, burned quickly and gave off no scent, at least at that moment. Ki scrunched up its ashes and rubbed it on his tongue. *My tongue will lead the way, and maybe I won't have bad breath for a couple of days,*

Ki quirkily mused.

One of the candle flames burned with a steady jet of solid fire. Never flickering, never dulling out, a pure embodiment of a flame, almost as if a divine vacuum was pulling the fire up into its holy kingdom. Ki focused on absorbing this flame, soaking it into his veins, and storing its power. He pressed his finger to a knife he got from the thrift store, and blood ballooned out into a nice thick droplet. Blood to find his mother's blood.

The candle flame morphed around his blood droplet, which fell through its center and gooed over its wick. The prevalent flame rose his blood at its base, and Ki sprinkled more Pennyroyal herb over all flames for all avenues of discovery. He placed his titanium fire ring below the angled focus candle, and a mixture of wax and blood dripped into the petite circle of security. He dipped the tip of his sliced finger in the hot wax to seal his cut.

Waiting for his fire ring to fill up completely with wax and blood, Ki felt like this was a good time to test out his abilities. There were a dozen or so people on the far side of the pond and a few passerbyers behind him, but all in all, it was sufficient privacy for being in a large city and amongst such a holy pond.

Toko Tuki became super small and drifted down to lounge between two of the prayer beads and under the candlelight. Being that it was night, the candlelight imbued across his ritual stone, reflected in the pond, and warmed the multitude of colors on Tuki's painted face and headdress. Ki wasn't a picture person, but this was an image he wanted to remember. Then again, Tuki most likely wouldn't appear in a photo… unless.

Ki closed his eye, straightened his back, and painted his surroundings in his brain. The trees hanging over the pond, the tops of the skyscrapers in the distance, people frozen in time, and the shrine island in the middle of the water, which reflected it all on its glassy dark water with stars sprinkled on its surface.

He steadied Bonez horizontally in his lap and maneuvered both hands into the indentations of the worm engravings. The moment reminded him of when his fourth-grade self liked to bite his pencil because of the soft malleability of its wood.

His unclenching right hand rested down on the staff, and his left was upright, ready to fluctuate through grip strengths.

Now his concentration beamed toward the candlelight. He was

so close that not only did he feel the warmth of the fire, but he felt its power of light transferring into him through his hands. He never thought of light becoming so liquified. It flowed in his veins like water running down a river.

Keeping his eye closed, he tried to track the flow of light through his body. Where did it go? Where did it want to end up? Would it leak out of him if he opened his eye?

He straightened his back again and flexed his body, hardening his grip on Bonez, and the liquid light rushed through him, spiraling around his heart, vortexing up into his brain, storing up in his sacral chakra.

Someone gasped behind him, and Ki opened his eye to see five strings of smoke drifting up from the extinguished candles. Toko Tuki stoically floated near the fire ring's perimeter at ease, as if it were a small cauldron; the ring full of reddish wax. He turned around and waved at the elderly couple staring at him in awe.

"Wizard." He told them, pointing at himself.

Ki picked up his candles, prayer beads, herbs, and lighter, and scraped off the melted wax on his temporary rock altar.

"I didn't know you could become so small, lil Tuki." Tuki floated up to him and squeaked. "Tuki."

It was rare to hear the tiki head's normal voice, making it even more adorable to hear it when he was so small.

Having let it cool, Ki finally picked up his fire ring and pushed out the dried wax blood from its center. Dual worlds lay in front of him, and a pod of blood and wax to conjoin them. Ki threw his ritual creation of dried wax into the pond, splashing in just before the Shinto shrine.

***

Having done enough exploration for the day, Ki decided to dive back into the Karaoke bar next to his hotel. He really didn't get to enjoy the comfortable lounge setting the night before, and thinking back at a mini Tuki chilling in between two prayer beads made him want to relax even more, imagining mini Tuki laying under a small umbrella still dripping with Margarita juice.

He found an ideally unsociable little nook in the back where he could be the scarred-face observer and not be watched himself. He sat on the ground surrounded by colorful, hard stuffed pillows and sipped his tea and sake, which rested on the stout table in front of him. The lights inside were reddish pink and created cosmos kaleidoscope patterns on the ceiling and walls.

From his vantage point, Ki could see the bar, front door, staff room, and pretty much the entire joint. The Karaoke stage was hidden from him; however, there was a grand mirror across the room where he could see the reflection of the stage.

Every other time Ki was around Karaoke, he always felt like he would have to sing next, which usually made him anxious. Here, he just listened with ease, with sake and tea and comfortable pillows around his knees. The jungle leaves and hanging vines wrapping around the pillars and ceiling also added to his isolated relaxation.

He noticed a cute little camera rotating ever so often in the corner. Sometimes it watched him, and sometimes it gave him privacy by rotating its lens to face the corner. Everything was so cute here in Japan, even their security.

When he looked back up to the bar, one new patron had sat down and was now receiving her first drink. The awkward feeling of being behind the bush and peeping in on a pretty girl overwhelmed him now. The wild nook had its faults. So he turned to the side and tried to get the attention of the cute security camera again. The walls were also fun to gaze at, and the Karaoke singers were entertaining.

The security camera swiveled this way and that, almost in a dance, and Ki nodded along, smiling to its jig, and suddenly like it was shy, it spun quickly to its corner again. Feeling like he was in a *Star Wars* cantina hanging with a droid, Ki took a sip of tea, then a shot of sake, and closed his eye and listened to the Japanese harmonies coming from the stage. He really could get used to this simplicity. Melodic tones and harmonious voices. He thought back on his wonderful ex-girlfriend Lexi, who simply wanted to be loved and to live a happy non-confrontational life. This would be the place for her.

"May I?" The girl from the bar came up around the ivy column. She wasn't really asking him, nor was she really looking at Ki. She was more pronouncing herself so she didn't startle him. She gave off tough girl vibes. Even if you stripped her down, took her dark eye shadow away and gave her a puffy pink dress, she'd still seem like the baddest lass at the ball.

"Aye."

She was surprised by Ki's choice of words and smiled with a penetrating look back at him. A smile he could have sworn he'd seen before. Her face was new to him, but her smile had pleasure and pain twisted all over the creases of her lips. She slipped off her Converse and sat beside him, taking a swig of her Asahi beer while watching the room's rotations.

Ki shuffled into the corner more and finished his sake.

"You need another?" She asked; her English was better than anyone he had heard yet.

Still very bewildered yet intrigued, Ki was beginning to have some fun. He responded again with what he knew made her smile.

"Aye."

A slight grimace formed on her lips, and she rolled her eyes. She blew out a cute little whistle and ordered another beer and sake. Ki used this opportunity to study her. She had great posture, at least her eyes said she did, and wild frost irises like beautiful crystalline ice fragments found in the depths of a forgotten cave. Her eyes made the kaleidoscope patterns on the wall seem bland. Characterized as Red Phoenix eyes, where the inner corners slanted down and the outer corners slanted up. Aside from the beautiful spheres, her fashion fit well with the Long Beach Californian gritty punk rock scene. She wore a too large black hoody with her hair twisted up in a flared out spiky black bun and tails of hair hanging loosely to the side. Based on her slender cheeks and defined chin she was thin. A thin and puffy full metal typhoon.

Toko Tuki rummaged through the tall plant by the entrance of the nook, finding himself a casual retreat along its inner stocks. Ki wanted to connect himself with Tuki and borrow some of his tranquility. This girl made his stored liquid light gurgle around in his sacral chakra.

He sucked in air through his broken nose, then exhaled. He inhaled again through his nose and found an intoxicatingly sensual flowery scent, his eye fluttering to a close. Darkness pillowed all of his inner light, encouraging him to pass his anxiety and unassurances through his breath. Until a whistle came that snapped his eye open. The girl laughed at him as she poured him a cup of sake. The whistle, he discovered over his next breath, came from his own nose.

Ki brushed his nose with his thumb and sniffed.

"You smell amazing."

The girl pushed the sake closer to him.

"You're in my normal nook." Her eyes watched him steadily, but her voice told him not to flatter or flirt with her.

Ki drank his sake and poured another, yet this time he pushed the cup right in front of her, gracing his offering with an open palm, a palm that held the skull and crossbone along with the scar Sokuru made for him with his Tanto knife.

The girl's eyes flared in anger for a millisecond, and then she settled back and air cheers Ki, downing her sake. With her chin high, Ki got a chance to look at her neck art, which, at a glance, seemed to be a similar style to his own skull and crossbone on his palm. Perhaps it was an image of a lady of the underworld.

"I have a question for you, stranger. You are mutilated and crippled like you've been through hell, and you are both Japanese and American. Your story intrigues me."

"As does yours… Miss..?"

"My name is Xillian."

Xillian gripped her beer bottle as she looked down at it.

"Your name?"

She asked in a way of forced politeness.

Ki hesitated and was glad he took a second to think before speaking. Yakuza were most likely still looking for him. They think he knows where the Ise-Shima National Forest documents are, and he killed off one of their leaders. This girl, Xillian, just appeared out of nowhere with tattoos on her neck, a thickened icy voice, and a rough attitude. She could be an informant to the Yakuza, and he'd be done for. But there was something special about her. The eyes, the attitude, the name, Xillian. Right now she was the hottest thing he'd ever laid his eye on. She was fire. He wanted to get close and warm his bones of solitude. He wanted to abandon light for a while and be pillowed in her dark attitude.

He didn't want to make up a name he didn't like or a name she might not find attractive. He gained more time to think on the matter by sipping more of his tea, his finger through the cup handle and pinky slightly tilted out.

"My name is Zepp." He had to stick with his favorite letter Z, and for some reason, the old Illuminati Zeppelin flying across the blood moon attached itself to him.

A small crack sound came from where Xillian was holding her bottle. Ki at least thought he heard a crack sound, though there was no leak in the bottle as she released it and stood up.

"Well, Zepp," She said slightly disbelievingly. "What happened to your eye?"

Ki itched his head a tad bit nervously, and Toko Tuki popped back out of his retreat. The feeling of calm serenity was gone. Questions brought in a hailstorm of possible answers, along with questions of his own. *How are you so cute but threatening at the same time? Why does it feel like you're about to sink knuckles down my throat? What do you do for a living? Where's your boyfriend? And, did you really just crack that beer bottle by squeezing it too hard?*

As if she caught up on what Ki was thinking, Xillian shook her head and weakly chuckled into her hand. "I apologize. Old war wounds aren't always fun to speak of… I'm going to sing a song. Will you still be here when I'm done?"

More hard questions. More sweet and sour attitude. Ki forced his shoulders to drop. He still wanted to play cool; even though he looked like a monster, he still greatly enjoyed a woman's company, dangerous or not.

"Yeah, I'll be here." Ki smiled, and the gap in his teeth made Xillian laugh again before she took off her sweatshirt, and floated over to the Karaoke stage. A light blue blouse with pink flowers hung loose around her hips and snuggled tight around her big breasts, revealing a fainting amount of cleavage.

She began to sing.

Now slightly buzzed and finally feeling alive again after being locked up behind bars with so many males; tears began to stream down both mutilated and soft cheeks. He didn't care who she was or what she wanted; her voice ground into his heart.

Xillian came back after her song and sat down next to him.

"Xillian… I." Ki couldn't believe it. He already went through what he would tell her when she got back. *Xillian you're amazing, your voice is so contrary to how you portray yourself, you're my dream girl.* Yet now with her actually sitting in front of him, her smell overwhelming his senses, planned words wouldn't work. She was a girl you had to watch, listen to, and wait for the opportune time to produce a relevant response. Telling her she's amazing and that she's a dream girl wasn't going to fly.

"I enjoyed listening to your voice. How are you so cute but so threatening at the same time?"

Xillian chewed over his last words. A slow draw of seriousness encapsulated her mood.

"Because it's neither cute nor threatening; it's just me. Also, stop being a pussy."

Another heart rhythm vibrated in his chest.

Pinky Boxer

Puke splattered on the backyard's cement landing. Jacklyn Poxer, A.K.A Pinky Boxer, rolled onto her back and looked up into the clouds. A piece of rice hung on the corner of her upper lip. The pillowy puffs of condensed water vapor visibly moved slowly across the sky. She gave an abrupt laugh, and the rice flew off.

A face of a small stone golem was carved into her caucasian features. Her squarish jaw was relaxed, cheeks subdued, palms unclenched, yet the essence of her gaze was marble.

Jack fit into her name pretty well. She had a competitive spirit out on the rugby pitch, her body was jacked, she liked girls, and her style always resembled an early 20th-century New York gangster. Pinstripe slacks, tucked-in white shirts, little body, small breasts, and curly dirty blonde hair that usually hung in her eyes.

Stranger's eyes tended to drift in her direction, picking up her unusually boyish manner of doing things, yet picking up that she was still very much a pretty girl with bright blue piercing eyes, always squinting mischievously.

She was puking in the late morning because she drank a lot the night before. At least for her, puking didn't burn or hurt coming out, instead it felt cooling. It was just a way to release her bullshit and to stretch her body. A metronome of cracks crackled as she rolled your spine on the concrete and finally stood up.

Tomorrow was the start of her six-day work week at her Refill Store. Thankfully for her, it was more like a dream than work. The only worky thing about her Refill Store was that she had to be there and only there. Locked away in her little dream whilst in her little box. She giggled in her palm, obviously pleased with her situation but making a joke of it all the same.

Poxer stood up and went inside to her Wicca altar in her bookcase. The books were displayed on the left side of the bookcase, and scarfs and tapestries lined three shelves on the right side. Crystals were in bowls, candles were tucked together in the corner, and an incense was on its last burn. She aligned some blue crystals with pinker ones, flick-clicked her zippo, and spit through the flame at the crystals.

Fire and water.

She raised her hands up to her face in a prayer grip. Her lips moved in a sensual lovebird whisper as she slowly crushed up the dry leaves she picked up from her rolly-polly puke area. Taking a deep breath, she released the leaves and at a second's fall abruptly constricted her face and blurted, "Way'oo-". Poxer sighed and spent a minute sweeping up her leaflets on the ground.

She waited a minute to try and get a sense of control over her toureettes. Ready to try again she released the leaves, and in mid-fall, blew the leaflets toward her altar crystals. A few landed in a bowl of tiny crystals, and she used a larger tourmaline stone to crush a smaller crystal into powder. She lightly blew the crystal dust and leaflets in a whirlwind inside her bowl.

Wind and Earth.

She sat there a while, absorbing the elemental energy of her altar, manifesting a great day ahead through her happy hangover.

A little later, Poxer went for her routine morning run down to the beach. She was only three blocks from Ki's house and still opening up her cracking joints when she saw Brock on the sidewalk ahead of her. She immediately rotated into a fence conclave and peered around its corner.

Brock and Mokes opened up Leia's side garden gate, speaking with their heads together. Jack Poxer knew an opportunity when she saw one. A tic came, and she gave a bird whistle and bop sound with the pop of her lips.

Being a scrum-half in rugby, opportunities meant victories. She stalked forward, then remembered it was broad daylight and stalking might attract unwanted eyes. She stood up straighter with a cautious look around and slowly twisted her way over to Leia and Ki's side gate. The meander made her feel like a penguin or a person that just crapped their pants, and they didn't want the crap to smoosh inside their underwear or fall out.

She peered around the front left corner of the house and just saw jungle. Plants, small trees, flowers, roses, bushes of herbs, Leia had it. Without Leia being around for more than a year, the jungle was a dwelling in itself. Tall and droopy, dark and muggy, the growth of the lush foliage was ever encapsulating.

Creating a canopy cover that blocked the sun, Jack Poxer had to really scan through the darkened shade before proceeding through the gate and after Brock.

At the next corner of the house, she could hear the testosterone filled boys' conversation. She took refuge in a dense Pride of Barbados, a Bird of Paradise shrub. She adjusted to be as cozy as possible, made sure not to leave any indentations of disturbance, and tuned her ears in for listening.

Brock was standing outside the shed entryway and Mokes lazily categorized empty pots and bins inside. This was where Ki tricked Yakuza Alisano with a hidden springtrap spike right to her dome.

"That 4th of July was so crazy for Ik. I can't believe Yakuza came after him." Mokes picked up an old herbal mixing bowl that made him think of Tawa. He slipped out a joint from his top coat pocket and gestured to Brock that he was going to Chief-Up the shed while he consolidated.

Poxer ticked, "Whaa'oo." She covered her mouth with her shirt, sort of stuffing it inside her mouth and closed her eyes.

"Yeah well…" Brock looked up at the powerline above where a few crows perched, then he casually went back to watching Mokes as he smoked.

"You know why Yakuza came for him right?"

The shadows deepened around dreaded Mokes, "I don't know. You said old artifacts and witchy stuff?"

"Yeah, real witchy."

"So you bought their house to look for magical scrolls?"

Brock laughed and then picked a golden flower. "I bought their house because it was cheap. Three deaths in a major gang-affiliated home…"

Brock snuffed and continued, "Someone hit me up a couple years ago. Someone I think my dad used to be connected with." Brock remembered the dark faces of the Illuminati that fateful night of Ki's interrogation. The night his father died.

"This 'anonymous entity' laid it out real simple for us. Find a magical Tiki head or anything of the sort and be rewarded like a King with all past family debts paid."

Mokes checked outside of the shed and quickly scanned the yard. "Where are all of Leia's Tiki garden guardians? Were they still here when you bought the house?"

"Yeah, well, I think they were. I found one with a large bull ring and another with a long face. I delivered those two masks, but I don't think that's what they were after… Something made that Illumin hesitate in shooting Ki in the head. It was like a ghost spooked the shit out of him."

"Well, that sounds like Ik. He has that kind of presence."

"Yeah… presence…" Brock turned in slow, pondering circles.

"If the Illumin saw this magical tiki brain when Ki was around, then it must still be with him." Brock shook his head.

"We need to find where Ki is… Mokes, do you have any idea where Leia would run off to when she sold the house?"

"Ahh, probably somewhere it'd be hard to find her. If Yakuza and the Illuminati were after me, I'd become a ghost too."

"Yeah… Lexi said on social media she will be in town the week before Christmas. I'll pay her a visit and see if I can get any information out of her. You need to stay posted here to see if Ki comes back home for any reason. We need to capture him, track him, or whatever it takes to find that tiki head and get him to the Illuminati."

Jack Poxer scrunched her nose, trying to lock in all the information she just heard. This was definitely something Ki needed to know. The Illuminati were searching for him and a tiki head. Brock Zendolini out to integrate their old girlfriend, Lexi. And Mokes completely flipping sides and betraying Ki. Poxer still couldn't believe the Illuminati were in on this, or for that matter, even existed. She'd have to find Pines and ask him for Ki's email address.

A tic came, and she blew a loud bird tweet and bopped with her lips. She closed her eyes again and crouched even deeper into the Barbados bush. A moment went by, and she caught a whiff of Mokes' pot overhead.

"I like staying here. It reminds me of home." Mokes murmured.

"Well, if we find this Tiki head or Ki, the house is yours Mokes… and the business is yours in Oahu. I have plans of my own after we sign off with these Illuminati freaks."

"Hmph'hm *Whaa'o*," Poxer's moaning tic caused a cough of smoke to billow out and over to the Barbados bush; Mokes was right in front of her looking for the whistling bird, but she knew her last tic revealed her. She steadily rose up in front of Mokes.

"Elo Mate," she said as she went to pull his dreads back with her left hand. She locked eyes with him and slammed him with a heavy right hook that knocked him back into the wall. She ran and used a palm to assist a jump over the wall.

Brock rushed after her, blasting through the sideyard's gate, and spun his head up and down the street, searching for which way she went. Not able to find her, he went back through the sideyard, pushing the broken gate aside, and was smiling on his strut back to Mokes. He wasn't happy about being spied on, but he loved watching a girl that knew how to punch.

"Who the hell was that Mokes?" He asked, slightly out of breath, his smile fading with the slow realization of his reconnaissance plans falling through.

Mokes held the front of his chin, his dreads covering most of his face.

"Pinky… Jack Boxer." Mokes tried stretching out his jaw and grunted in pain. "Jacklyn Poxer, but they call her Pinky Boxer. She's a Mermaid."

"A boxing mermaid, eh? Well, we couldn't have done anything if we caught her. Do you think she will tell Ki what she heard?"

Brock was annoyed yet still enthralled by the little bouncy blonde that had just snuck under his nose.

"Yeah, she'll tell him. She's a diehard." Mokes was bummed, all his plans of security, wealth, and fulfillment of dreams slipping away from him.

Brock walked on Mokes' other side and peered toward the sideyard gate, arms crossed over his chest.

"Well, I guess I'll stay here too then. No sense in hiding now. And maybe this Pinky will try sneaking up on *me* next time." Brock's grin returned.

Mr. Zen's Secret

Six months after Sheriff Worden's Siege on the Zendolino Warehouse, Brock was released of any affiliation with his Father's Crime Syndicate. Leaving the courthouse, Brock felt more alone and uncertain about his future than he had ever before. He felt alright about not being criminally affiliated, but broken-hearted that his whole Italian family was either dead or in prison for life. He walked with his hands tucked in his fur coat pockets, kicking leaves and wood chips off the sidewalk.

The walk went on for half an hour until he stopped in front of a tattoo parlor. Never having gotten a tattoo before, he played with the idea of having the stabbing physical pain to distract him from the ache in his heart. Brock looked at the art on the walls and watched the inked-up Billys and Roxies move around the parlor, until he sensed someone closing in on him.

He suddenly turned with his fist cocked at his waist and ready to swing. It was only Mokes, with his hands in his hoodie pocket, watching Brock with a burning joint hanging from his lips.

"Watch out, your dreads might catch-a-fire."

Mokes moved the joint to the center of his lips and took a big inhale. Along with the cold air, his smoke endlessly billowed out like a dragon exhaling to the moon.

Brock relaxed his fist. "What you want, huh?" Brock was annoyed. He just wanted pain.

"I wanted to talk to you about your Father."

Brock quickly revealed his fist again and rubbed his knuckles under Mokes' chin. "Give me an excuse, and I'll let her fly."

Slowly, as he did everything in his life, Mokes removed his joint and snubbed it out in his palm, grimacing with the heat of the ember. Sheriff Worden made it look so cool when he did it during that Earth Day festival.

"I have a letter Brock… from Mr. Z." By the look in Brock's eyes, that wasn't enough to stop his fist from taking off his head, giving 'high as a kite' a whole new meaning.

"Here. Just take it, and I'll leave you be."

Mokes slowly pulled out a letter from his jean's back pocket and handed it to Brock. Brock grabbed the letter and Mokes turned and walked away.

Before reading, Brock looked back inside the tattoo parlor and saw that most of the Inkers were watching him with unbefitting eyes. He turned around, using his backside as a wall, and read.

Moments went by, and as he reached the end, three tears simultaneously dotted the letter, flooding his Father's inked strokes: '*I love you, Son.*' Brock whipped his eyes and reminisced. He stood there for a long time, watching a lamppost, thinking.

He turned back around and walked into the tattoo parlor. "I want a big letter Z on my back, Hawaiian tribal style."

The girl behind the counter was lost for words and just stared at Brock with her mouth ajar. As Brock's eyebrows curiously tilted down and upper lip frustratingly curled up, a big gorilla with his whole body tattooed walked up beside her.

"We're closed." The spider web under his eye pinched in on itself. Brock looked around the front room where customers were waiting to get tatted. He inhaled a large amount of air like a wolf about to blow the little piggy's straw house down, but for him, it was just to calm his nerves.

"Maybe I can make an appointment."

"Naw, we don't like your energy, man. You have to leave."

Maybe it was how he said 'Naw,' or possibly the growl the tattooed gorilla had after he told Brock to leave. Whatever it was, it didn't sit well.

Brock smiled at six inkers, now all taking a break from their work to watch the entertainment of him getting denied.

Another tear ran down Brock's cheek. "Well… Fuck you," and with Big Popa Z, his Father's letter, balled up in Brock's fist, he grabbed the tatted gorilla by the collar and began a slow waltz of destruction to all that wanted a piece of him.

X Marks the Spot

All tied together and hidden under his hood, Mokes' dreads pillowed his head against the car's headrest. Brock waved the lingering smoke away from his face and tried leaning back as far as possible to get away from the encroaching headlights coming towards their parked car.

"Alright, I think that was them. Grab your flashlight, and let's go."

Brock pulled a face sleeve over his nose and mouth and got out. Halfway up the driveway, he looked back and saw a huge cloud of smoke around their car.

Under his breath, Brock whispered to Mokes, "You ever going to quit that shit?"

Mokes looked back at him and put his finger in front of his mask. They were approaching the house, and silence was crucial. They opened the back gate, checked all the windows and doors and sat back on their hunches in the shadows.

Brock whispered to Mokes again, "You need to be my lookout if they come back. Call my phone if you see anybody coming, alright?"

Mokes nodded and stalked out of the yard and back to the front. Brock rolled his shoulders and tried again to force the kitchen window open. When it didn't budge, he slammed his elbow through the door window and let himself inside.

In his adrenaline, he didn't know if the red light on the ceiling was blinking before he came in or afterward, but he didn't have time to wonder; he needed to search the house. He pulled apart the mattresses, looked in all the drawers, and even looked in the bathroom cabinet and refrigerator, but had no luck finding what he wanted. He felt abnormally paranoid and unfocused. He searched the refrigerator again and grabbed a chocolate pudding cup, downing it like Poppie would his Spinach.

"Thanks Mokes, now I got the munchies…" He growled.

***

Mokes sat back in the car and smoked another joint with one

finger hovering over the call Brock button on his phone. As he puffed, he decided to listen to some music while he waited. He just needed his eyes to be on lookout duty anyway. He giggled at the congruity of his position.

Really getting into his tunes, Mokes began to close his eyes slightly and bob his head. Old, loving reggae beats imbuing his soul. He could almost see the light blasting up from Marley's guitar.

Mokes' eyes powerfully flicked open like he had to break a layer of glue holding his eyelids shut. Headlights raced down the street in his rearview mirror, and he fumbled with his phone. The screen went black and locked on him as soon as he was ready to open it. His sweaty finger kept missing the quick password pattern swipes, and after the third failed attempt, he was locked out.

"Ah, Fuck."

***

Pines drifted his little four-cylinder into his driveway and sped up to the front of his house.

"I got the guy in the car. You good to check on the house alone?" Adam Vander pulled back the slide on his pistol and let it click back in place.

"Yeah, I got it bud."

They both chuckled and exited from their vehicle, leaving Zoo Za'mara inside. Adam charged for the house as Pines slunk against the gate and covertly paced down the driveway to the mischievous guy sitting in the unknown vehicle.

***

Brock itched at his belly, still murderously hungry, and sat on the couch looking around the room. Surfboards, skateboards, and motorcycle frames were attached to the walls like artwork. A sword was propped up on its point in the corner, and clutter was scattered on their table in front of him. Then, he saw, under a tall melted candle, a map of Japan with an X on Ise-Shima National Forest.

A car screeched to a stop, and doors slammed closed.

"Time to bounce." He had the backdoor halfway open as the front door blasted open, and Adam was there hunched over his iron cross.

"Don't move. You're busted."

Brock smiled, still facing the backdoor. He knew Pines and Adam from high school, and he knew Adam didn't have the guts to shoot.

BANG! A bullet went right by Brock's left kneecap. The collision of sound echoed confusion. No more words could be heard with the ringing in their ears, so it was time to act. Brock needed to run, but at the same time, he didn't want to lose the ability to run forever.

Being secondhand high, Brock probably made the worst decision and jetted out the back to hop over the closest fence.

***

Pines snuck all the way to the inconspicuous car and readied his fingers under the door handle. To him, this was the best way to catch the possible burglar lookout. If it wasn't a burglar, he'd just apologize, and the guy might not come back to his street again. If it was a burglar, he'd have him. Confident in his Jiu-Jitsu submissions, he opened the door and simply looked at who was inside.

"Fucking Mokes. What the hell you doing stealing from me now, eh?"

Mokes was quiet with bloodshot eyes and let Pines pull him out of the car and submit him face down on the road. Mokes and Pines were always close, which made the interaction pretty awkward. The two guys from the islands who also used to like to smoke together, were now like two stoners wrestling for the last spam musubi.

Adam raced down the driveway. "I lost Brock. Seems like they were looking for something because the house is a mess." Even with Brock's face sleeve, Brock was Brock.

Pines spoke to the back of Mokes' head, "We don't have anything Mokes, so what in the world could you be looking for?"

Mokes moved his head to the side with his cheek on the asphalt.

"We are just looking for Ki man. People are looking for that Tiki head he has."

A blur rushed out of the bush and ran Adam over, throwing his gun to the side. Then Brock quickly walked up to Pines and bashed him off Mokes with a forearm X slam.

"Get in the driver's, now!" Brock yelled.

Mokes scrambled up to his feet and turned on the car. Adam and Pines recovered from Brock's hits and blocked his way to the vehicle.

"I've been waiting for this moment. The battle against Zero's goonies. Time for you to weep-" Pines slid in close and produced a half dozen quick jabs up Brock's torso and to his head. Adam came up on the other side to slip in heavy, one-two swings during openings where his buddy Pines was out of the way.

Adam hadn't been in a fight with Pines for 4 or 5 years, so he had forgotten how quick Pines was and how he liked to dip and dive around in circles to spin his opponent into a daze. Back then, it worked well against the drunks; now, however, Adam wasn't sure about the dexterous slab of mountain tracking Pines' every move. Masked burglar Brock would catch Pines soon enough, and based on the way his arms flexed with ripped muscle contour, Adam feared for his best friend's safety. Promptly, Adam jumped onto Brock and tried to hold his arms back from punching. With a seconds break, Pines stood up straighter and studied Brock's green eyes.

Pines took in the moment, for there was much to take in. During his transgression into reality, Brock's stillness relaxed the air. Alas, inside Brock, all cells vibrated with an escalation of energy, and with a wolfish exhale, Brock power flexed Adam off of him, sending him stumbling back for only a moment. Adam came back at him, and Brock then winded back and let the incoming Adam have a five-fingered mega punch right on his nose. He turned on Pines.

"Tell Ki I'm looking for him." He charged for Pines and used his elbows as spear shields to trample him over.

"Let's go Brock!" Mokes yelled from the car.

Helpless, Pines tried to piece together how Brock knew about Toko Tuki, but a beast hung over him with a massive fist, and Brock let one more fly, knocking Pines out cold.

"You stoney dingdong! Where was my phone call!"

Brock got in the car, and they headed out.

Poxer's Warning

Jackyln Poxer needed to tell Ki what Brock was up to. Spiritual entities being the talk of the town, Illuminati after him, Mokes' betrayal. Ki was in deep trouble and unfortunately she still had to run her new Refill Shop. Her clients were counting on her, and she was still trying to do her part to help save the planet. She kept itching at the back of neck when she thought of how urgent it was to get a message over to Ki, like his ventures were catalysts for strange resolutions.

On paper Ki was a bad guy, and maybe he was considered criminal in many eyes, but not hers, not the planet's, and not Pines. Pines fought with him against the Yakuza, he must know how to reach him in Japan. Jacklyn had so many questions now, and getting a hold of Ki might be the beginning of answering a few.

She worked, she waited, and she even directly messaged Kavika Pinederosa on Instagram. When the clock hit 6:00 p.m., she locked up and drove straight over to the outskirts of Ellipsis where Pines lived.

Arriving at 6:30 in the evening couldn't have been planned better. Happy hour, a time when work was finished and feeding time began.

Feeling clever, Jacklyn Poxer walked up Pines' driveway and found him crying through the kitchen window. She went over to his door and knocked. A bark came first then Adam answered with a bent nose and two black eyes.

"Hi." Adam looked around Poxer for a cart of Girl Scout Cookies.

"Hi. I'm here to speak- *You Cunt* -with Pines… sorry."

Pines came up, wiping the tears from his eyes. He looked a little confused to see a hardcore lesbian at his door, but joyful to see a friendly face. "Hey Pinky, come on in. Sorry the place is a mess. We had a break in last night…"

"Oh wow, sorry to hear that. Was that why you were crying?"

Pines laughed, "No No, I was just cutting an Onion."

"Well, I will- *hm'hmff* -make it quick. I just need to get- *hmm'ff 'pop'* -some urgent information over to Ki. What is the best way to reach- *Wha'ooo* -him?"

Pines looked intrigued and shared curious glances with Adam.

"His email would be my guess. You ready? It's Earthbiatch at gmail.com. Haha, I love that one… And what do you need to tell him? Maybe we can help."

Pines sat down on a bar stool, and Adam came back with a glass of water for Poxer. They'd both love it if Poxer would stay and chat all night. Anybody would.

Poxer eyed Ki's friends up and down. They were helping get ahold of him for her, the least she could do was tell them a bit of the reason why.

"It's about Brock; he's planning something against Ki, and Ki asked me before he left to inform him if Brock was doing anything suspicious."

Adam laughed like a hobgoblin. "Ohhh Brock is definitely fucking suspicious. First, he bought Leia's house, and then he was caught trying to break into ours. Fuck that guy."

Poxer's mouth dropped. "No way!" Her head tilted up in a tic contraction and she whistled, popped her lips and clicked her cheeks three times. "-*Fucking Cunt* -I was listening to a conversation he was having with Mokes, and he- *Whe-oo* -said he was looking for a- *hee'mph* -magical tiki head. He must have been looking over here for- *ah'ff* -that!"

Pines and Adam gave each other that dreadful look again and Pines ran away. Poxer and Adam just watched and waited for him to return, while Zoo Za'mara laid her head on Poxer's foot. When Pines came back, he had his laptop open and his fingers quickly tapping away.

"Sit, sit. Write your message now. He needs to know now."

"Okay, I'll- *Fucker!* -opps that was a bad one- *fuck wee'ou* -sorry. I'll sit but I have- *whey* -email on my phone. And I want to know more- *shit ass* -" Her cheeks clicked with a long closed eyed tic. "About this Tiki ghost when I'm done."

A Swirling Gut of Monarchs

Every time Ki pulled a zipper around in a binding arc, Tuki followed, floating from right side up to upside down to right side up, miming the bend. After melodically organizing the last of his travel gear, Ki zipped up every pouch of his big backpack. As he stood up, he found himself face to face with Toko Tuki.

He had this new untarnished connection with Tuki ever since his Mother Leia left his old worm-engraved staff in his prisoner belongings box. It hadn't been too long since Ki had been out of prison and free to roam the world, and he knew this fresh feeling of freedom was what gave him a rejuvenated exhilaration throughout the day. However, there was something else that lifted his spirits and gave him a cloud of energy.

Being away from Uka Buka for three and a half years, peace solidified over his body and soul. Even while locked up he could concentrate on tranquility. Half of the reason he was so at peace was because he had nearly died during the Fourth of July Yakuza break-in. Then he just coasted through his prison time. He was beaten up, half-blind, and no one in the cells wanted to mess with a quiet cripple.

There's something in the human anatomy which allows a period of attunement for victorious warriors. From studying magic and natural manifestation with his cellmate Irking Caldor to crip walking the block, Ki was a ghost; he was untouchable. This was why Irking liked him so much; he was a replenishing spirit with a juicy survival rate for his close proximity rituals.

He figured being untouchable and rid of the demon Uka Buka brought him his newfound happiness, this enlightening sense of peace. But now, standing face to face with Toko, he knew that rainbow eye of Tuki's stood for something important.

Love and complacency were the feelings he held onto these last four days out in the free world. He needed to hang on to this feeling and remember it, for it was Tuki, the rainbow eye, the kind warmth of love and compassion that Earth needed to rise above all else.

Ki stretched his hand out in front of him, and it simply went right through Toko Tuki. *Truly a spirit of the divine Mother,* he thought. *She is always here with me, guiding me toward a path of planetary righteousness.*

"Alright Tuki let's go find Suga Duka and Mom, eh?"

Tuki bobbed a nod. Feathers slighting bouncing, headdress half evolved into its ancient planked wood, large squat eyes of green and yellow, and at times an array of all the colors in the right light.

Ki was glad they were leaving the big City of Tokyo. There were too many eyes to catch sight of the Japanese American, who obviously had a story to tell. He felt dumb being so reckless in his showcase. In the land of your enemy you had to keep a low profile, not frolic around like a kid at a Japanese arcade.

He put on his face mask and continued his long clunky walk through the station.

"If you have energy to spare Tuki, keep that rainbow eye of yours on me. I don't always make the right decisions." Ki huffed out a snicker through his mask.

As he walked the streets, he occasionally looked down at his side in anticipation of seeing if Zoo Za'mara was still there following him. The feeling came from years of her by his side, and he guessed Toko Tuki filled that area of companionship during their time apart from each other.

Down into the subway and onto the train to the main Tokyo hub, Ki breathed a sigh of relief at being on the right path and able to take a break from walking. Only to be suddenly pomelled with an old lady's bag, shooing him out of the subway train.

The doors closed and his train took off, cars filled with only women. Ki saw pink stripes on the gate, then looked down and noticed he was standing on a pink square with small italicized print, *Women Cars Only.* Another train would be there in ten minutes. Japan was righteously efficient.

Finally making it to the Tokyo hub and getting on the bullet train into Kyoto, Ki sat down and closed his eye. He wore sunglasses today, which he thought made him blend in a bit more, covering up his missing eye and concealing some of his scarred cheek.

Wanting to watch the speed of the train and land pass by, Ki scooted over to the window and helplessly closed his eye again. He thought he could feel the speed and imagine the fast landscapes moving around him through the eye of the Sun.

He chuckled in his drowsy fantasy. *Maybe…*

Ki rubbed his thumb along a lengthy worm-engraved canal and began to believe light was filling his mind. His thoughts slowly formed into illustrations of fields and towns interwoven between hills and forests. Rivers and mountains glistened and reflected from their running water and powdered snow. The images formed in his mind bled with so much color he felt like he was on a psychedelic trip.

Were these images of his creation? Was Toko Tuki doing his subliminal bidding and flying alongside the train to connect his eyes with Ki's? Or was it truly the Sun's light, a luminescent eye in the back of his head, showing him the magical land that worshipped its spherical sol power? Before he could begin diagnosing the power within him, a fragrance smacked him in the nose and jolted his heart up into his throat.

"Do lights dance wherever you go… Zepp?" Her voice wasn't deep but definitely self-assured and a little sarcastic.

Ki kept his eye closed, not that she could tell if it was open anyway with his sunglasses on. He wanted to tease her, test her. She was always so rough with him that it was time to play with her. Lighten up her mood by first pissing her off. Ki wondered again if that was such a good idea, but it seemed right for the moment. How'd she find him anyways? Was it destined in the realm of synchronicity that they were on the same train to Kyoto a day after drinking sake together at the Karaoke bar? Or was she actually following him? A hot undercover Yakuza girl tracking him till he found his treasure.

Anger gurgled inside her growl and she nudged him with her forearm. The scent of her engulfed him at that moment, causing him to gulp for breath. Her air was right under his nostrils as if she were trying to look up into his shades.

"Why does light always flicker when you're around, huh?" He could feel her reaching for his sunglasses. *A test.*

Ki surreptitiously went for her wrist and bent down to kiss her thinly lined lips. The embrace was longer than he anticipated, skewing his test and scrabbling his brains. He was expecting a knife to his throat, a slap to his face or at least a moment of repulsion and discontent. The kiss was long enough that he risked readjustment for more lip succulents, but the move caused Xillian to retreat.

"You Inu…" Xillian's voice softened as her slackened gaze pulled away from him.

"How is it that we are on the same train together?" Ki asked nonchalantly as if that kiss hadn't filled his heart with more light than the sun previously had.

"I'm traveling to see my Grandma in Ise-Shima Forest. I told you that last night."

Ki rubbed at the bridge of his nose. Drinking always made him forgetful. He also vaguely remembered her saying something like that. Their paths were so close to each other; it was unbelievable to him that fate wove itself so close to one's heart. Was this how true love happened? A majestically woven destiny of two souls. All differences cast aside, all problems a mere distraction of truth?

"Did I tell you where I was going last night?" Ki asked Xillian, a little embarrassed.

Xillian was waking up out of her shock, and Ki could tell her ferocity was strengthening up again.

"Nope. You did call yourself a gay butt pirate, and gay guys don't kiss straight girls like that." Xillian exerted dryly.

Ki also had a history in telling girls he was gay when he had too much to drink. Gay guys had an easier time getting into straight girl's rooms.

"Ah, I…"

Again, Xillian's voice was dry, rough, and direct as she interrupted him. "If gay guys all kissed like that there would be no straight men left."

She created a side-long grin, obviously not used to such a break in her face. Her hair was fully pulled back today, but she still had her spiked up little black knot on top of her head, held together by a Japanese flower pin. Her eyes were shadowed, and she wore loose dark fitting clothes that made her look cozy as ever. Her feet were propped up on the chair in front of her, not caring about normal formalities and train etiquette. She was so cool he couldn't believe just a moment ago his lips were pressed to hers.

"So the train lights were turning on and off?" Ki took off his sunglasses and faced her, leaning back into the window to try and seem half as cool as she was.

"I was five cars up and lights flickered on and off in the same rhythm they did last night at the Karaoke bar, almost like an S.O.S beacon. I was curious to see if you were on the train… following me, and here you are. Not so sneaky as you thought, hmm?"

"I was taking a nap. And I'm not following you, I'm just…" Ki's mind started swimming in an underwater library, searching for what Xillian's frosty eyes reminded him of.

"You're just… Where are you going then, if you're not following me?"

Ki didn't remember telling her where he was going last night, and he did give her a false name. If she was a Yakuza member how would she know he was the infamous Ki La'dori?

"I'm just going to Kyoto for some sightseeing. Tourists shit." Ki looked away from her penetrating light blue eyes and outside into endless lush green forests and hills. Xillian usually looked away from him when she spoke to him, what changed? He wanted to sneak in another kiss. Maybe he'd kiss the queen of the underworld on her neck next. She deteriorated his composure and broke his discipline. He had to look away to not act like a fool.

"Interesting." She responded a moment later.

Xillian sensed his restriction, leaned over him, and pointed at a massive snowy mountain with its peak above the clouds.

"Fuji Mountain." She breathed robotically in his ear.

She was everything Ki loved: beautiful, dark, isolated, independent, tough, mysterious, kind, in her own way, and smart. He thought of Lexi and how he was close to settling down into a simple, slow life. A life of love and bliss. Could he redeem that past? Could he catch a girl with a name as badass as Xillian?

It was good she was so easy to talk to. Maybe he could get more information on Ise-Shima to pass the time. If her grandmother lived there, she should know some stuff.

"What's with your land rights here? Why doesn't your government own the National Park?"

"They do and don't… Here let me explain. The National Park Act demonstrates the authority to uphold the public interests of property rights, mining rights, and national land development. Upholding these interests is called the pro-development principle, a loophole and possible problem in National Forest conservation, if manipulated.

"The reason for having this obscure principle is because of the high risk of natural disasters in Japan and the necessity of heavy equipment and private organizations available for repairs. Basically a Pro-Development Principle.

"The Minister of the Environment can designate incorporated foundations like non-profit organizations, to promote nature conservation and 'proper use'. Something called the Protection of the Scenic Area Protection Agreement.

"Complex protected areas or biodiverse areas will inevitably require partner-centric approaches to reconcile with complex land ownership, overlapping laws and institutions, and vulnerable administrative resources for conservation authority. However, failures in partnerships or collaborative approaches often happen.

"Conservation authorities will inevitably seek more partner-centric approaches for the efficient use of government resources and synergizing area management. Hence the government owning a small portion of the land and Japanese citizens owning the rest.

"The Ministry of the Environment of Japan only owns 42 percent of the land. 27 percent belongs to local governments, and 58 percent of Japan's land is privately owned."

"Those percentages don't add up." Ki noted smartly.

"That's because the 27 percent of publicy owned forest is also part of the 42 percent of National forest, just managed by the local government."

Xillian's response outsmarted Ki by a million, mostly because Ki was awestruck with his mouth open. Xillian gave him a moment to settle in the information she gave him. Ki looked back out the window watching the cloud formations.

"Looks like a storm is coming into Kyoto."

Xillian leaned into Ki again to look at the clouds.

"It does."

Why was such a simple response so powerful and much more meaningful than a scientific synopsis of a subject? The only thing Ki gathered from Xillian's snational forest political landright speech was that it is owned by both the government and regular people, and that a lot of Japan is inhabitable forest.

Ki readjusted his focus. "So the government can't touch privately owned land rights in their National Forest. That seems risky, right? What if the owner's mistreat the land and environment?"

"Japanese people aren't like Americans. They don't mistreat their environment as easily as your people do. If there was a problem though, like illegal harvesting or environmental degradation, then the Forest Governance would step in and regulate or seize land rights.

"The Ministry of the Environment and Landscape protection agreements are all set in place to have a pretty strong environmental protection policy."

This chick was a nerd underneath all those baggy clothes and dangerous frowns. Ki wanted desperately to show her the tricks he could do and the spirits he had as friends, but he reserved himself. The Japanese were masters at having unbreakable discipline, so it was time for Ki to harness some as well.

"You are very well informed. Thank you." Ki bowed his head a little in appreciation.

"You know, my grandma and I could use an extra hand at her cabin, if you want to come with me. Then I could show you the Japan that's mostly untouched by loud foreign boot heels." She winked at him and then looked out the window. She was a rough one, but not too rough to stay away from. Ki thought he could learn some more from this girl, and it was starting to sound like he'd get to spend one or two nights with her, and in a storm at that! *Discipline took time to master,* he thought. *This felt too good to pass up.*

***

Later, when they were both squished close together awaiting departure from the bullet train, Xillian stared at Ki, going back and forth between his eye patch and his open hazel eye. He stared back at her.

"How'd you turn the train lights on and off?"

Another rush buzzed through his brain. Her questions were like a drug to him.

"Magic." Ki kept it simple and completely serious. Maybe his simple mysterious response will stir her up like it did him. It was funny to him, and he wanted to laugh, but the adrenaline pumped his muscles with ecstatic petrification. Magic was a part of his everyday life now. It felt good to say it out loud and actually mean it.

Xillian took a moment, still watching his eye unfazed and very present. Ki ambiguously calculated over twenty-five years worth of Xillian's thoughts and character developments. *Who was this courageous woman? What happened in her life to make her, so her?*"

"You got any money, magic man?" Xillian smiled while leaning into him more.

Ki never had a beard, absolutely no hair ever grew on his face, but while he was so flabbergasted at the specimen inches in front of him, he subconsciously created an itch right below his mutilated and scarred cheek, right at the edge of his defined jawline. He always preferred to have a deeper jaw, but it was a hair too shallow for his liking. So he will have to unhinge and drop his jaw, just enough not to look mental. Pensive was what he was going for, not doo doo brain, where'd Dumbo go, dumb.

He rubbed his earring between his fingers and the train finally came to a stop. Xillian pressed closer into him, and she gave him those, *we are going to be lovers*, eyes. The eyes that said it all. Ki dreamt of those blue spheres before. He remembered to worship and absorb their power. Filling him up with pure energy. He could feel their rays even through the rain clouds. Manifesting the light from above to within.

They followed the crowd out, walking amongst the exodus of people, popping open their umbrellas, and skipping along for cover. Xillian and Ki made it under a long, upwardly curved corner of a thatched roof. The wind swaggered a line of orange lanterns hanging on the bamboo framed perimeter. *Rural*, he thought. *Old world*.

"I have money." And like the wind, Ki added some swagger to his head. Having money was no big deal.

Xillian looked down one street and then the other. She put her head just far enough outside the roof's protection that water plattered down her face and over her lips.

"I'm going to get a car. Maybe you can pitch for gas."

This was the time for him to get out while he still could. Safety First, right? But he didn't want to be safe. He wanted to risk everything just for the love of being around Xillian.

This was a whole different fight Ki had not been used to. The battle within, and having to make the choice of following your ethereal heart, your rational mind, or the Monarch migratory cycle of your gut.

Kudarimiya

Thrusting the stick shift forward, an X tattoo revealed itself on the top of Xillian's wrist. An X disguised as a serpent.

"Can I call you X?"

She nodded, still watching the road.

Ki had never met someone this interested in him and yet so complacent with the little he told her. She hasn't asked him any questions other then, how he turned off the train lights and whether he had money for gas. You would think there would be a lot of questions for an American with an eye patch, scars engulfing his hands, and a cane to stagger around on.

He thought about her immense mysteriousness as two of her fingers stroked her tan skin through a tear in her jeans.

Did that mean she wanted me to touch her like that? Was trying to call her X a bad idea? He loved calling her Xillian. He only asked her if he could call her X to try and squeeze a story out of her. But that was just like Xillian, piercing eyes one second and stonewalled the next.

Thousands of bamboo shoots covered the hills overlooking a river of light blue water. As they approached the coastline, hundreds of tunnels cut through the mountains, breaking up the scenery with immense forests to darkened passageways. The clattering rain transitioning to a hum as they zipped through the long wormholes.

Ki knew islanders liked to drive slow, but he wanted to drive really really slow through these areas. The environment was ever-changing. The storm, the forests, and the dim dens of the mountains were all illustrative flawlessness.

There was enough space between the trees to see beyond, creating great depths of beauty in one frame.

He imagined a national forest being somewhat of a protected grounds of just forest; however, there were towns, harbors, plots of land, and farms amidst the jungle. Xillian did say the land in the national forests were mostly privately owned, so the people had to live somewhere.

He wondered about Hattori Honzo's land rights and why he had given them to his lost father Asagaio. Now that Ki was in the actual forest, driving for multiple hours, he understood that his land rights were only a small portion of the forest. A relieving discovery to an otherwise overwhelming comprehension. Wherever the paper rights were to, the land must be unmistakably magnificent and valuable to have Yakuza still searching for Asagaio's family twenty-five years later.

"X," Ki asked if he could say it, so he might as well use it now. He also liked it because his old nickname was Z, and now he had met X. A name like that doesn't get any seXier.

"I read there are many holy Shinto Shrines here in Ise. I want to know about them all, but for time sake, how many look over the ocean?"

"You mean the Kami Sanctuaries? Man-made places for our gods to await men's prayers? There are many Shrines in the Kii Peninsula..." He instantly regretted asking her anything, but how was he to know she got grumpy over shrines.

"The Kami are the world around us, this is true. They manifest all elements and all natural things. If humans all pray together in one *sacred* location, the energy of that area builds, and the Kami perhaps are more attuned to listening." Xillian looked over at Ki through his silence. His pensiveness ignited another flame in her.

"The Japanese Goddess is a corpse of the underworld. Killed by birthing our fire god and outcast by her husband. Maddened by the lack of her husband Izanagi's compassion, she cursed this land with death..."

Xillian had a menacing curdle to voice.

"And I don't believe Izanagi, a male god, birthed the Sun, Moon and Storm Gods by washing his eyes and blowing snot rockets. Try to remember that there are shrines everywhere throughout Japan, probably around 100,000. We show our respects, though it's what the Kami represents which is most sacred. So don't go basking in the glory of the shrine itself; you should be releasing yourself to the Kami, focusing on the spirits of our land. Which is without question, all around you."

In his arousal to combat her anger, Ki choked on his spittle. He didn't know how his question led to him becoming a gullible dumb tourist, but he desperately wanted to tell her what he was really looking for. He could spend weeks on the coastline searching.

However, maybe that was what his mother intended. Connect with the land before fighting for her.

"I'm looking for some connection between those three gods, actually. Facing an enshrined leap towards a rocky reunion of Sun, Moon, and Sea."

"A stupid riddle," Xillian shrugged. "I'm in no mood for such things."

She gave him a side-long glare, curious about his new inquiries but angry enough to have to tell a foreigner the secrets of her land.

When they got out of the car, she tried to shake off her bad mood, "Welcome to the land of the Kami. Shrines for all walks of life…" She rolled her eyes.

"I'm going to meet with my Grandmother in that temple."

She pointed at ancient Japanese architecture.

"You should look around and become more acquainted with where you are. I'm not your tour guide or your investigator, so try and find a map."

Still hurt from the jab at his mother's first clue, Ki wanted to give her something special before she stomped away. Something to remind her he wasn't just a tourist. Bonez pulled him closer to Xillian.

"What's up with your grandmother then? She lives with the Kami?"

Another dumb question, but sometimes words spill like wine.

Xillian scrunched up her face in annoyance. By doing so, Ki could see several puncture holes from piercings, all bunched together in the center of her face.

"Buddhist Temples house only death. Shinto Shrines hold a life force. The cycle of Death and Reincarnation."

Ki limped even closer; Bonez was off the ground and at his hip. He looked into Xillian's eyes; some epic loss hollowed out her stare, burning with fire. She was still alive in there but broken somehow. He nodded for her to take his staff.

A softened gaze rolled from her forehead down to her chin. Another breeze blew through the surrounding trees shading ancient soil, setting Xillian at ease, finally graced with the blessing of the forest.

She grabbed at Bonez indifferently, and suddenly, a woosh of air blew up around her. Lifting her loose strings of hair, almost flipping up an eyelid and rippling over her baggy clothes, fluttering her bandana tails wrapped around her elbow. The wind felt like it was coming from every direction, all at once. Her dark clothes seemed to radiate with kindness, instead of grunge, even though they retained the same hue.

The wind only blew her up for a moment; then her emotions were next to explode. A tear came down her filibustered cute face, and her spikey bun hung loose and off to the side. Xillian passed the staff back and quickly walked away towards the Temple. Her feet were light off the ground, and the defined mass of her thigh formed through her black jeans.

She'll be alright, Ki thought.

Some people stopped and looked down with a wary side glance as she passed, and others further away seemed troubled by her appearance. Ki thought it must have been some sort of cultural Japanese Elder and Youth exchange. The only person who seemed to be unfrazzled by her was a man leaning on the side of the Temple's front door. A well-dressed man who looked straight at Ki with obvious contempt. Ki guessed he himself was indeed a site for sore eyes.

As soon as she entered the Temple, Ki's hand was scorched by Bonez the Cane. Instantly, he flipped it and grabbed Bonez by the apex stone, glad it wasn't wickedly hot as well. Toko Tuki rocketed out of his hand holding the stone and did a huge vortexual spin up in the misty air. Up and up and up till the only thing Ki could do was look into the sky and wait.

Xillian must have pinched a nerve on the drive there because she seemed so villainous. Voice gurgling with anger and eyes boiling with hate. It was a complete contrast to how she was behaving before they got in the car, that was for sure. She was pouty before, but not contemptuous. Ki decided she'd be transfixed with questions soon, and unable to be angry by the recent influx of pure *magic* which literally exploded into her face.

A flash of perspective appeared in his mind of what Toko Tuki must see above the forest canopy, and then he got an idea. Toko Tuki of course! Toko Tuki could find Suga Duka. A rush of love for his tiki companion filled his heart. He kissed Bonez on the stone and continued waiting for Tuki to fly back down.

Like sand falling into an uncharted crevice, five minutes went by. Ki wondered if he looked strange staring up at the gray mist.

He settled in and crutched over to a path that opened up to what looked like water under a bridge and blue sky elapsing through a sliver in the clouds. During his long trek to the bridge, he reviewed his new plan…

Suddenly, a bell rang to the North, and Ki turned to look down at an odd, heavy, foreboding stone in the mist, inviting curiosity to its darkened descent. Limping over to the top of the stone steps Ki looked far down into the shadow. At the bottom was a looming shrine. How he felt a looming presence, Ki could not decipher, the shrine had enough power to seemingly look down upon him even when he was high above and it was far below.

"Kudarimiya," an old lady said while walking up and away.

Fog swirled around the horizontal beam set as the shrine's top.

Before he knew it he had made it to the bottom of the stairs. The feel of a dismal vitality flourished in the misty air. Ki looked down at its base and saw Japanese lettering written in the dirt. He turned to a man wandering around, looking up into the trees.

"Sumimasen, sir. Perhaps you might know what this means?"

The man gently strolled over to him. "Ah, Kudarimiya…"

The frail man half raised his hand to point up the slope that led down to the shrine. He finally looked into Ki's eyes intensely as if to increase the impact of what he was going to say next.

"Descending Shrine."

Right then, Toko Tuki rushed through the canopy and flew by Ki's ear. Wary, Tuki floated up a few stone steps and then a few more, probing Ki to follow. He gave his Arigatos and walked up and out of the shrine's gloomy hole with Tuki.

"Wrong energy, eh Tuk?"

Toko Tuki looked at him sideways.

"Your spirits will pick up once we find Suga Duka." Ki said this like he was trying to lead a horse with a carrot.

"Suga Duka Tuk. Don't you want to find Suga Duka?"

Tuki went back to looking like his gregarious little puppy self. Zipping around looking behind trees, over rocks and finally, as they made it closer to where the sun was just poking through the mist, under the arched bridge. For the time being, Ki was just glad Toko Tuki was happy and not mad at him. Ki could have guessed Tuki might have been disappointed in him by passing Bonez over to a girl.

Toko Tuki popped up from a haystack, seeming enlightened, and rocketed back into the sky and towards the sun.

Ki didn't wait for Tuki this time. He went to the middle of the bridge and watched the river pass under him. The high-arched bridges allowing space, not just for the majestic light blue water to flow through, but also for an expansive amount of air. Japan encouraged their environment to breathe.

Everything has a spirit, she said. Everything has life.

The rush of a spirit blew behind Ki, and Tuki flew straight over to a large wooden plaque standing up at the base of a trailhead.

"A map. Brilliant."

When they made it over to the plaque, Bonez the Cane picked itself off the ground and slammed its butt onto the wooden chart, creating a loud thunk. Toko Tuki licked Bonez twice and his floating bobs slowed down into a mellow fulfillment.

Ki removed Bonez from the plaque and read, *Meoto Iwa Marriage Rocks.* His mother's clue came back to him; *To help find Suga Duka's secret location, she will be facing an enshrined leap towards a rocky reunion of Sun, Moon, and Sea.*

These Meoto Iwa Marriage Rocks were a little offshore, with a shine on top of the larger rock of the sea. Aside from Bonez and Tuki clearly pinning Suga Duka's location, Leia's clue also made sense.

Ki took a deep breath of relief and put his hand up for Tuki to give him a high five. Tuki tilted its head and closed his mouth in confusion.

He wanted to give someone a high five and hear the euphoric smack of triumph. It was time to see Xillian.

***

On his way back, Ki looked down at the Descending Shrine and found Xillian alone in meditation. The mist hung low in this part of the forest, as if creating a barrier around the shrine to protect the sky.

Ki looked at Tuki in surprise to find Xillian at the eerie spot they had encountered earlier. Toko Tuki, on the other hand, glared at Ki when he started to descend the steps. Bonez went red hot again, and Tuki suddenly vanished. Ki, as silently as he could, pulled himself down the steps, holding onto his mother's cool stone handle.

Was Tuki jealous? Did he not like being around Kudarimiyas? Or did he know something about Xillian that Ki overwhelmingly didn't want to know?

"Watashi Wa Xillian kara Musuki Island, Watashi wa kamigami

to sono deshi-tachi no karada kara koboreru mizu o nagashite imasu. Watashi wa anata no kekkan o nekkyo-teki ni sosogi, watashi no chi no aganai ni yasuragu o ataete kudasai. Naze anata no chikara to hikari ga watashi o kon'nani kuraku suru no ka oshietekudasai. Shojin o onegai itashimasu."

Xillian paused as if accepting what the shrine had to give. "I am the serpent of Kusakabe Yoshini."

Ready to wait all night for Xillian to arise from her prayer, Ki leaned over and tried to absorb the total feeling of the area. He remembered the power of darkness. Dark power was, after all, a being of imbalance. Ki used to enjoy that life of chaos.

Finally, she stood and turned around right to him. She seemed to know he was already there. No shock passed over her mellow-cheeked face.

"Thank you for showing me some light on such a gloomy day." Xillian eyed Ki's walking staff, and Ki nodded.

"How's your Grandmother?"

Xillian's eyes peered down, and she started to ascend back to the main road.

"She's fine. How's your Sunny Moon in the Sea thing?" She said this with a mouth full of distaste and assurance that he had not found anything useful on the matter.

Now annoyed with her constant sourness, he answered only to prove her wrong. "Well, I found it." Retaliating back with a little of Xillian's fire.

Xillian didn't seem to notice. And she didn't seem surprised at him finding it either. *A hardened cookie always left crumbles*, he thought. Being too hard was an obvious mask for something. He had to be careful.

"I'll make you a deal. I'll take you there if you tell me what kind of trick you played on me with that… staff." She playfully punched him in the shoulder and did another one of her uniquely beautiful smiles.

Ki tightened and stood up straighter, beginning to see how she played this game. She did want something from him. Yakuza or not, Ki was also down to play the game, especially if he had the upper hand. He had Toko Tuki on his side; he could deal with a little Yakuza spy.

"Okay, for starters. The staff's name is Bonez. Bonez the Cane."

From there, Ki and Xillian set off to the Marriage Rocks on the southeastern side of Ise-Shima, and Ki did what he forbade himself from doing. Bonez became so hot that Ki had to set it on the backseat.

Xillian consumed some water and birthed wet, juicy words.

"I've heard of monks doing some incredible things in the past, but it only seemed like fairy tales and myth. Then you, from the far shores of fast food and television, come in contact with a godly appendage?" Xillian seemed totally bewildered by the idea.

"It's hard for me to believe, yet…"

Ki now assumed whenever Xillian played the kind and curious sweetheart, she was faking herself. It was all a ploy to get closer to his mother and find the Hattori Honzo's land rights. He best make her believe she was on the right trail.

"Yeah, I am Zepp, the wielder of magic appendages. Hear me roar."

A flash of Xillian's true self appeared from his humor, and fire ignited in the rearview mirror. They both looked back to see that the back seat was on fire with Bonez' engravings illuminated with a cool blue igneous.

Pulling over with smoke billowing from the windows, Xillian took off her sweatshirt and snuffed out the flame. After Ki saw that she had the fire covered, he grabbed Bonez and looked around at where they had stopped, knowing right away that Toko Tuki had set that fire for two reasons. One being Tuki was pissed Ki was revealing so much, and the other being a sign that Suga Duka was close by.

The sun was setting fast beyond the treeline, giving a beautiful orange glow to the ocean water. The entire sky surrounding the sunset held storm clouds, yet rays of light beamed through the thinner wisps of mist as if the burning sun was cutting through the storm. A drizzle tickled his scarred cheek and nose.

Ki left Xillian and walked the oceanfront path to two massive dragon stone guardians. An unknown drum in the vicinity thundered full of bass, filling Ki with a tribal instinct, filling him with so much power he wanted to hug the sun itself. Powerful yet bewildered, he searched for the slow melodic boom over the coastal railing and found that it was the swell rolling into a metal gate used for damming the estuary. *What a beautiful sound made by water and steel.*

Frog sculptures lay beyond as the shrine overseer and god. He continued past the dragons and followed amazing natural hues of smooth breakwater boulders that looked like hardened ocean swells themselves. No one was around except the dozens of interspersed human-sized frog sculptures secured around the rocky coastal bend like it was their little village. They really were deep and far away from civilization, even though this coastal shine area was at the foot of a small village, not a soul was to be seen.

Ki moved with one hand pushing Bonez into the ground and one hand sliding over the smooth boulders of the break wall, meandering around a bend to finally find the two mystical rocks tied together with a sacred rope. A golden green toad wedged in with the boulders as their wedding officiant.

She will be facing an enshrined leap towards a rocky reunion of Sun, Moon, and Sea. Ki's eyes went from the frog shrine up to the shrine on top of the larger sea rock, then to the moon rising over Fuji Mountain far off in the distance, and then back to where the sun had been before moving along its path of regional slumber. He turned around and mused at his mother's cleverness, lazily searching the area.

He marked the trees, studied the shore's water line, and listened to the water drum on the river's gate. Then, as he turned in the degree not yet studied, he saw Toko Tuki face to face with a hollow in the cliffside and past the sacred frog cleansing station with mountain water running down bamboo shoots out of three frog mouths.

The hollow went deep and Ki had to stretch his legs over a few barriers and climb some boulder blockades to reach it. Tuki watched giddily as he laboriously did this, then shot a look over his shoulder. Ki turned around to find Xillian walking alongside the waterfront. She stopped at the Meoto Iwa overlook and Ki ducked behind a boulder.

Waiting for a moment, he slowly rose to watch Xillian more covertly. Mist was rolling in fast around her as she rubbed the golden toad between its eyes.

Satisfied she wouldn't find his hollow, Ki turned around and crouched deeper into the cave. Below a trickling spring, the tip of a red chin with a golden line running down its center poked out from a clump of moss. Moving his hand into the shadow he moved the moss to the side and found Suga Duka inanimately waiting for him; the tiki head that hung in Leia's garden for as long as he could remember.

One day, Leia used Duka to explain a lesson to Ki and broke her in half, only to put her back together with a Japanese-style gold binding called Kintsugi. Showing that anything could be mended with the golden light of love.

A long golden line ran down Suga Duka's face, splitting her in two. Ki picked her up and found a note with the location of where he could find his mother, *Nachi Katsuura, first cabin past the waterfall.*

Xillian frustratingly called for him, competing with the clatter of rain, "Zepp, Zepp, I'm leaving. Have fun in the storm."

Ki watched her and effortlessly began to imagine her with a sword in her hand and barking orders to kill. She stood there in her tucked in white T serenely taking on the cold of the mist flowing in heavier and heavier.

Without the sweatshirt, she not only looked like a Yakuza, she looked like their damn boss.

"It's getting dark. I know a place around here where we can crash out. I think the car should air out before we drive again anyway."

Ki automatically began to inch up and Toko Tuki froze him in place with his rainbow eye. *Discipline Ki, no sense sleeping with the enemy,* he impressed on himself. He will wait for her to leave and somehow find his own way to Nachi Katsuura.

His backpack was still in her rental car, full of thrift store goodies, but nothing of importance. A parting gift to cushion his Irish goodbye.

Xillian, till we meet again, my little demon light.

LEX

"**D**on't call me that, Brock," Lexi told Brock while glaring into his eyes. The name was from another lifetime ago. An old high school relationship between a star linebacker and a popular sweetheart lovebug. Lexi hated the name because Brock used to say it as a dull-headed rhyme. Sex with Lex time to Flex.

She pinched the bridge of her nose to try and forget, inhaling a breath to relax. "I'm sorry about your father, Brock. It is good to see you after such a long time."

After talking with Mokes in the backyard of Leia's old house, Brock hit up Lexi on Instagram and set up a tea time to meet up when she got into town for the Holidays. Lexi was a permanent resident in Barcelona, Spain, so when she visited back home in Ellipsis, her time was pretty much always filled with catching up with old friends.

Today, outside on this chilly December morning, they sat at a cafe across from each other, both dabbing their tea bags in their cups.

"Thanks, Lexi. It's been tough, and that's actually kinda what I wanted to talk to you about." Brock leaned his big body over the table with his hands engulfing his cup to keep them warm.

"You… want to talk about your dad?"

Brock knew he had to be careful; he needed information about Ki, but in his heart, he also knew Lexi loved Ki more than him. He frowned in jealousy and heartache.

"If you'll allow it Lexi, yes, that is what I wanted to talk to you about today… I wanted to tell you about the night he died and how it happened."

"Ahh, okay…" Lexi rocked back and forth in her chair, not knowing whether to lean forward in a consoling manner or lean back defensively and ready for the unexpected. She studied Brock's sad eyes.

"Okay Brock, what happened?"

"Three and a half years ago, my father got into a composting partnership with an environmentalist group in town… The leader of this new environmentalist group was your old boyfriend, Ki La'dori." Brock paused. He had to be so careful around Lexi. She was much brighter than he was, and he didn't want her to catch him in a lie and walk away.

Lexi's eyebrows curled in angrily. "Mr. Zendolini was charged with running a criminal syndicate. How does trying to help the planet and breaking kneecaps for money correlate?" She leaned back defensively, cup on the table, and ready to run.

Brock laughed, "Yes, Popa Z, got caught up in bad things, but he was trying to change for the better. Little did he know to what extent Ki would go to get what *he* wanted."

Lexi cut in, leaning forward again. "Ki only wants what's best for the planet, Brock; you're the one that beat him up all those years ago. So, what are you trying to say? Ki got your father killed?" Lexi steamed in the brisk winter mist.

Brock rubbed his teacup handle with his thumb. It was time for his lie. He looked at Lexi and flushed. She was already so beautiful, but when she was angry and quick, Brock's heart wanted to beat out of his chest and lay in her lap for all eternity.

"Lexi, Ki tried to save my Father. He tried to get him out of the crime house and away from the bad people who wanted my Father dead… Ki was even there that fateful night Popa Z was shot…" A tear ran down his cheek and Lexi relaxed and inched out of her defensive posture.

"I was there too, but I never got a chance to thank Ki for trying… for what he did. That night… We were all together celebrating the 4th of July, and… My father was attacked. I still don't know who attacked him, but it was probably because of some mafioso crap he was involved in. They came in with suits and started gunning my family down."

"Oh my gosh Brock, I'm so sorry."

"Ki tackled the first hitman, which saved my father for a moment, but there was only so much we could do…"

Empathy turned to confusion on Lexi's face.

"Ki was charged with burning down Oil Derrick Harmony that night… How was he *celebrating* with you?"

"He vanished right after the shooting, and I have no idea why he set fire to Harmony. Maybe he thought the hitmen were associated with the Oil industry. I'm really not sure Lexi. Ki and my father worked together for months before this all went down. They talked about things I'm sure my father kept from me…" Brock steadied himself and leveled his eyes on Lexi's.

"This is why I wanted to talk with you today. Supposedly, Ki was released from prison a couple of weeks ago, and I want to find him, thank him, and talk to him about my father and what they were doing together."

The fog rolled in heavily within the last five minutes, an elemental veil. Brock put his cup to his lips to hide his smirk. He felt like he was the fog now, unstoppable, mysterious, and gray. His eyes watched Lexi over his steaming cup.

"That is so crazy." Lexi was lost in piecing it all together.

"Lexi, can you tell me anything about where to find Ki or maybe how to get a hold of him?"

She twirled her long brunette hair around in a temporary braid, thinking of what could help her old boyfriend find her other old boyfriend.

"Well, I have no idea Brock. Ki and I broke up a long time ago. Gosh, probably five years ago… I know he loved it here, in Ellipsis. Maybe check in with some of his friends, or maybe he's just at his mother Leia's house."

"I checked his house, and I checked in with his friends." Brock rubbed at his head, still bruised from all the punches Pines and Adam had given him.

"All I got from them was that Ki might have gone to Japan…"

"Japan, eh? Well, I know his mother met his father in Japan. Maybe he is just visiting there to get back to his roots."

She bought his story and was trying to help him now. Brock felt like he had her, like he could ask Lexi anything.

"Did Ki ever talk about anything magical he was working on? Anything supernatural?"

"Haha, that's funny you ask that question, Brock. Ki's whole life revolved around the magic of literature and poetry. Always keeping journals of his extraordinary journey and the magic within it."

The magic of literature and poetry… Brock cracked his knuckles and openly smiled at what Lexi had told him. He had found his clue, and he knew exactly where to look next.

Lex

NIGHTMARE

Lava slowly oozed its way over the purple plains and tannish rocks. Long fuming shadows of two masts and ribbed sails bobbed above the river of molten core. A starch white forearm reached up for the mast pole, identical to their bare bones.

"Hoist the Halyard! Heave. Ho. Heave. Ho." Clusters of clattering bone shapes moved around the deck like a blur. Yet, clear to the eye of the beholder, the scout on the topside mast tower rang down to his crew.

"Citadel Ahead!"

The Citadel was tall beyond the gigantic stone castle walls.

Suddenly, the memory warped into a sea of stars and then, in a psychedelic blink, flashed back to the colossus Citadel, only this time, it was collapsing backward into the pitch of night, bordered by a fiery halo.

The fiery halo was like a warp cylinder, burning, brightening, cooling down, and solidifying as a golden ring, quickly, or perhaps slowly, moving through the starry sky.

As the halo moved through space Ki's stomach irked and flipped upon itself. He had nobody here, and the burden of weight held no meaning anymore. An eye through the past and future was his lucid gift. Nothing else mattered.

Stars and planets zoomed by like trees on a highway. A ring, a halo, a portal falling through space. One sphere after another passed by his spirit eye until a blur occurred over his vision, until a recognizable sphere of yellow appeared in his path. Through his haze, a watermark Ki recognized as a tear during his sight recovery, gently solidified into a blue, green orb. His Mother lay waiting ahead for his return.

The halo rapidly warped through the cloudy atmosphere and plummeted down onto a tree covered mountain. Finally connected with its end was a ring of light with four flames. Beyond the firelight was a path lost amongst the shadows. A ghostly spot in the darkness, where ghosts whispered to your fears.

Ki landed in the center of the ring and bowed to the universal portal for its galactic transport. Helpless of his movements, Ki then floated over to one of the four bonfires with a moat of water around it and scooped up enough water with his invisible limb to watch it fall back down as lava.

Ecstasy ran through his transcendent floating eye, vibrating with tranquil amusement.

A hungry wind picked up from the opposite side of the ring, and Ki noticed again the path that led into flat darkness. His spirit blinked inside the hollow for a moment, and the night's stars showed enough light through the surrounding trees for him not to be transfused back into an ambiguous dimension of space.

He blinked back and continued floating down the path. A serpent wove its body over the freshly cut vegetation and meandered ahead at a speed Ki did not want to contend with. The world was at peace, and there was no reason to rush through nature.

As if his ease summoned a balance to bliss, a howling wind burst through the branches and cast his spirit to the side, where he was captured by a platoon of vines.

The idea of being a fearless spirit blew by him with the wind as shadows encroached on his position. Even though there were no faces or laughter, he felt like the shadows were doing a ceremonial dance around his captured soul.

As he conjured enough thought to wonder why a spirit could not escape earthly vines, the vines grew in girth and turned into the serpent that coiled him back against any attempt to get away.

Then with a *whoosh* of understanding, Ki knew what was to come. He had felt this way before, in the waking world. He had felt the anger, the hate, the fear of something over his shoulder, watching him. With the gales of wind seen as gray spirals through the night sky, a bubbling laugh creaked out of the woods, and suddenly, a tree in the middle of the hill in front of him came to life and rushed right for him. The knots turned, and its bark twisted around and around like a psychedelic trip until a face appeared, now inches from his spirit eye.

Teeth clunked out of the wood as it grew wide and split open. Heat escaped a fat knot above a mossy lip, and green eyes slowly opened to stare into his. As the face inside the tree morphed around in its babble, Ki's encapsulating serpent stretched forward and into the tree face's mouth, surrounded by jagged, blocky teeth. The slithering slide seemed to take up an eternity of time, yet finally its head poked through the tree's knotted nose and yawned a great fanged mouth until the serpent's tail made it through the other nostril. Now, with just a little space between the head and the tail, the great fangs leaned forward and bit down on its own end. An eternity snake as Uka Buka's nose ring.

Complete, the awakened tree of Uka Buka moved to the side to reveal a dark hole from where it unearthed, and Ki uncontrollably floated over to its voided being. For the hole swelled with a heartbeat and had an eternal feel.

Ki began his fall through the ring of slumber, falling with no direction. Down, down the rabbit hole he went.

Ki awoke from sleeping face down on his right arm. When he rolled to get his right arm out from under him, he stopped midway through, rolled back to his stomach, and then waited. If he rolled further on his right arm he felt like his arm would possibly break because he had no feeling in it. This could be the case with his left arm as well since he couldn't feel that either. Really, he had no idea what was happening, still drowsy and half asleep.

He lay there face down with a thin mat between him and the hard wooden floor, trying to reflect back on the dream he just had… *The dream, the dream.* Ki usually remembered dreams by the main color they were in. If the dream had a picture frame around it with lights in the corners, what color were the lights?

He looked over at Toko Tuki, who was still sleeping face up in the other room. His silhouette contour was so clear in the moonlight against the Japanese shades. Ki squeezed his eye shut, rolled his forehead on the sleeping pad, and tried imagining color.

Black, dark space. Darkness. Darkness and… red… fire. It was cold then it was hot, then it was cold. It was black water, then it was lava. Purple mountains under purple sky. Yellow. A halo. A snake… Uka Buka.

Lacking grace, he did a full somersault forward.

Arms both dangling at his sides, Toko Tuki had arisen and blankly looked straight at him through the shade.

Ki had found some kind of unoccupied dojo and settled there for the night. He went a long distance to escape prowling Xillian, who searched vigorously for him around the car and the Meoto

Iwa Shrine. He would have loved the spontaneity and adventure
of staying in a small, cozy room with a girl he had just met, but he
would probably have *woken up* as a skeleton if he'd gone that path. He
remembered then, a s*keleton crew on a skeleton ship, riding on a river of lava
into the gates of Hell.*

He remembered alright, and his mouth became as dry as the
bones that made up that ship.

Ki wagged his arms, ironically feeling boneless.

Tuki drifted back down to get horizontal, and Ki thought he'd
do the same. Tomorrow, he'll deal with Uka Buka, but tonight, he
needed rest.

After Ki found a spigot, he laid down again and closed his eyes.

He imagined a broken skull of smoke slowly pulling its natural
surroundings into itself and manifesting into Uka Buka. It was then
that he realized when he blew out that smoke at Adam and Pine's
house, it was Uka Buka who showed himself. Still a little inside of
him. Still a little alive.

Zero's Weird Sonnets

Mokes even asked if they were looking for magical scrolls. Brock cringed at his past ignorance and then cringed again at his present inconvenience of having to decipher through Ki's magical conceptions versus his actual magical experiences.

Brock was never attached to books. They were always there but had never cared to open themselves up for him. Now, however, he was surrounded by Ki's journals, notebooks, and sheets filled with words that made his head spin. When he first figured out that Ki's secrets were, of course, written down, he was exhilarated. Now the idea of Ki's secrets made him want to puke. All these words, all these rhymes that made absolutely no sense. Reading was Brock's least favorite thing. Reading his sworn enemy's poetic thoughts was downright torture.

After he skimmed through the first couple of booklets, he decided to categorize Ki's works. If he organized them by the time he had written them down, he could focus on his most recent stuff first.

As Brock unpacked, he found one moldy old book, *Treasure Island*, with a map tucked in as a page marker. Opening it up, he inadvertently skimmed to the back and found Ki's handwriting. He then reluctantly started reading the first sonnet on the page.

A Sonnet of the Sun
Aye the breeze of a blazon ray,
Let float a belly of plundersome weight,
To tarnish the wreckage of the once worrisome reap day.
Bring forth the light shall we end up on winter's hate.

As ignorance and wellbeing both make kin weak;
The angle of the transcendent Sun, peeps, mayhap for weeks.
Whence thy own chunder doth drag feet to go meekly.
A crisp mess of moony leaks.

"There!" A being calls, "The son to Sun arises in thy smoke."
Curious looking, "We hope they all don't choke."
But the Sun knows things, it hath the spectrum of heat;
It grows wealth whether be veggies or meat.

The Sun can't run, the Sun won't hide,
The Sun never hesitates in an up and down stride.

Brock gritted his teeth. "Man this sucks." He moved the map to the side and half-heartedly, almost without any thought behind the words, read the next sonnet.

Sonnet Toko Tuki
Tuki, a mark of elemental functionality,
Sentenced to few repeated blurps of thy legacy and title.
Hung in rainbow feathers on top of ye planked face of mortality.
Never wilting in flotation, nor written on Tuki's bridle.

Storms thy give prismatic energy, once circling the halo'd name.
When mountains rumble and winds gust,
When oceans roar and fire erupts.
This is the storm of rainbotic hovering lust.

A vortex keeping thy Uka Buka lineage thin.
Blizzard in thy mind, a tsunami falling down on thy body;
Quake in thy soul, forgiveth the reasons for thy sin.
Worthy in God's eye, but Uka sings with no grace in his rhapsody.

Patterns of nobility broken by a duki.
The fabric of thy jungle protected by chants of Toko Tuki.

The words here were written differently than the other writings he had. The letters were scribbled on top of each other like he was shaking and writing in the dark. Brock reread it, this time trying to decipher more of each line's meaning.

Planked face of mortality. Never wilting in flotation. That sounded super close to what the Illuminati was describing. Alive and floating like a tiki faced spirit. Singing of legacy and lineage… This Toko Tuki and Uka Buka seemed like ancient beings. *The fabric of thy Jungle.*

Brock's mouth hung open, drool puddling up in the pocket of his lower lip. He set the book down and opened up the map. X marked a spot up in their local mountains, in the elements… in the jungle.

"Gotcha Mother Fucker."

***

Water slapped Brock's face like thousands of tiny little elemental palms. Clapping his shoulder for his victory, washing his pride off into the drain, and refreshing him for his next task. It pained him to be working with the secret society that killed his father, but in order to honor his father he listened to him. *Always keep your friends close but your enemies closer.*

At the time Popa Z told him that, Brock thought he understood. Keep your enemies close so you knew their next move, and you can prepare better for what was to come. Now, having an actual enemy, he truly understood.

If he denied the Illuminati, not only would he possibly get merced but he would never know where to find them, never really able to get close. So, for now, his number one enemy was the enemy of his enemy, and he was getting more and more information day by day to settle this redemption of his. He would wait years, maybe even decades in order to strike efficiently. But why wait? Might as well slap a melon while it's fresh.

He got out of the shower and sat down at his computer. The anonymous email that initially briefed him on what to look for was pulled open. Subject being: Magical floating tiki head bounty.

Brock thought he found the beast, but what would he do with it once he was there? Was it invisible? Would it kill him right then and there? He wanted to simply go and find it for himself, but the repercussions were too extreme. He needed a little more guidance.

Enter, clicked on the keyboard, and his message was sent.

Found the whereabouts of where Ki initially came in contact with the 'Uka Buka' and 'Toko Tuki'. What's our next move?

He got up, put on his slacks, white button t-shirt, and his pinstripe vest. While he was straightening his collar, a ding came from his computer.

New Message:

Mr. Brock Zendolini, we are happy to hear you've found the possible location of what we have been searching for. If you could send us the coordinates, we will send a search party and significantly compensate you for your discovery. Thank You.

Brock cracked his knuckles. *Keep your friends close, but your enemies closer.* He was about to be let off, but he needed to get in close, and he also wanted to know more about what these cryptic spirits were.

How did Ki get so lucky? Why did he get all of the paranormal, supernatural abilities?

He slowly typed out his response and reread what he wrote:

Anonymous Society. The coordinates are vaulted up in my mind. I will be the guide for your search party. This will ensure I know if you have found something substantial or not. Here is an address where we can meet before the backpacking excursion. When can I expect them?

677 Cliff Dr. Ellipsis, California.

Brock sent the message, rolled his shoulders, stretched his joints, and anxiously welcomed another notifying ding from his computer.

New Message:

Tomorrow.

The MotherLand

Ki made it into a Family Mart and hand-signed his situation to the clerk. When he first entered the mart, the clerk had long, greasy hair and a scowl, and Ki quickly identified him with the lowlifes who worked in convenience stores in his hometown. However, this man's scowl turned to rays of sunshine when Ki began to deliver his dilemma. The clerk understood everything Ki had signed and just as easily handed him a free water and told him in English his Taxi was on its way.

Ah, yes, English. Ki rubbed his head awkwardly, "Arigato gozaimasu."

The taxi picked him up and dropped him off at Nachi Katsuura's epic waterfall. He wanted to show up to his moms on his own. He made it this far; might as well finish wearing the right hat.

He sat at the fall for a bit, soaking in its visible mist colored by the blue skies sun. He thought of the clerk's helpful demeanor and smile when Ki started their *interaction.* Life was what you made of it. Life was grand, life was about helping each other and making things better. It all made sense when looking into that clerk's eyes. Why was destruction and hate on the tip of so many tongues? He remembered the feeling of destruction in cahoots with the feeling of accomplishment. The feeling of gratitude for having the ability to put something to an end. *What a weird parable.*

Maybe I can think about it more on my walk up this mountain.

He began his crutch up the empty road, pondering if he was a bad person. Pondering if destruction was even a bad thing or merely another annotation of life itself. If everyone was like the Family Mart clerk, things would be too perfect, and everyone would be too similar if not the same.

Boring, Ki thought. *Unrealistic and boring.*

Rounding a long bend in the road, he was gifted with another waterfall on one side and an amazing view of the town Nachi Katsuura far below. His mother really knew how to choose a hideout, beautiful scenery, and absolutely no traffic; it was as crazy as the river of sweat pouring down his shoulders.

"How much farther Tuki?"

"Tuki." Tuki indifferently said, distracted by his surroundings.

Ki continued up and up for two more hours, and just as he was getting tired of seeing beautiful view after beautiful view, he saw a different beauty that gave him a spurt of energy, smoke rising from a chimney.

Trying not to scuffle too many leaves on his way up to the cabin door, Ki saw his mother Leia peep through the blinds of her window. A muffled yell came from inside.

"Ki!" She exclaimed as she opened the door and ran to her son.

"Oh Ki, you made it!" She hugged him and looked him over. Ki rose Suga Duka in one hand and Bonez the Cane in the other.

"Hi Mum." He beamed.

"That's all you brought with you?" She asked the question while checking on his facial scars. She even popped up his eye patch and gave his grotesque socket a look-see. Leia deserved this much, and Ki watched her happily. For some reason, she looked even younger than she had in Ellipsis. What a magical woman, filled with secrets of her own that she held to her chest with tight strings of charisma.

She brushed her hair to the side. Her old blue strip now extended up to a section of her bangs.

"So, you little skeleton. Tell me. What happened to all your stuff? Is this really all you brought with you?"

Ki clapped his mouth dryly. "I'll tell you my story over water and a comfy couch." He was a little alarmed that his mother called him a skeleton. For one, he had gained twenty pounds of muscle in prison, and for the other reason, Ki just had a deeply significant dream as a skeleton.

Leia took him inside and sat him down on her velvet blue couch. A table swung in front of him, then a beer, a water, and an unopened bottle of sake.

"Okay Son, I'm listening."

Ki put a few fingers around the Sapporo beer. Fish, Tawa, Alisano, Sokuru, Prison, Baggan's grief, the realization of a great country he never thought to explore… and Xillian… they all came to him then, just as Leia lined up his drinks, his emotions followed set, and Ki began to cry.

Tree Spiking

Leia presented two dozen nail spikes in the fold of her hands. "Tonight, I'm taking you tree spiking."

"*Tree*…spiking?" Ki knew what it was, but it was shocking coming from his mom's mouth.

"Ohhh yeah."

"It's December 28th, the middle of Winter. You have a jacket for me?"

"Yeah'p"

"… I'm going to have trouble keeping up." Ki twirled Bonez the Cane in the air, then looked down at his leg.

"I made this." Leia went to the food cupboard and pulled out her drill and a hunk of metal with a hollowed out pocket in the middle.

"Let me see Bonez son."

"Ahh, yeah sure, Mum." The handover was hesitant.

When Leia took it, her veins popped outside her tensing muscles, and a wave of tension through her body put her on her tippy toes, as if she were about to float away. It was almost like Xillian's experience, but the heavy wind blew inside of Leia. Ki also realized how ripped his mother had become.

"Powerful stuff." After taking a moment to soak in the cosmic discovery. She touched Bonez on her forehead and told Toko Tuki a simple word. "Peace."

She began drilling out the bolt in the stone ontop of Bonez.

Ki looked over at Toko Tuki, and Toko Tuki looked back at him with not a care in the world. Behind Tuki, red and white Christmas lights hung around the house, making Ki feel warm inside.

Leia put the triangular tannish stone on the counter, grabbed the hunk of metal for replacement, and finished fastening the bolt.

"A sleeve hammer Ki!" Leia exclaimed happily. "You can have a free hand for spike prep, and your staff can be your hammer while you're not crutching around from tree to tree.

The heat of his tea relieved a small bit of his anxiety.

"My hand can't grip… I won't be able to swing the hammer."

"Use your good hand for your crutch and hammer then, silly." Her smile solved it.

"My offhand is now my good hand." Ki said regretfully, but with a definite air that he was still going to try.

Leia ignored him and began preparing clothes, food, and tools for their night out.

"Let me brief you on what's going on. Yakuza want the land in order to sell the timber and make room for half a dozen Onsens and a golf course. They seem to be trying to Americanize the forest that's presently, as you can see, mostly untouched by greedy fingers."

Ki pointed at Leia's computer, and she nodded, "Password is skeletonkey."

Before she continued talking about the Yakuza's plan, Ki murmured his reflection on Leia's password. "You know I had a nightmare Mum."

"I didn't know hun." Her smile added to her sarcastic reply.

"I started off as a skeleton, actually. Part of a skeleton crew on a ship made of bones and sailing straight for a wicked looking Citadel on a river of lava."

Ki ignored her exclamations. He felt it last night, but he knew it now. This dream had meant something.

"Then I fell through space, zipped through the universe, and landed on a mountain that I used to backpack to. I landed in the middle of some kind of ritual *for* Uka Buka, and when I saw him again, it seemed like he was guarding some kind of portal…"

Leia frowned and furrowed her brow in worry. Earlier, after he was done crying, Ki showed her Toko Tuki and a bit of the light magic he could produce with Bonez the Cane. In prison, he tried to explain Uka Buka and Toko Tuki in letters, but he stopped because he thought supernatural ideas from prison made him seem crazy, even to his mother. Now, actually able to see Toko Tuki, he could explain the earthly spirits.

Ki focused down at the computer, "Ah oh."

"Ah oh, what? Not that anti-virus protection crap again?"

"Jacklyn Poxer sent me an email… I'll just read it to you."

Hello Dear Ki,
I regret to inform you that Brock has invaded your friends, Pines, and

Adam's home in search for anything to help him find you. The day before this break in I followed Brock and Mokes into your mom's backyard and overheard them talking about the Illuminati looking for you and this floating tiki spirit? Zooza and your friends are okay. Just wanted to fill you in. Hit me up if you have any questions.

    Cheers

    Mer'cerely, Pinky Boxer

Ki pushed the computer to the side and rubbed his hands over his buzzed head. "I can't believe it. My dream… The snake, Uka Buka. The Illuminati want to use Uka Buka for an interdimensional portal? I can't believe it. This is crazy right?" A glaze of tears began to swell over Ki's eye again.

"This… That is crazy, Ki. *Almost* too crazy for me to wrap my head around, but there are hidden forces amongst us and so much history of our world I need to enlighten you with."

The glaze in Ki's eye turned to stern conviction.

"I *will* tell you son… soon, but first we must concentrate on our mission tonight. We can get a lot done with the two of us. Why don't you respond to Jack's message while I make us a midnight snack for later."

He was okay with doing one thing at a time. It did seem like everything was suddenly piling up on them all at once. It was good to take a breath in moments like these. He slid the computer back over to himself and thought of another question he'd been meaning to ask his mother.

"How do we know these Hattori Land Rights are even still credible Mum?"

"I checked Son. Hattori Hanzo paid his property taxes for up to 50 years. The paperwork is almost ready to be signed over to me as well, but I was waiting for you. Signing the land rights over will expose me, so I need a wingman watching my six while that's happening." Leia continued, speaking over Ki's sudden outburst of argumentative squabble.

"It's not outrageous Ki, it's a numbers game, and a dangerous game, as we know." She could tell that didn't sell Ki on the idea. His eye patch haunting her from that night long ago.

"When are you going to get that missing tooth filled in?"

Ki shrugged and Leia smiled and shrugged as well. Of course, knowing there was no time for cosmetics, yet still entertained by her ruffian looking son.

"After I turn in an application to simply register for the property, the Yakuza will, at the very least, know I'm in town and will be trying to sabotage me. The most dangerous time will be while I wait for this registration certificate and the real estate due diligence review of the property seller's documentation before the final agreement. Aside from watching my back at the local post office, there is also the high possibility that the Yakuza found a way to deem themselves eligible to contest the land rights. If they contest, they won't win because our names are literally and legally on the paperwork, but it will allow them time and information on where I am, how I get my mail, and where I will be to conclude my land certificate." Leia tossed Ki a heavy flannel jacket and a green hoodie.

"Meanwhile I've been tree spiking almost every night." She watched his reaction midway from putting a long nail spike into a thick leather quiver.

"If we lose Ki. If. We. Lose. I want to break as much of their shit as worldly possible. We spike enough trees, and their *whole* plan collapses. If a chain saw breaks that's good, but if the machine saw at the lumber mill gets damaged from every piece of timber they try to cut, that's even better. That's why we put the spike high enough in the tree so the chainsaws miss, but the mill saws catch. They will lose time and money fixing saws and machines, hopefully to the point of abandoning their traitorous idea of chopping down their majestic forests for uncultural and unethical retreats. Of course, this is… if we lose. If we win, our forest's trees will simply have metal spikes in them. No harm done."

Leia gave Ki time to write out his response email and came back later with a short blade and sheath. Ki closed the laptop and snickered at her final tool.

"Expecting trouble?"

Leia shook her head, "Naw, just a precaution. It's hard getting a gun here. It was even hard getting this!"

***

Ki gripped one of the nail spikes in his working hand. It felt good. A super solid spike of steel. Long enough to go more than halfway through 2 to 3 feet of trunk.

Much like Ki's ankle brace that kept his foot from flopping

around, Leia had a metal brace with a rod and a small hydraulic tube attached to the outside of her calf.

"Watch me first."

Ki smiled. He was proud that he had such a savage environmentalist for a mother.

Her free foot pressed down onto her other heel like she was about to slip off her work boots, but instead the hydraulic rod pressed her up a good foot off the ground. Fully stilted on one leg she casually pulled a spike from her quiver and placed the tip at an upward angle on the trunk of the tree.

"We want to hammer in the spikes at an upward angle to cover more space, more possibility of their saws slapping against our bars of protection." She adjusted her body and gave five solid hammer strokes to the spike, slipping in a couple of inches every hit.

"Try to fully embed the spike and cover up the hole so the tree harvest scouts can't find them." Leia pulled some moss off the trunk of the cedar, concealed the hole, and retracted her rod stilt back down to the ground.

"Do 2 or 3 spikes every tree with a foot of separation. I'll take this line of trees, and you will take that line. We will pop out to the next tree line every 200 feet, so every 60 trees or so… Okay, let's get started."

Leia walked up to her second tree while Ki threw the spike he was holding from his good hand to his temporarily magnetic one; he then crutched over to his first tree, paralleling his mother. Toko Tuki watched, a little awe-struck and a little tentative, for trees were his ancestral brethren.

The magnet Leia strapped to Ki's hand worked out pretty well. Because he couldn't grip with that hand, the magnet held the spike enough in place to await Bonez's swing. The new sock of metal bolted on top of Bonez anchored back, and suddenly, a flash of light, lit up the worm engravings, and Bonez hammered the spike so hard it went through the entire tree trunk shooting out into the forest.

"Whoa… Hey, there's not even light around. How'd you do that?" Ki looked at Bonez and back at the hole it made through the cedar.

"What's that hun?"

"Come here. My *hammer* blasted the spike right through with unattainable holy power."

Leia strutted up and calmly put a kind hand on the cedar's bark.

"I see. To Bonez, these trees are like his ancestors or parents. Bonez probably *thinks-*" She shook her head incredulously at a fallen branch thinking for itself. "Thinks that it is harming its own by embedding metal spikes. Possibly Bonez also has reserves of light stored inside of it for emergencies." She hummed, satisfied with the cane's ability.

"Can I see Bonez again Son?" Ki handed the cane to his mom. She hugged Bonez in the nook of her arm and closed her eyes. After a moment, Leia's hand glowed slightly, and the sap began to seep down in the fresh gap through the tree, followed by wooden strings weaving themselves together like rapid growing vines. She picked up Bonez and showed the worm-engraved staff that the tree was healed and that everything was good. Light again flashed across the trunk as if checking on its recovery. Toko Tuki floated next to Leia and gave her two huge, long, wet tongue spirit licks on her face.

Not knowing what Tuki had done, Leia rubbed her cheek and gave Ki a look that said she'd explain her powers later.

"See Bonez, the tree will heal over the spike and cause no harm. The spike only acts as a protector for its wooden kin… Tuki, can you tell that to Bonez if it didn't sink in. It's time to get to work."

They worked all night, mostly tree for tree. Where Leia was quick on her feet, Ki was quick with his hands. Little flashes of light imbued the spikes as Bonez popped them in with one tender kiss.

Working up a sweat all day and night, and finally doing some productive vigilantism with his mother, Ki felt extremely happy. He stood at rest watching Leia finish another tree and peered around at the vastness of the forest.

"Hey Mom, it looks like there's some kind of dwelling over there to the East."

Leia walked over to him as she checked how many spikes she had left in her quiver. "We did pretty well. Let's go eat our midnight snack and check it out, Ki. I worked up an appetite."

As they slowly moved East, Leia spun up a conversation, "Kumano Kodo is a web of shrines and pilgrimage trails. Kodo to me means, *the primal source of all rhythm*. These shrines on this path, deep in the forest, away from the populace, and honored by the truly devoted, definitely tell of a Japanese story song long ago. Up ahead, I'm guessing, is one of the shrines that are a part of these routes, which help people travel more easily from shrine to shrine on the Kii Peninsula."

They reached the shrine, and to Ki's absolute amazement, it had a beautiful view of the wilderness, Nachi coves, and the Pacific Ocean.

Leia clapped her hands in glee and began unpacking their sandwiches and snacks.

"We are very lucky today, for this is Amaterasu... the Goddess of the Sun and Universe, the Chief Kami Deity in the Shinto Pantheon. She is considered to be one of the three most precious children of their Father Izanagi-no-mikoto, the primordial god of creation and life. Him and his sister wife, Izanami, are manifestations during the awakening between two worlds, heaven and earth. Their union is said to have birthed Japan and its kami spirits. Their other children are Tsukuyomi, the Moon Goddess," Leia pointed to the moon over the water, "and Susanoo the God of Storm." Leia pointed at Ki and herself and giggled.

"We seriously need to protect this land Ki, or these amazing shrines holding their ancient gods will be lost. We need to be the storm that pushes back the plague." Leia pointed at headlights coming up the mountain.

"Some active rangers or even National Park advisors are with Yakuza. Routinely checking up on Hattori Honzo's land."

"What? I thought rangers had more environmental backbone than that." Ki asked incredulously before taking a big bite out of his sandwich with two strawberries on top.

Leia smiled at her son's creation. "No, Ki. You know how the Forest Service is in America. They are the ones responsible for industrial development, roads, oil exploration, logging, all that. No countries are protected by a high ranking stewarding association. It's a system based around tribal people honoring the land, people who see the land as their community, not a commodity. Unfortunately, honor has no teeth. The system can be manipulated by greedy men. Money, power, and signing contracts, right as the common people are distracted by something else. That is what has control over our forests.

"A partnership between a nonprofit organization and a private sector, designated by the government and the forestry service, is what Yakuza wants. They just need some nonprofit to request a massive scenic repair for the *well-being* of the ecological grounds, which they will get through loopholes and use of confusing words and articles as their pardon to do so.

"A golf course is considered an Effective Conservation Measure and the Yakuza could be trying to clear the forest to, sell the trees to Cargill, the worst palm oil company in the world, and then plot their Onsen Hotels around the golf course. Most of this forest will be wiped out, and his beautiful Amaterasu Shrine will be moved, completely disrupting the Kumano Kodo." Leia seemed like an Onsen herself, steaming hot mineral water from the belly of their Mother.

Ki gave Leia a moment of peace, then asked, "How do you have the power to heal trees Mum?"

Leia's shoulders visibly lowered and she comfortably eased herself into answering.

"There are people beyond normal loyal stewards of the land Ki. An ancient bloodline of people that were blessed by pure descendants of Mother Earth. Like angels of our world, the descendants are called the Sky Sisters, and there are Six of them. They enchanted a few devoted families with extra abilities to help preserve our planet. Unfortunately, there aren't many of us. However, I am one, and you, of course, are one as well…" Leia studied Ki's slack jaw, mutilated face, and the magical cane he held that had brought him the Earth spirit companion Toko Tuki.

"Yes, Ki, you without a doubt, are a Totem Clause Sentinel."

Fairy Ring

Jacklyn Poxer rolled onto a pair of titties and checked her phone for new messages. Tit to tit, armpits cuddling ears, and soft hairless skin warming inner passions. Poxer relaxed when she found Ki's reply. Her job was done. Ki counted on her for information and she delivered. She wanted to bask in the glory of her achievement, and what better time than the present.

The girl under her was the real estate agent who found out Brock Zendolini bought Ki's mom's house. She also had other things Pinky Boxer liked. She rubbed her tits on the other girls, slightly nipping them together for a tingling sensation down her spine and into her vagina. They smiled at each other and started making out, pressing boobs together and running hands along the sides of their soft, athletic bodies. Feeling each other twitch with pleasure.

Poxer loved her nickname just as much as she loved what it meant. As soon as Poxer was the age for socially acceptable sexual interaction, she started with the box and never went shaft. Being very hands-on and having a little more muscle on her than other girls, Jack was perceived as the pants-wearing lady in most of her relationships, especially because the girls she liked were skirt-wearing, pinky-brained, barbie girls. Hence the name Pinky Boxer.

When her girlfriend left, she threw some water in the kettle and finally allowed herself to read Ki's email while she waited for her tea.

Hi Pinky,

Thank you for finding that out. I don't know how you did it, but thanks a bunch. Since you already know the briefest snidbit of what is going on, I want to tell you the whole story. But, the whole story is mind blowing, out of this world, crazy freaking shit. I hope you take me as seriously as I think you do. I, for one, trust you and honestly think you're the only one who can help me with this next task.

The secret society that killed Brock's father is now looking for me to get to Uka Buka. Uka Buka is a floating tiki head that I once thought was just a figment of my imagination, but it turned out to be much more. A supernatural floating tiki spirit of Mother Earth, a child of hers empowered with the influence of destruction and rage.

It first found me when I went up to our local mountains with rage bursting out of my pores. The night I stumbled across its hovel, I must have awoken it strictly based off of how pissed I was, and then it attached itself to me. That night grew ever foreboding, and I could feel darkness creeping into me, but Mother Earth had created a balance to its darkened spirit and made a staff that I found near Uka's hovel. This staff, which is the one I carry now, imbues a magical light of love and another tiki spirit, Toko Tuki, the spirit of empathy and kindness.

Four years ago, the night the Yakuza took Tawa and Fish's life, was the night when Toko Tuki and Uka Buka fought. Uka Buka was defeated, but now I believe Uka restored himself and resides back in its hovel, awaiting another angry soul to attach itself to. I fear Brock is desperate enough to find this Uka Buka, and with the Illuminati's help…

I had a dream Jack, a nightmare just last night, that I floated back to Uka Buka Mountain to find ritual fires and a doorway underneath Uka Buka's tree. This doorway could be the very thing the Illuminati are after. My nightmare hinted at a far-off galaxy with skeletons and lava and scary fortresses. This… Galaxy of the Dead could be what that doorway leads to. Based on my old Illuminati discoveries, they did prove to be pretty satanic.

Here is what I propose to do. While I was in prison, I learned about magic rituals and portal building. If I make a magic circle at this sacred shrine in Japan and you make a magic circle at a holy site in Ellipsis, I may be able to transfer over Toko Tuki to you. Once Toko Tuki is with you, he can help guide you up Uka Buka Mountain, where you and Tuki can destroy the tree in which Uka Buka resides and bury that doorway into hell…

Wow. I told you this would sound out of this world crazy. If you're up for it, here is what you'll need to know for our portal ceremony.

First, you'll need a natural essence to secure your spirit circle. I think I will use rocks. Then, once your artifacts and energy-infused items are set and your desired fragrances of smoke are lingering in the air, begin with the manifestation of us succeeding in our quest, opening up a portal, and transferring a spirit of our Mother, who is most precious to her. Slowly whisper louder and louder these latin words, which mean, 'hear my soul ancient being of spherical wisdom, hear my breath of your creation, to transfer your spirit across to another, a friend of truth and no other', until that belief, your belief, triumphs over all other emotions and thoughts.'

I truly believe my voice and your voice can be heard across the world.

Bring all things that harness magic in your eye and be ready to die for it and *the world, for the planet does not react well to those who seek complacent life.*

Once the portal is open you will need various pieces of driftwood or sticks that you think will be able to harness the power of Toko Tuki's loving light.

I suggest using sage for wetting your staff and preparing it for a spirit transfer. Herbs as well are nice to cast about as offerings to the elemental gods of our world.

Find your sacred area outside.

Overview: Secure our ritual space, ease into our incantations, which will eventually link up, and open up the portal to help Tuki find a new staff to transfer into.

Also try and bring some human bones with you, Toko Tuki really likes those. I think you might be able to find some at Baggan's cemetery. And don't worry, Baggans knows all about Toko Tuki. He should be ready to help, with a little nudging of course.

Time is short, let us conduct the portal ceremony in exactly 24 hours? Being that it is on the midnight transition into the New Years, which should increase the spell's magical properties.

Remember, the Illuminati want Uka Buka probably for some bullshit, Earth destroying reason. We have to keep that in mind and stay vigilant.

Let me know what you think and if you have any questions. Haha, Good Luck and may the Force be with you.

She exhaled a spell of air and leaned her forearms on the kitchen counter. The kettle whistled with heat. Poxer will have to get working if she was going to make that timeline. Maybe she'd even conduct the ceremony at her Refill Store. Work was in the next 24 hours. Ki would be doing his ritual at midnight, but she would be smack dab in the beginning of New Year's Eve day.

The refill store could run itself with little supervision, she hoped.

Tea splashed into her cup of hot water and Poxer went for a run. White shirt, hoodie, net bag, yoga pants, everything she needed for the beach. It was five blocks away and a hundred steps down, not too far away, and she could always run back.

Poxer smiled. She always liked working out on her days off, and now she could work out and have fun looking for magical sticks. She felt like she was the luckiest girl in the world.

At the time Poxer sunk her toes in the sand, excitement overcame her, and she began her search by scurrying around like a crackhead looking for a pearl.

It was still early enough in the morning that there were only a handful of regular beach walkers out. She stuck a finger in her ear, feeling the power of the ocean in her lifted armpit, and pulled her finger out like she caught her berserk with a hook and flung it to the sea. She wanted to soak in the good moments in her life.

Bad moments always seemed to linger around, slowing down time and making the sufferer ever more sleepy whilst under the dark cloud. Good moments went by in a flash. A day's celebration and you're back on the grind for your next dopamine hit. Good moments could be tarnished by a millisecond of an unsound decision. Your guard is down when everything is just dandy, then boom, real life comes back and smacks you on the ass.

Relatively, it was all good, but why not demand better? Why not fully encapsulate these magic moments and meditate on what was happening to her, giving her time to decipher how she wanted her future to unfold. Again, it only took a millisecond to make a wrong decision.

Poxer crossed her feet and bent her knees to the side until she sat on her bum. The yellow sand ran clean down to the shorebreak and the sun glistened a blanket of rainbow shimmer on the calm ripples behind the breaking waves.

Damn, was the water always this beautiful? Did it take a prime event to see the beauty that was always there?

She closed her eyes. Now, her ears picked up the crash of waves and grains of sand blowing in the wind. Her lip curled up in another smile. She wasn't even aware of the wind before. What other gifts did Earth have for her today?

Another deep inhale and exhale, and she switched her senses. The smell of an ocean. Salt, yes. Tar, yes, but there was another smell, wood, wet wood. Driftwood, yes. Poxer breathed again, this time ballooning her chest out and sucking her stomach in. This was her time. This was what living meant, and she didn't want to forget it. The freedom, the ease, the absorption of power in a natural essence.

Islands, Sea, God of driftwood. Bring me to what you so cherish so I may indeed cherish it as well. Give it a story that it so suavely deserves. Let us connect. Let us live as one and embark on this wooden quest. Poxer invoked the expanse of the Pacific Ocean.

Still with her eyes closed, she got up and walked ankle-deep in the water, crouched, and blew her little button nose in her hand cupped with ocean. She stayed at a crouch for a couple of wave sets, then turned around, opened her eyes, and closed her eyes in a tic, then opened them again and began drawing a large pentacle in the sand. Still acknowledging it as a cute star or the powerful Seal of Solomon. Even though a true star triumphant overall, it was just a little too pink for curly-haired Pinky Boxer. A Seal fit her energy lingo a little better.

Standing in the center of the pentagon, she caught woody smells in the wind. A sorcerer's pentacle readying her for the hunt.

For a mile, piles of logs, driftwood, and sticks were all bundled together at the base of the cliff. Poxer managed her walk with a conscious heart and focused nose. She looked under vast amounts of perceived rubbish to find the right stick. Some were smelly, yes, some knotted and gnarled, many thin and smooth, and a few holey and etched in curving wooden patterns.

The sticks that made it over her shoulder were thicker logs, the length of her leg, and had all of the characteristics in one. When her bag was full of cool rocks, and her sticks began to jostle out of the bundle on her shoulder, she wondered if she would find any human bones on the beach. Even if she had, she didn't have enough room on her shoulder for this trip, so she ran up to her house and quickly returned for more.

Finally she found a really special piece of driftwood she thought would do good for the upcoming ritual. Its surface almost looked like a long bone, but it was holey and worm-engraved with its top pocketed just right with three wooden curled fingers, perfect for holding a stone or clump of moss.

After her second fill, she thanked the Great Sea and headed home for her next phase, preparation of the sacred space.

She went home, grabbed some pots, and snuck over to Leia's house, which was pretty much like a nursery. Poxer hopped to see Brock or Mokes there. She prayed to be able to pinky box those dumb ears of Zendolini's. Reminding her again to keep her cool and stay in Zen. These plant transfers wanted a calm and happy pot transition, and one mistake could ruin this magical experience she was going through.

Poxer took clippings of the the large plants in Leia's garden. To her, it wasn't stealing, it was propagation. When she took the entire plant, she excused herself of wrongdoing by the basis of protecting them. If she ever saw Leia, she'd say she saved her flowers from the mad Zendolini man. Plus, they were so beautiful, they didn't belong in the care of a brute. They needed a delicate, carrying touch of a box hound.

Poxer always wanted an excuse for Leia to notice her. The hot mom that Poxer always dreamt of helping in the garden. Now her excuse seemed heroic, helping her son make a spirit portal and saving her plants from the villain. She smiled at Leia's presumed reaction.

After she had enough plants for her fairy ring, Poxer set them out in front of Leia's house tucked behind a grand Oak, and ready for a quick pickup. The plant and flower pots filed in nicely in the front-middle portion of her jeep, leaving enough space in the back for her sticks and rocks.

She definitely would have had the portal summoning at her house, but dreaded work had to be a top priority. In this case, she would take everything to the very small but very zen back patio or her Refill Store. She also felt it was a good idea because the Refill Store was a successful manifestation of her dream in helping the planet. Maybe Toko Tuki would sense that. It was all about appealing to the spirits right? *Well, let's bring on the magic.*

Aside from being stoked to finally be able to tap into real witchery and witness real occultism, she wanted to be desired by this new spirit. She wondered if it was a religious dearth that made her feel this way. A lifetime of lacking belief. But she believed in the Earth, and that's what excited her. Religion at its finest: chants, natural things, elements, beliefs, all rhythmically flowing together to create a warp hole for their God's literal descendent, the spirit Toko Tuki.

Once the jeep was packed with flowers, plants, crystals, intricate bowls, scarfs, candles, and two bundles of potential magical staves, she headed out to her shop. The steering wheel rubbed against the inside of her palm.

She always wondered why she felt a special connection with Ki, a connection she'd never felt before with anyone else. It must have been the probability of a fated transcendence. Taking the path parallel to Ki's was like a slow merge with destiny. The intertwining of paths and the unraveling of time had finally brought her to really believe in the holy spirit. Every relationship is an opportunity that will alter your life. She was happy to have chosen Ki as one of her important links. Now all she wanted was for the spirit to believe in her and to create a destiny link with Toko Tuki.

"Wow..." She exasperated out loud. "This is- Ball Stick - cool."

The sudden urge to jump out of her automotive *machine* and roll into a field of flowers was staggering. Luckily, Leia's orange yarrow was sitting next to her, and she massaged its stems to put her at ease with her earthy connection.

As thoughts of Ki faded, his mother Leia rose into her imagination, like rubbing the plant stem was like rubbing a genie lamp that held a seductive lady of the forest inside. A Stewarding Ranger in uniform with a wispy foxtail. It was a lusty wish that gave her a tingling explosion above her car seat. Again, she desperately wanted to be out of this man-made concoction. The sensuality drove her with power which could be a useful form of magical energy to manifest before the ritual.

Power, magic, and the creation of a welcoming setting. Desire morphing into passion, passion into an intense feeling. It all circled back to the magic. It was the connection of objects and the bonding of natural things, the elemental dialog towards a creation that every atom desires, love.

Moving all her trinkets and natural talismans into her Refill Shop's back patio was a relief. Finally she was where she belonged. A sanctuary of worship, love, and peace.

The potted plants created a thirteen-foot circle with only an inch of space between their bushy ends. The Fairy ring's main piece, completing the outer portion of the circle, was the Willow tree that rootingly stood in the center end of her patio. The Willow's earth protruding roots spiraled around in a fashion that was prominent and elevated just enough so she could kneel within the rooted pockets and bow down to its space as a sacred landing.

Next was her planetary tapestry that usually rested on the ceiling above her bookcase altar. She cut a big circle in the middle of it, attached its border to the trunk of the Willow's small twigs, knots, and branches, and tied twine tight around the tapestry and tree for additional security. If they were going to transfer a spirit across the world she'd need a portal on her side.

She placed the tapestry cut out of the center circle in the center of her ritual space and then laid her favorite staves around the tapestry's perimeter.

In the grooves of her rooted altar space she delicately organized her candles, herbs, trinkets, and gems.

A matchbox opened, and with a flick, the first flame inside her circle lit the tallest purple candle. She used that spirit flame to burn the end of her sage and lavender, then walked around her circular plant wall perimeter. She blew the cleansing smoke in between the branches and leaves of her natural guardian.

Colorful scarves were hung from Willow branch to Willow branch, sometimes tied on a branch at one end to hang loosely and flow in the wind.

She stood back to look at her sacred ceremonial fairy ring and noticed the black plant pots. Plastic in the realm of magic didn't vibe. She grabbed her gilded dagger and cut open the pots, letting little roots hit the floor.

"Don't worry little Earthlings- *fuck'n bitch* -I'll repot you tomorrow after our portal party. Enjoy- *ahaa, ahaa* -the air on your bottom side." Poxer gave a motherly smile at the cozy unbalanced plants securing her fairy ring, the driftwood circle in the middle, and the spherical Willow portal she had created.

Dirt sprawled across the patio haphazardly, and plants tilted into each other, now standing unnaturally on roots and clumps of soil. This felt right, and she began to feel good about tomorrow.

While locking up her Refill Store, an undercover establishment for her fairy circle space, she went over everything Ki told her in the email. It was getting dark and the lack of people around the plaza seemed eerie. A fitting time to remember the last thing she needed. It was time to journey off to the cemetery, where Baggans cocooned himself as the Keeper of Bones.

Keeper of Bones

The mostly full moon cast its white on the mist above and the yellow streetlight that bled across the ceiling of fog. Poxer was outside the cemetery and threw up her hood in a subconscious way of keeping ghosts from kissing the back of her neck. She opened the thick ancient door of the entry building and walked in. It was quiet and cold, and Baggans wasn't behind the main desk. She got the irking feeling that she would have to search for him in the scary movie cliche of a misty graveyard, difficult to see even five feet before you. Staying around in this cold empty room wasn't much better though. It was as if the dead outside gave more life than the empty, dull office she was in.

Jack Poxer started her meander around the tombstones with eyes glancing side to side for any kind of movement. Walking along a narrow path amongst the graves, she eventually began to rotate her torso more as she checked over her shoulder at every other step. As she continued her walk, a white mass stood prominently in the gray haze.

'It just takes a little bitty belief in the supernatural, and they all rush in to- *bop, ahh* -greet me on my day of transcendence." She noted to herself, slowly putting one foot in front of the other. Poxer wanted to yell for Baggans at this point. 'Hey Bags, where the hell are you, big guy?' But that might be rude to the spirits around here, and if she was going to have a little Tiki spirit puppy by tomorrow, she better get used to having goosebumps.

The white mass was a grand mausoleum with open-winged bird sculptures engraved in the corners of its roofs. Candlelight illuminated the edge of the entrance, and she slowly peeped around the doorway, expecting the undead of conducting a seance ritual.

Suddenly, a hand clapped onto her shoulder, and Poxer flew inside, manically throwing off her hood to see what was behind her.

Baggans grumbled echoing laughter. "Jack? I gotchu good you scallywag… What are you doing here?"

Still coughing out her excitement, Poxer put a hand to her chest. "I- *wha' whoop 'bop'* -was looking- *fucK* -for you. What are *you* doing all the way out- *'bird whistle'* -here?"

Baggans shuffled inside, picked up a lit candle on the ground, and lit a torch in the corner of the mausoleum.

"Well, I'm working." He laughed again. "Gotta make sure the souls are at rest, you know what I mean? Rest In Peace and all that. Gotta make sure there's no gravediggers…"

Baggans turned his jolly brows into a piercing stare. "So, what's up Jack?"

Her mouth dropped in her realization that she was exactly what Baggans was looking out for. How could she possibly ask him for a pile of bones?

"Well, I'll start from the top. Ki wanted-"

"Oh, Ki sent you, eh?" Baggans leaned back against the wall with the torchlight flickering in his left eye.

"This oughta be interesting."

"Yes, yes, very interesting indeed," Poxer huffed with a tense tic that twisted her neck upwards in a hard angle. She brushed her curly blonde hair out of her eyes and looked down at her Converse on the stone tile.

"We need… Bones." She started gathering her confidence, the worst part was over.

"We need- *Cunt!* -bones for a spirit ritual, Bags. He said you'd understand."

Eyes bulging, Baggans picked himself off the stonewall and started to pace the room with a family of dead bodies drawered up all around them.

"This is exactly what peaceful gravekeepers don't do Jack. Why do you need bones? For that little Tiki spirit he has, I'm guessing?"

"You know about Toko Tuki?" Poxer's heart lodged itself into her throat. Belief overwhelmed her, flushed her with warmth, pigeon-toed her feet, and made her stroke back her blond curly hair even more. She wanted her eyes even though all of her feeling was in her heart. Poxer believed before, but now she really really believed, especially if Baggans had already seen the spirit.

Baggans nodded with a smile. "Yeah, pretty crazy, huh? The first time I saw Tuki, it pulled three bones out of a crypt."

Excitement brimming, Poxer stepped closer in her adamant

sincerity.

"Wow, the spirit can actually- *Bop, Bam* -" Poxer blew a kiss as her tic. "Touch and move things in our realm?"

She thought about it almost stupefied, while rolling back her shoulders to start tying back her blonde hair inadvertently. "Ki was going to- *bugNUTS* -transfer Tuki over to me in a full moon ritual tomorrow. He said to gather things Tuki would want to attach itself to or feel welcomed to."

Baggans' face twisted in dissent.

"Bags, I heard Brock- mother FUCKer -talking about finding a darkened tiki spirit up in our mountains, and- *wee'o, 'click'* -we think he will use it for evil stuff. Illuminati stuff."

Baggans remembered all the blood in the lower den of the Zendolini warehouse that 4th of July. He remembered that feeling of evil in the halls. Illuminati escaping, Yakuza killing his friends. He shook off the pain of the night.

Poxer's stomach rumbled, echoing as well as their voices did in the mausoleum.

"Let's go get something to eat Jack. You can tell me more about this spirit transfer stuff then. I don't want to disturb the peace of the dead anymore than we already have here."

Poxer nodded weakly, and they headed out.

Portal Ceremony

The next day held a beautiful open blue sky and sunny rays. A brisk chill still clung to the air, but melted over Poxer's skin in fragments as she did the final preparations under the stark branches of the Refill Store's Willow Tree.

Smoke rose all around her as she knelt in a Child's Pose prayer. Four herbs, damiana leaf, echinacea, hyssop, and valerian root, burned in bowls around her. She straightened up and did long smokey herbal inhales as if the smoke itself were the spirits she so desired.

It was 6:30 A.M. in California, meaning it was 11:30 P.M. in Japan. A good time for both Ki and Poxer to be away from loitering eyes and still in the presence of the same day.

Poxer and Baggans had devised a plan where he would be upfront watching over the Refill Store while she conducted the Portal Ceremony in the back.

Poxer felt at ease within her fairy ring sanctuary and even more secure with a friend working her shop. She couldn't imagine explaining the science behind the organics of her refillable soap and its efficient distribution in barrels while summoning a tiki god through a portal in the back patio.

Nothing manufactured was inside her fairy ring. She was ready, and she wanted to begin her incantations early because she had no clothes on and no clock. Chilling excitement swelled over her and it was time to warm this baby up. Ki had told her to start sooner than later, and she guessed he would probably be early as well.

***

A plum of mugwort smoke twirled up past a scarred cheek and a dark green eye patch. Ki was late. He also didn't think about the tides when planning Tuki's ritual. Two days before, when he was observing the Meoto Iwa rocks, it was low tide and easy to walk to from the shore. Now the tide was high, so high the ocean water submerged the entire beach and a large portion of the old walking path.

Smoke blew out again, making the shrine on top of the larger rock look mystical. Ki snubbed out the mugwort and sage joint and swallowed the rest down. He would have to swim across the channel of water between the Meoto and the Northern coast of Ise-Shima National Forest in Ise Bay.

The Meoto Iwa were two sacred sea rocks connected with a beautifully intertwined thick ceremonial shimenawa rope that acts as a division between spirit and earthly realms. The actual shrine itself was posted on the peak of a 30 foot-high jagged sea rock.

The loud rhythmic booms of the ocean swell hitting the steel gate dam of the nearby estuary pumped him up for his swim in winter water, and then after his swim, he'd have to climb up the treacherous rock, and all without losing his spark. All he needed up on top of that rock was fire, and a 15 minute swim swashed in his way.

While crouching down next to a Kami frog sculpture, he looked around for a boat, plank, or even a log, but Japan was so clean there was nothing to help him across. Ki slid Bonez the Cane behind his belt and plopped his sock in his mouth, a lighter wrapped inside to keep dry. He had 30 minutes to get up to the shrine and begin the ritual.

Toko Tuki bobbed in front of Ki looking curious at him, wondering why he was being so secretive and slipping in the freezing ocean water in the middle of the night. Ki looked between the two Meoto Iwa rocks and stared at the snowy peak of the ominous Fuji Mountain. What a beautiful world he thought. The weirder his journey got, the more beautiful life became. Because of this moment he had no regrets. Shivers ran down his spine, and he began to limp into the water, finally slipping in with his chin up high and a sock stuffed in his mouth.

Finishing his frog stroke, he ascended onto the rocky ledge of big Meoto and was thankful he wore his shoes. Even then the ledge was so steep that he had to use his hand to pull him up on most of the inclines. One foot being limp as a dead fish, dragged along the rocks, and one hand unable to clench, made him have to pull himself up with his forearm and thigh while finding deep groves to fit and stabilize himself with his good hand and foot, slowly inching towards the top.

Once achieved, he knelt on the cliff's edge before the epically isolated Shinto shrine. Water filled his eye, fire burned along his body. It was an interesting feeling of warmth after his polar plunge.

He thought perhaps it was the workout from his climb, yet when he looked down, he discovered he was only half right. His shirt was torn, and his arms bloody, so bloody a pool of blood puddled up in between his knees. Nevertheless, the warmth of the blood felt good, and he decided now was a better time than any to get started.

Bonez came out and helped Ki around to slowly pick up loose rocks and stack them three or four high in a circle formation. He made thirteen stacks coming off the shrine as its centerpiece. He pulled out a wooden bowl from his bag, two candles, and unraveled his lighter from his sock. He slowly removed his clothes while Toko Tuki zipped around the high rock edge, almost creating a breeze in his merry speed; as if Toko Tuki were playing with the invisible spirits of the Meoto Iwa Kami.

Ki's heart wrenched together as he wrung out the water and blood from his shirt into his wooden bowl. He felt like he was abandoning his puppy, which Tuki seemed to resemble more and more every day. Always there with him, always happy, always loyal.

Naked now, Ki threw his clothes in his bag and set it outside his stone bordered circle. While his blood was still wet, he dotted and clawed tribal markings over his body and face with it. He caught a weird feeling of deja vu from the Zeppelin Blood Moon night as it was time to make fire.

Five minutes went by and his lighter wouldn't light. He was sure it was dry enough when he unraveled it from his sock, but it just wasn't sparking up. Anxious at the time, Ki grumbled at Toko Tuki to stop racing around.

Maybe Tuki's playful gusts were stopping the flame. "Tuk, Tuk, slow down. Take it easy… Toko Tuki, come here now!" Tuki flew over with a grand and colorful smile after Ki set his parental order.

"Tuki, I have to tell you why we are here." Tuki tilted its head, then turned and looked off towards Fuji Mountain.

"Tuki?" He asked as if the beautiful mountain and midnight venture had already explained the reason.

Ki bowed his head, watching blood still drip from his forearms. He made sure to catch it in the water bowl if he could. He looked back up to bobbing Tuki.

"Tuki, something very bad is coming and I need your help." Tuki became stern-faced and dashed a little closer to Ki's nose.

"Uka Buka," Toko shook its head wildly as Ki voiced the name.

"Yep, Uka Buka is coming back. I need to transfer you to a friend of mine to help her find Uka Buka before the really really bad people do."

Toko Tuki looked disappointed in Ki and turned its head again to distant Fuji Mountain.

"Tuki…" Ki didn't know what to say. He took a breath and went back to trying to flick on his flame. He thought the flame would come now that Toko Tuki had stopped flying around. Alas, it did not, and without fire, he could not complete the elemental bond that was essential for any kind of spiritual magic.

Ki dropped the lighter and bowed his head, defeated.

"I am a La'dori, born in Ellipsis, and vanquisher of evil. May you and yours be blessed on this night. For outer spheres of light make your coupled Earthly presence renowned and holy."

Toko Tuki looked around at the shrine, the rocks, the blood on Ki's arms, and then slid under his kneeled legs to peer up at him. Somberly, Toko Tuki closed his eyes in a sort of meditation.

Ki watched his chest blood dribble down and splat onto Tuki's wooden face. Embracing the calm serenity of the moment, he closed his eye too. Embracing the world in which he had no regrets in.

Another form of heat warmed Ki's right thigh, and he opened his eye to see Bonez the Cane, imbued with extraordinary light, shining out of the worm-engraved patterns. Ki dipped his hand in his wooden bowl and grasped Bonez, anticipating a singe of burning heat, but the light, the heat, flowed into him, coursing through his veins, becoming one with his cane.

Ki looked from Bonez the Cane to the candles and finally back down to Tuki, who was still meditating between his thighs.

"Bonez, fire?" Ki asked, feeling weirdly like a caveman sorcerer.

Toko Tuki opened one eye, sparkling from the moon overhead with all the colors of the rainbow swirling together, the swirl softening the shock of seeing an eye that color; and a moment after it closed again, Tuki softly spoke, almost as an intriguing whisper, a word that Ki had never heard before.

"Taloonka…"

Ki repeated the word, "Taloonka." The top of Bonez sparked up with an orange flicker. "Taloonka…" He said a little more confidently, and the spark encompassed the entire top of Bonez. There was no more hammer sock nor triangular stone on Bonez tonight. Ki and his mom thought Bonez should just be organic Bonez for this ritual. Ki shifted side to side, then pointed his index finger at one of the purple candles in front of him.

"TALOONKA!" He ordered, and a flame shot out of Bonez and scorched the candle in a splurge of wax, alas lighting the wick.

"Thank you Toko Tuki. Brother of my God." Ki stood and a massive gale of wind picked up from the SouthEast. The wind was so sudden and steady, so fierce yet calm, that Ki believed the only explanation was that Jacklyn Poxer had begun her incantations.

It was time. Toko Tuki flew up and faced the wind, its headdress feathers blowing back. Ki crutched over in front of the Kami shrine, square to the North, and framing Fuji Mountain. Bonez, still illuminated, rose above Ki as he put his arms up as if to encapsulate the sky, and spoke more prominently than ever before.

"Taloonka!"

He sensed the twin flames behind him and closed his eye, silently moving his mouth to whatever flow the world had cast for him, eventually voicing the unknown yet intuitive language. "Sha ku lamaki naki ruu sinapolofrono ke pa nini no so ni ruu… Sha ku lamaki naki ruu sinapolofrono ke pa nini no so ni ruu…" As he repeated his chant, Toko Tuki's chant, he felt a shroud form above his stone stacked circle, and the elements of wind, water, fire, and blood twisted together in front of him, splitting, growing, morphing into an interdimensional hole.

He opened his eye and saw Toko Tuki's eye, yet Tuki was still facing East. This new eye floated in the shrine's center as the portal coalesced around it. The eye melted into a whirl of melding colors.

Floating eight feet high off the rock and facing the shrine, Toko Tuki hypnotically drew himself between Ki and the portal. As the wind ripped around them, Ki's blood from his cuts began to elevate and pull towards Tuki. The blood from the bowl rose to meet the other bloody streamlines, twisting in a helix and slowly wrapping around Toko Tuki in the shape of a bandoleer. Ki persisted in his chants and felt his way around the sounds of the elements.

"Ol La Utu Uta lanye Calm Walke shinsuku lani uzz blapper boosuru. Kano Ka to me sarru katagura lili ke ke."

Gray daylight beamed through the center of the portal. Toko Tuki's blood bandoleer morphed into a rotating boomerang that spun revolutions around its plank feathered head, then solidified and became an orbiting bloody hula hoop.

Throat fatiguing from long moments of chants, he finally caught a girl's harmonic voice, singing her intuitive incantations and assembling the elements in a blizzard of gray on the other side.

***

A rustle of leaves shifted and ch-chattered as a wave of wind rolled around the perimeter of Poxer's Fairy Ring. It's been half an hour of repeated and refined incantations.

"Help bringeth the light inside thy cherished tree. Make her glow with- *Way'oo We'op* -an indigo hue. The power within burns to be free. Light in this way, spreading on through. Light in this way- *Fff* -spreading on through.

"We, the green Earth disciples, welcome your floating spirit. Space- *weep* -available through a wormhole in time. Stars could not free it. Shine beyond the darkness, dear- *'whistle'* -friend of spherical proportion. May my worth gander no illusion-" The ceaseless breeze flattened Poxer's resolve. At first, it blew in from the West, but then it shifted and blew straight at her from a crack in the bark of the Willow Tree.

She picked up again with a steady eye on the Willow, "Guide my- ASS -soul into your Witchcraft now. Make a portal big enough to fit a cow-"

Poxer laughed as the bordered tapestry flapped, slapped, and blew right off the little branches that held it up. Poxer looked around at her trinkets and gems sprawled amongst the tree's roots and picked out a pointy piece of obsidian and a large hunk of tourmaline.

She scurried over, grabbed the fallen border, and hammered in the obsidian with the black hunk of gem. She raced back, grabbed her vine-gilded hilt on her dagger, and pulled her arm back behind her hip before stabbing the tapestry border to the lower part of the tree.

Poxer hesitated and felt like the plants securing the circle branched a little taller, giving off an air of hope. Maybe they believed her to be a transcended soul of protection and kindness. At least, that's what she wanted them to believe. *Fight on little Greenlings.*

She brushed her hand over the Willow's bark and abruptly wrapped her arms around the trunk in a T fashion. The trunk being too vast to even come close to an integral hug. Time didn't exist in moments like these. Doing what was right was like undoing time because universal flow turns into an acceptance of fluidic destiny.

Fire instantly ignited behind her, and a stick of driftwood caught flame, charring the cutout portion of the tapestry lying in the center of the Fairy Ring. Turning, Poxer stumbled forward as she got caught up in the trees' ever expanding exhale and pounced on the flame, patting out the stick but unable to help the circular piece of tapestry. The center slowly burned out to the edges with unusually high flames, and she hurriedly collected all her staves together that bordered it. She watched the apex of the flame twist around in a red whirlwind.

"Water!" Poxer yelled.

Baggans was surprised to see the Refill Store so busy at 6:30 in the morning, but he was even more surprised at Poxer's yelp for water.

He handed back a jar of salt to a beautiful older woman, "One moment please," connecting his apologies with the other two people behind the salt of the earth woman, he ran to the back patio. When he opened the curtain, his eyes widened at the scene. A gray whirlwind storm was encapsulated in Poxer's Fairy Ring, with a red flame tornado'ing at its center and glimpses of colorful scarfs swirling around like dragon serpents trapped in a squall. The amazing part was how Leia's little plants and flowers contained the storm and didn't completely rip apart. The elements were working together.

There was a small gap between two of the plants.

"Water incoming!" Baggans yelled at Poxer while rolling a large metal water container through. As soon as it bumped over the clumps of soil and one stringy root, it vanished from sight. He only waited a couple moments after to see the center flame descend in its uprising.

Baggans rushed back to the front. "Okay, I'm back. How can I help you?" He was a tad askew, being it was very early in the morning, and he was a graveshift guy now. He was also used to working with the dead, yet now he was surrounded by angels. And finally, he really hoped Poxer would be alright in the eye of a spirit storm.

Another woman now stood next to the smartly curious older lady with long salt and pepper hair. This woman was young with punk rock energy, her long pink hair tied up in a spikey flair and checkered sleeves on her sweatshirt.

"Is everything alright back there?"

Baggans just stared for a moment. He wasn't expecting them to ask any questions. The morning chaos jumbled his mind so much that it tricked his mouth into telling the worried angels before him the truth.

"The owner of the shop is doing a spirit ritual in the back… It's just a little wild at the moment, is all." He broke them a dubious smile as their mouths opened in shock.

The old woman chimed in, "Can we see? It sounds like a blizzard back there."

Baggans gave her an unsure shake of his head.

"We won't disrupt the ceremony… please?" Six angelic eyes now fluttered at him. All seemingly very concerned yet steadfast, behind their charismatic eyes.

Baggans slowly turned around and opened the curtain to the back patio.

***

Through the blunderous wisps of the clenched winds, Jacklyn Poxer could hear Ki's voice calmly babble out his incantations. The wind from Japan carrying his voice through the Willow. She scooped the ash from the tapestry and dropped it over her head, sticking to her naked, sweaty, slick skin. Then moved in closer to the portal opening.

Stupefied, Poxer watched the portal like it was the best clip in a film she had ever seen. Toko Tuki was floating at its center with a ring of blood circulating around its tiki head. A nice chunk of the moon was peeking through Tuki's feathers, and a massive snowy mountain sat in the distance to his side. Tuki looked back at her in the windy night sky. A seemingly ancient image in a brand new day.

Within Ki's chants she could hear formations of the word Staff.

"EmbarKo Levioso Kat Ti O Laff shino kuro Stafo. Pinni ey steye, pinni ey stye, pic opn the staf. Show Tuki the staff." The voice growled in the end.

Face elongated in a flash of sudden acknowledgment, Poxer twisted around and grabbed two potential wizard staves. Toko Tuki was as unmoved and stoic as ever. She dropped them on the Willow roots and grabbed two more. Unmoved. Two more. Unmoved. Two more, unmoved. Until there was only one staff left, the one that had caught fire.

Poxer held the one staff above her head like it was undeniably the champion of sticks and slowly turned around to the portal. Toko

Tuki held its hardened face and floated further and further back.

As the tiki head hauntedly floated away like it was restrained by a large rubber band, the portal expanded, and Ki finally came into view. Knelt down on his shines, head bowed low, his chants still plundering on. He looked ravaged.

Torn, naked, and bloody, Ki grabbed his worm-engraved staff, which was completely illuminated with golden light, and held it with two hands in front of him. He looked into Poxer's world, then gave her a wink.

"TalOONKA!" And all at once, everything erupted. The staff blasted out a nova of fire light and Tuki slingshot forward through the portal and right past the staff Poxer held over her head. The fairy ring plants collapsed outward, and the storm ceased…

She watched the Willow grow its bark back over the midnight portal on the other side and slumped her shoulders in relief. She had done it. The feeling escaped her. The best way she could describe her feeling was that she yearned for the storm to come again.

"Jack?" A beautiful voice ground down into Poxer's soul. A voice that remedied her whole body of syndromes of pains, maladies, and tensions.

When she turned around there were four people in absolute awe, jaws unhinged and hands masking or capping their heads in disbelief.

Poxer eyed them for a moment and giggled, eventually causing the third woman with reddish hair and freckles on her high cheeks to chuckle out a coughing laugh. It was contagious, and everyone laughed together. Poxer began to cry hysterically, laughing so hard her tits bounced soulfully.

***

Ki stood up and looked towards the moon, then down at its reflection on the water below.

"So, how am I going to get down from here…"

In the shadow of the smooth rock cliff on shore, eyes watched a naked man silhouetted in the moon's glow. Silver glinted under the covert patient eyes, swinging a rope in one hand and a towel in the other.

Portal Ceremony

The Lot

Sitting on the one couch in Leia's house, smoke curled and wove itself around in the air in front of Brock and Mokes, waiting on the so-called Search Party. The secret society's message said they could expect the search party in one day, but as of now, it has been two. Their backpacking gear was ready and set by the front door, food was packed away, and anxiety bristled on end.

Mokes was also there that night the Illuminati came into the Zen warehouse with their perfect suits and flat uncaring eyes stuck on their mission. Mokes guessed that was what this search party was going to be like. A grip of suited-up murderers hoping to spill another gallon of blood.

"What's keeping these guys from mercing us once we find the tiki spirit grounds man? We will be up in the mountains, a day's hike away from civilization, and alone with secret society monsters able to turn invisible and untrackable within a moment's notice." Mokes bit at his nails and watched Brock longingly for a reliable answer.

Never being a stoner of any kind, Brock puffed on the weed Mokes had rolled up for them. He didn't like this day anymore than Mokes, but something called for him, pulling him towards the mountain. Even if his mind and body weren't ready to go, his spirit beckoned him to go.

He puffed at the joint again; it helped with his 'search party anxiety', and it helped soothe his excitement about discovering an unknown magic masked by Earth's creation.

"I don't know Mokes, we are just going to have to hope for the best. I was thinking this search party was going to be more nerds and scientists than hitmen. Mr. Z did business with these guys for decades, and they hold true to most of their deals." Brock cocked his head to the side, "Ah, but they might want to keep us quiet too. Hmm."

He passed the joint to Mokes and cracked his knuckles on his chest. Moke's face went white.

Brock knew he had to be more reassuring for his partner. "I'm sure it'll be fine bud. We will catch the vibes and puzzle out what to do later."

The day got later and later, the intensity boiled, and their contained molecules of energy became too much to stay put. Brock spent his time doing pushups and eating, while Mokes spent his time smoking and eating. Eventually, Brock fell asleep, and Mokes went outside to walk around and watch the stars. If it was going to be his last couple of days alive, he wanted more star time, making him feel small in a universe so big.

If he left this planet, maybe his soul could travel to another galaxy. He wondered about the possibilities out there. He wondered about the possibilities he'd have here on Earth, his home, a place and time that felt like heaven. He wondered his way over to his van. He wondered. The van was put in neutral and the wheels rolled it forward to the next house.

Mokes turned over the engine and got out of there. He didn't want to die yet. Not today.

***

A knock came from Leia's front door, and Brock woke up. "Mokes?"

He moved over to the door and opened it. Rugged earth-toned shapes blocked the driveway, and Brock had to arch his head back to see the big fellow's face and squint low and around to pick up the others behind him.

"Ah, glad you could make it." The time was 11:45 p.m. December 31st.

"Aye, there Mate! Names Moorendo. Could we come in?" The big African muscle carried two duffle bags and a large camping backpack. His voice rumbled inside the entry room with a vibration that was surprisingly calming.

"Yeah."

Moorendo pivoted back a step to make room for a darkened maiden of the cauldron. Just by looking at her, Brock could tell she was a witch. She had long black hair that went down to her waist and entangled itself in multiple twine pendants and a green and brown scarf. A bag was slung across her shoulder, and she held a bouquet of herbs. Past the bag strap, she wore a very open, revealing blouse that showed a black and white flame tattoo covering her sternum.

The only part of her body, other than her face which revealed skin. Her clothes were droopy and ragged like her hair, and many strands of her clothing held dark earth-toned colors to them. She was like a bundle of long, weathered rags fit for a witch's ball. It must have been her confident glare that made her seem so elegant. Her hazel eyes studied every bit of the situation while her mouth twisted and pitched together like she had nothing to worry about. She nodded at Brock and walked past him to the couch in the living room.

Then came two roughly robed ninjas with Persian-style monkish clothing and Greek skin. Short cut ropes were tied at every joint to eliminate any drag or baggy clothed inconsistencies. They both wore deep hoods, but Brock could still tell one was a guy and the other was a girl. They carried interesting old leather bags on their backs with what looked like ancient scrolls poking out of the drawstring opening. The couple had definitive jawlines with muscles etched out and their visible wrists thick with strength.

Finally, Moorendo came in, squeezing himself through the doorway.

"So, you must be the search party," Brock said hiply.

The monk ninjas looked at each other, and the young girlish witch turned around from looking at the couch.

"Are you Brock Zendolini?" Her British accent was rough, but her tone was sweet.

"Yeah."

"Packed for two are ya?" She nodded at the two camping packs next to the door.

Brock wondered where the hell Mokes went. "Ah yeah, is that okay?"

"Yeah, we don't care."

Brock was taken aback. She sounded so petite and kind. It was a strange contrast to the square scientist he'd been expecting all day. What came through the door were a bunch of druids, monks, and witches. It almost felt like their venture was going to be fun.

They did bring the search 'party'.

"*You're* with the Illuminati?" His curiosity rang through the air.

"We're just hired by them. Subcontractors, if you will."

Brock laughed. Of course, his dad, Mr. Zendolini, was a subcontractor for them too. That's how the Illuminati got their business done, by having other people do their bidding.

"Well, help yourselves to whatever. Two of you can sleep on the couch, and there are a couple of open rooms with beds for the other two."

The witch continued analyzing the house and lollygagging around while her team just stood there, still holding their bags and waiting for orders.

"Alright. We are ready to leave now. No sleep needed tonight."

Again, Brock blinked in surprise.

"It's about a 17 mile hike from the car. That might take us 7 to 8 hours... in the dark." *Blessid be, it was ten minutes to New Years. What a strange way to celebrate.*

The silence was like a void of unknown nothingness; however, in nothingness there left the potential for expansive exploration and creation. Hadn't the universe begun out of nothing? The Witch mulled it over, trying to find the opportunities in unknown space and time.

"I want to some spend time at this... what are you calling this spiritual site?"

The words fell out of Brock's mouth uneasily. "Uka Buka's... hovel." Excitement flared up in the witch's voice. "Ah, interesting. Well I want to spend time at Uka Buka's hovel during the day to get our bearings and set up camp without *distractions*. Under the light of the stars and moon is when spirits have the most control over our reality. Additionally, our client is the One World Order, so speed and efficiency are of the utmost importance. The moon is pretty full tonight, so we will have plenty of light to at least get us there. And a complete full moon tomorrow will be ideal for the summoning." The witch finished with a spry skip and grin.

"I'm going to go out front for a minute and call on our ride. Look through the pantry for any extra food you might want to bring." Brock jostled out, looking back to see four blank faces watching him.

As Mokes' phone rang, Brock slapped together a quick text. *They aren't the suited-up Illumi monsters you thought, Mokes. They are cool. Come back over. We leave in 20 minutes.*

The moonlight cast a creepy fluidic shadow to his right.

"Is everything in order?" The voice matched its shadow's ghostly creep, and this time Brock jumped. He was a guy who never flinched nor was ever startled, but this little chick with black wispy strands of hair hanging in front of her face easily did him in.

There was something friendly about the druidic search party but also something very scary. At least they didn't give out murderous vibes. The vibes that came from them were more haunting. Brock guessed it was because they had worked with spirits before, a phenomenon still entirely incredible for him.

"Yes, everything is cool. I was just calling our ride. He'll be here in 20 minutes…" Brock answered while unable to take his eyes off of her shadow.

"Why…" Chills flushed and froze up and down his spine.

"Why is your shadow doing that?"

The girl's shadow's edge was wisping around like the wind was blowing against it, but there was no wind, and the girl's actual clothes were completely still. At least the umbra of her shadow was consistent with its owner, extremely ominous, exotic, and unknowingly terrifying. Its flat black gaze told him every scary movie he had ever seen wasn't as frightening as this little girl's sinister immortal shadow.

The witch looked down at her flowing gray outline.

"That… is a long story. I will tell you this, though, you are not crazy. My shadow is much different than any other. We, the gathering set before you, all have special, possibly unsettling, abilities. Because of these abilities, we are here to find this spirit you speak of. What did you expect?" The witch stood straight, flat, and unmoving, proving the shadow was a separate entity from her own.

Brock walked to the girl's other side and a little further away from her shadow, then looked back at the moon. The flood of moonlight filled his spirit, and a strange power was delicately merging itself into his future. He thought these kinds of people were only to be found in fairy tales and ancient fantasies. This Uka Buka was slowly becoming more substantial to Brock.

They both stood before Leia's garage, looking at the moon.

"What's your name anyway?"

"Moorendo calls me Gem." She answered absently. Brock looked over at her and she was moving her lips while looking at the moon. A prayer, perhaps, or incantation for safe travels.

Without interrupting her focus, Mokes pulled up in his van and looked at Brock through the passenger window with eyes that screamed he wasn't getting out. His dreads draped around his shoulders like pet snakes.

He yelled out, voice cracking a bit. "I had to get gas… Load em' up and let's get on with it weh."

***

The moon leaked its light throughout most of the trail. Under canopies, along mountain ridges, and even over terrain completely shaded by topography, the moon's light found its way through to brighten their path. Their hike was no ordinary walk and talk waltz up a prairie either. The group, which Moorendo called The Druids of Crete, was always tinkering with vials, herbs, scrolls, crystals, and some unknown device that clicked louder and louder the more the moonlight hit it.

Gem spent at least half of her time walking on Moorendo's heels, playing with her trinkets in a wide open fold-out pouch in Moorendo's backpack. The pair of them were very cute together. Brock didn't think they were together together, but it was obvious Moorendo was Gem's ward and socialist, which allowed her to stay focused on her tasks.

Moorendo was a chatter bug that kept long conversations with anyone that would indulge, and because the other two monks were utterly silent, only shooting whispers and hand signals between themselves, Moorendo's main conversationalists were Brock and Mokes.

At least Moorendo's blabbermouth made Mokes feel at ease, and for Brock, it was kinda fun getting to know actual druids. Who else could call on the moon to shed its wandering light, casting serpentine shadows that had a sense of their own…

About ten miles into the hike there was a fork in the road. The female monk removed her deep hood to retie her interesting hair bun. The sides of her head were cleanly shaven with ram horn tattoos that spiraled above her ears. When she flipped her hood back up, she noticed Gem's shadow entranced by her. She suddenly spread her limbs out like a starfish and made the shadow explode in surprise, looking like it was hit by lightning. It retracted to its normal form and gilded back to its solidified embodiment for safety.

At this point, Gem was up ahead with Brock discussing which path to take on the fork in the road. Her music at her hip still played harmoniously, creating a buffer of sound that made it difficult to hear their voices. Moorendo was already talking with Mokes about his previous life as a Shaman and drug counselor slash lucid dream enthusiast. So it was a good time to ask another intimate question, especially after they both witnessed the shadow spark up and wisp around unattached to its host.

"Endo. What is that?" Excitedly looking at Moorendo as well as terrified at shadows being able to move on their own.

Moorendo looked away from Gem and back at Mokes.

"I think the question is Mokes, what are they?" He nodded at the Monks off to the side by themselves, always in the back of the group and always shady. He chuckled and bumped Mokes with his elbow, bringing his voice to a low whisper. "I'll tell you Mokes, if you'd share some of that Marijuana you got. We don't have anything like that in Greece. I can tell by its smell its grade A ganj."

Mokes slipped a joint out of his chest jacket pocket and lit it up. "Your wish is my command, big guy." Mokes put on a curvy smile with light gray tendrils of smoke curling up the corners of his mouth.

The joint was halfway gone after Moorendo's long inhale. He coughed out a cloud of smoke and Gem glanced back at him.

"Ah, she caught me." He giggled out, hunching his shoulders in as if to mask his voice from carrying too far.

"Alright ol' Mokie boi. Little Gem over there is a super powerful witch; some might even go as far as to say a necromancer…"

The two monks creeped up behind them in a crouch and took off their hoods. Moorendo gestured to the joint and the male monk nodded. The joint was then passed around as Moorendo whispered his story.

"Gem is short for Gemini." He looked a little off to the side of Gem, where light had trouble penetrating.

"Her sister died during their birth. A balance of life and death in one womb. Even though one was mostly lost, they say her spirit attached itself onto the living soul of her sister. When Gem became a rebellious teeny witch, she wanted to test out a resurrection spell she'd been reading about. This dark spell nearly ripped her to shreds. I was there. It was actually how we met.

"I was guiding a couple of kids on a Peyote trip, and we came across her bloody pulp, torn to shreds by the wind cycling around her lone body. A super powerful spell attracted our Peyote hallucinations. Honestly, I'm sure anyone around would have felt it, but we especially. We were out on a deserted plateau overlooking the Mediterranean. Lucky for Gem, we happened to be camping out there, or she would have been completely alone, well isolated from human beings anyway.

"Her new shadow was ravenous when it was freshly resurrected, and it took me a long time to heal Gem because I wasn't sure if I was still tripping on Peyote, dreaming, or really witnessing a living shadow.

"Conjoined as their spirits were, Gem became an even more powerful witch because her shadow could communicate with the underworld, and Gem maneuvered and manipulated reality. Yin Yang twins at its finest, mate."

They all *umm'd and awh'd* as they stared at Gem and Brock looking over a map in the moonlight. Arguing as they were, they also seemed very close to one another. Only a sliver of moonlight cast between their lips as they disagreed over the correct trailhead. Intimate as the scene was, they caught Brock's words after yelling over Gem's music, "I hold the map witch!"

The female monk cringed at the argument beyond and passed the joint over to Mokes. Mokes took a moment and asked, "What are your names?"

The girl answered after a long look at her partner. "This is my brother Crum, and I am Cid. We-"

"Getting acquainted, are we?" Everyone jumped out of their skin. The joint flew up and away, and Moorendo sprawled out in fright, knocking Crum into a toppling somersault. Little Gem stood amused with her sisterly shadow. The sound of her pocket music didn't even alert them that Gem was coming, like they had just whispered into existence.

Mokes tried to instill the memory of her popping up like that. Later, he might disassociate reality with the weed haze in his mind, in everyone's mind now. Was everyone that high already that people could teleport next to them out of nowhere. Gem definitely had a powerful aura around her, a living aura of her own shadowy kin, but she also had enough mischievous twinkle in her eye to tell she had a whole bag of tricks up her sleeve, as well as a bag of magical spells.

Gem looked them over for another minute.

"We go left, into the forest and away from the moonlight."

Ahead, the fork in the road was clearly visible. The right fork cut through a small thicket of trees and then opened to a very lit-up moony pathway curving around the outside face of the mountain.

The left fork went straight up a dense incline with a forest canopy, which blocked out the moon. They picked up and continued their march.

Mokes quickly stepped ahead to reach Brock at the lead. The path at that moment turned very dark, and Mokes almost came to a halt because he had lost his depth of awareness. He didn't want to falter before the team, so he kept Brock at his cuff while he let his eyes acclimate to the darkness. Sometimes, when leading, you just had to keep putting one foot in front of the other for the benefit of the pack. Either dark or light, the path was the path.

"Well, what a freaking adventure, eh Brock? Feels like we are in a movie or something… Did you know Gem's shadow is her twin sister?"

"What? No. Gem told me those ram horned monks are part of an ancient cult of exorcists! The Illuminati either overdid themselves in this search party, or we are wayyy out of our league."

Brock's voice was in a whisper, but Mokes could tell Brock was bemused at finally being out of his league. Being around an irrefutable higher power only made one stronger.

"It can't be that bad if Ik came up here all alone."

Gem returned behind Moorendo, turned on her ticking moonlight device, and began mixing herbs in the light of a mini lantern hung on Moorendo's backpack strap. Moorendo wasn't just a ward or a mule, they conversed and analyzed the mountain together. Discussing their current human biological frequencies and the energy the environment was exuding. It seemed that these factors played a big role in their mixtures of organic concoctions.

Still speaking softly, Gem gave a small wooden box a couple of super hard shakes that tumbled her gems and crystals together. As she set it aside she grabbed a bundle of sage and watched the smoke float up and over Moorendo's backpack lantern. She listened to the ticks of her moonlight device and smelled around her herbs and burning sage like a hidden fragrance would reveal itself betwixt them. A very busy little bee during a mountain hike in the pitch of night.

Then, up on seemingly the apex of the mountain's ridge, darkness grew ever solemn, and their pace slowed to trickling cautious steps on top of a narrow ridge.

Gem whispered, "Adow, stay close."

The Southern side of the ridge showed the 1000 foot slope down

Uka Buka Mountain, cuddling up to a vast lake and lush beginnings onto another mountain 30 miles away. The Northern side declined into wicked darkness. Gray trees holding a doomy world behind its pitch black curtain.

The moon had set, and the loom of the sky showed a sun about to rise.

Gem stopped and looked down the Northern bank. She smelled her bundle of herbs one last time and threw them down into the darkness. With her free hand, she reached for a pocket, extracted a pouch of her fragmented, shaken-up gems and crystals, and poured them into her palm. She then snuffed out the sage, mugwort, and lavender into her palm of shiny aggregate. She shook the ashen crystal mix like dice to spill onto a gambling barrel, creating a really natural chiming lullaby noise to it.

The hypnosis lasted just long enough for Gem to slip into the darkness without any confrontation with the others. Her hip instrumental beats tuned out, and the sound of her crystal shakes seized. The deafening thumb of silence encapsulated the Druids.

Difficult to decipher the time that went by, it had been long enough for Moorendo to begin moving down the bank after Gem, and simultaneously, Gem reappeared, creeping out of the dark. Her continual instrumental beats grew louder as she climbed back up the bank. Her music was like African Viking ritual chants set in a Yoga studio.

"You alright Gem?"

Gem had to rifle through her pockets to turn down her tunes. "Yeah, Endo."

Only knowing her for a night, Gem seemed like a melancholy adventurous little kid. The most relaxed, unexcited adventurer out there. She looked around at everyone, then back at the darkened void within nature.

"Brock, you mentioned that this Uka Buka spirit might still be with its host?" Gem politely asked.

"At least when the Illuminati came across it, it was. But that was about 4 years ago."

"Ah huh. Well, I believe it came back to its hovel." Again ominous silence.

"Sign says there's a campground half a mile in. Should we establish ourselves there, Gem?" Moorendo was checking Gem for any marks or signs of harm, then turned her around when she didn't respond.

"Gem?"

She looked up at him out of her trance.

"Full preparations Endo. It's a good thing we brought the Exorcists, because this Uka… Buka is pissed the fuck off."

The Bone Brigade

It was the morning of January 1st, New Year's Day, and a full day after Toko Tuki's spirit transfer. From that time, Jacklyn Poxer had cleaned up her back patio, repotted Leia's plants, and put colorful eastern cushions on the roots of the Willow tree, creating a nice and shady sitting area. She lounged on the center cushion with her black hood up and over her blond curls, resting a wrist on a bent knee. Her other hand rotated a charred staff with three wooden-fingered branches at its peak.

She had the staff of elemental power, but she could not use it. She thought she had Toko Tuki, but she could not see him. She was a puzzled little Poxer.

Two other women sat with her. One had long pink hair and a checkered-sleeved sweatshirt, who was reading an old book with a deteriorated bidding, and the other had naturally reddish hair with freckles on her cheeks. Goosebumps embossed her skin where her flowing sundress did not conceal.

Poxer rubbed her goosebumped thigh and leaned in to kiss her on the lips. The woman with the reddish hair was Sloan Sullivan, the most recent Secret Sauce to Poxer's life, her real estate girlfriend.

On the day of the spirit ritual, Sloan went to the Refill Shop to see how Poxer was doing. It had been an entire day that Poxer went without responding to Sloan's text messages. Being unlike Poxer, Sloan went to her work to bear witness to whatever was keeping her so busy. An encapsulated storm summoning of a Tiki Head. Since that moment, the three women who witnessed the rise of their now *high priestess*, have devoted themselves to Poxer, for she was a Goddess in their eyes.

Poxer, Sloan, and Punk Rock, pink-haired Laney, were all brainstorming on ways to release the Toko Tuki spirit from the charred staff so it could lead them to Uka Buka before Brock. The beautiful older woman with long salt and pepper hair was working the Refill Store's register up front.

"You are all very sweet, and I enjoy your company, but I think I know what I have to do." Poxer said while looking into Sloan's blue eyes.

Laney looked up from her book and sat up from her loll.

Poxer's voice was sincere and kind. "I feel like this spirit isn't revealing itself because too many of us are around. I'm going to leave for a little while and try a couple… isolated ideas."

Truthfully, she needed some space. After the spirit summoning ceremony, life was very lavish and exciting. She had three extremely beautiful women drooling over her, and had just done something she had never dreamed of doing.

Was I a soccercess now? Should I accept being worshiped and revered as a goddess?

She definitely wasn't used to it, and her petite belief that Toko Tuki wanted a little space as well made up her decision.

Laney opened her mouth in protest, but Sloan gave her a short smile.

"Jack, do as you need, Love. One of us will look after the store for you while you're gone. It's best not to strangle the freest soul we have ever met…" Sloan gave Laney a kind yet telling stare.

"Plus I think we three still need to digest all that has happened these last couple of days."

Poxer kissed Sloan again and rose. The three women started to believe they were a representation of the Triquetra, falling together by the gravity of fate. Triquetra was the ancient Celtic name for the triple goddess, the Maiden, the Mother, and the Crone. Symbolizing the sublimeness of the number three. A never-ending cycle, a balance greater than two. The beginning, middle, and end. In this case, they depicted it as the different stages of a Woman's life and also the different realms of our world: Heaven, Earth, and the Underworld.

Siggy was the oldest and wisest by far. Sloan had no children but was fully developed and ready to nurture the ones around her, and Laney wanted all the experiences, all at once, in order to blossom into the flower she was fated for.

Yet fantastical prophecies, ancient theories of triunity, and age equilibriums meant nothing compared to the connection the women felt when together. All the rest was just words. What mattered to them was their immediate bond with each other. A knowingness inside of them that being in each other's presence was what they needed to do. They had a fixation to spiral around each other until destiny guided them into triumph.

They were Poxer's limpid lucky charm, as Laney put it in the simplest terms.

"Okay. Call me if you need anything or have any questions." With that Poxer brushed a hand over the Willow and left the patio with her staff in hand.

She knew exactly where she was going first… Taco Bell. Then, to the cemetery. Poxer had a bone to pick with Baggans.

***

"Baggans!!" Poxer yelled as she strode through the cemetery gate. The pathway lawn was kept neat, and there were piles of leaves in the larger open areas, fallen from the Oak trees overhead. A thick head and Hawaiian shirt collar popped out from behind one of the leaf piles near Poxer.

"Hey! Toko Tuki needs-" She ticked and 'bopped' with her tongue releasing from the roof of her mouth. "A bone. We've tried everything else to get him out of hiding. Even this." Poxer rose the charred staff above her head, "Os Sesamoideum Bone to your- *Fuck* -Domeum!"

Baggans laughed, "You really taking this High Priestess thing seriously, huh?"

Cheeks blushing in the shadows of her hood, "The Illuminati ruining our world with a Uka Buka chaos spirit guarding a gateway to hell is pretty serious. Throw me a- *wee'op wee* - bone already."

Feathers, wood, and tribal paint all camouflaged in with the fall leaves. Toko Tuki barely stuck its head out of the pile behind Poxer and Baggans to see where this conversation was going.

Baggans chuckled again, "It's not like bones are scattered around the yard here. They are in the graves. They are with their people."

Puffs of leaves blew out of the pile behind them, and they looked around for the corporate. While looking out in the vast expanse of the tombstones, Toko Tuki sniffed the back of Baggans' head and wagged around like a dog with a nice calcified bone in its mouth. Poxer turned around, and relief morphed into her eyes. She leaned on her staff and nudged Baggans with her elbow.

"See, that's all he wanted…" Poxer said slowly, basking a little in her amazement of the funny floating spirit in front of them.

Heavy, bushy brows bowed on Baggans' head.

"Oh wow, I can only see the bone. Tuki is invisible to me without the light of Ki's cane… Okay Poxer, after we are finished with taking down Uka Buka's hovel, the bone goes back to its rightful owner."

Tuki was ecstatic and flung the bone out of its mouth, where it flipped around a few rotations, then slid into a freshly created hole under its nostrils. Tuki's face still held the Japanese characters running down one side of its cheek, and Ki's blood splattered across the bridge of its nose.

"Alright Tuki, show- *wee'op* - us the way to Uka Buka."

***

The Cadillac Deville trailed Tuki as he swished and soared over the high noon road, occasionally rising high above the trees and becoming a silhouette of a feather-capped plank against the first sun of the year. When Tuki saw a fork in the road, he'd fly back down and guardedly guide them through the dense forest terrain.

"Do you think anyone else can see him?" Poxer asked while leaning back with her foot on the seat and leg lazily bent up.

"I don't know… I saw him fly out of your fairy ring with Sloan and the others, but now I only see the bone he has."

Poxer gave Baggans a forbidding peripheral stare. "There was- ahuhh -a lot of energy in that moment. In that area… Those women are…"

Baggans tried to help, "Smoking hot?"

Poxer punched Baggans with her left, and the Caddy gently swerved back and forth, then floated over a bump. It was Baggans' turn to give the disagreeable stare, though he was impressed at the weight behind her little arm.

A moment was taken to watch Tuki soar through tree trunks and around a bend on the mountain's edge.

"Special somehow. It's almost as if they have- *fuck ass* -found their purpose, or maybe just finding each other has given them purpose. They give me the feeling like finding me was just- *wee 'bop'* -the beginning for them, but having each other is more important in some way."

"Like they are Sisters, huh Jack? Strangers one day and Sisters the next."

Poxer nodded and watched the trees.

"What's up with Sloan?" Baggans asked while taking a big right turn. Tuki turned around and nodded for them to veer off the main road and onto a narrow dirt path.

A smile twisted on Poxer's lips, and she straightened out one of her blonde curls. "I'm- *'whistle'* -glad she saw. I just hope she will still treat me like an equal instead of some *high priestess*. I need some- *fucK* -fight in a woman. I don't want pussy handed to me on a silver platter."

"Ha, yeah, digging for it in the bush is way better." The Caddy came to a stop, and they smiled at each other. Baggans still wore his Hawaiian shirt, and Poxer her torn jeans and hoodie.

"Let's grab our stuff- *Wee'ouu* -and head out."

As they headed up the mountain, a glint from the reflection of the sun showed on Baggans' heel. Feeling the heat and the call of the sun he turned around, only to see his Cadillac sitting alone in the parking lot. Little did he know the sun was trying to tell him something else, for its glinting message was from a hidden van concealed by a camouflage tarp deeper in the offroad bramble.

Four Flames

At the camp, high up on the mountain near Uka Buka's hovel, a snare pounded rhythmically to an elvish pipe twiddling happily like a songbird amidst a piney background. The exorcists, Cid and Crum sat facing each other with their legs intertwined, drumming and piping along on their instruments lightly enough for the others not to become distracted and heavy enough to motivate their hearts while doing their chores.

In Mokes' case, it was nice to hear the flowing rampant beats and hums of the camp, so he didn't get lost in the wilderness. Gathering firewood all day seemed much easier than what Brock had to do. The poor guy had to clear a path from their camp to Uka Buka's hovel, a ramshackle of dense underwood on a relentless slant.

The thick growth of the untarnished forest was darkened and daunting. Brock's machete would be swinging back and forth, back and forth all day, up the hill and to the spirit they were after. A frightening chore Mokes thought as he cheerily picked up fallen branches and placed them in piles. He decided hanging out in the forest smoking weed and picking up sticks would be a new hobby of his.

Gem was also out and about in the trees, searching around the forest floor for herbs, roots, and anything else she could use for her Seance later. The way she bent down with her dark drab and closed her eyes as she waltzed through the forest grounds was intoxicating to Mokes. Gem may have been a witch, but she was young, world-centric, and uniquely cute as ever.

Moorendo stayed around the camp with the exorcist musicians and prepared the ceremonial area.

"Wha in your bag, Cid? Pounds of garlic with scrolls on top?" Moorendo wrinkled his nose as he dug out a small moat around their western flame space. There were four fire pits Moorendo needed to build. The one he was currently working on was the water flame pit to the West. Just before that, he finished a large stone pit to the

North for the earth flame and a wind flame tipi with just enough twigs to support a fire from the winds of the East.

Brock's trail began between the fire and wind pits. SouthEast area. Gem had a plan to pull Uka Buka over to them and then catch Uka's spirit into Crum, the Ram Horned Exorcist. They said he'd held such a spirit in his body before so he could do it again. Him and his sister Cid just needed to smooth over his spirit enough before letting in such a force. Readying him to be used as a vessel for their Mother Gaia.

The Northern earth pit took all morning because Moorendo had to test out the vibrations of each stone. There were levels the stone had to pass before it made the cut. First, he'd hover a hand over every rock, then he'd tap the stone on his tribal-painted sonorous rock. It didn't matter if the connection of stones made a clunk sound or a chime; there was something else Moorendo was listening for before he tossed it into the final pile.

Still having to wait for Mokes to come back with a half a dozen more loads of wood to finish the largest of bonfire structures to the South. Moorendo relaxed and took his time with his moat to the West. Clay was nearby on a western bank, which Moorendo used to coat the moat, slapping it down and smoothing it over.

Cid stopped playing her flute and playfully pushed Crum's shoulder back with her toes as she unwove her legs from his and crawled over to Moorendo. Crum's snare beats still rhythmically resonated over the grounds.

"What were you listening to?"

Moorendo pointed to his ear as if he wanted her to explain her question in more detail and busied himself with rolling up a lump of clay in a coalescing ball.

"The clinking of stones? Why?" Cid asked again while taking a piece of garlic out of her pocket.

"A ritual like this requires stones that will have a better chance of repelling this Uka Buka spirit. We don't want stones flying around hitting us in the head because of objective spiritual possession."

"Ahhh, that is very interesting. Possessing inanimate objects." She took a bite of the garlic and chewed.

"Aye, Natural spirits linking with natural, dormant, things." Moorendo plopped the ball of clay in front of Cid to help him coat the other side of the moat. Curiously looking at her chewing mouth.

Garlic bits spit out into Cid's palm, and she seductively started rubbing out her ball of clay. Salubrious time passed, pawing the clay down and soothing it out into the moat with kind hands.

"This is like what Crum and I are doing, you know. Coating his soul with love so the spirit doesn't cause him harm. A pillowy cell embodiment. Love is a great sigil of protection from the Underworld, you know." Concealed mostly by long, baggy brown monkish sleeves, her hands smoothed the clay like it was her own baby's skin.

"What is the Underworld… to your people?"

She laughed, "To my people? The Ram Horned Cultist, the most ancient Demon Slayers in our living world? The Underworld is the same for all. A far far away Galaxy of the Dead." Her eyes brightened with the excitement on the topic.

Moorendo looked pleasantly intrigued. Staining his chin with his amused clay fingertips. "If the dead rest in another galaxy, why call it the Underworld?"

"The dead do not rest until they die again my good man. The double dead fly off to ghost moons where they can finally sleep." Cid noticed Moorendo's questioning brow.

"We, the ancient Ram Horned Cultist, have sent our own to possess demons, you know. Some of our elders have been to the Underworld. I guess they call it that because the dead ceaselessly try to rise up to the living, for the living are the ones that bask in this radiance that so resembles *heaven*." She smiled and pretended to take a bite of the ball of clay in her hand.

A shadow came across the moated fire pit, and Moorendo saw Gem making her way over into the encampment with an arm full of bushes and herbs. She set them down in the middle of their ritual space, center to the four elemental pits.

Moorendo smiled at Cid, then went over to Gem and waited for her to survey the area.

Gem nodded at all four points of the compass and riffled through her black robes for a few minutes, finally finding three Gem sized handfuls of mushrooms, only filling one large palm of Moorendo's.

"Separate these and hand them out to everyone. Crum and I get double the amount of everyone else. At sunset, we will all take them and begin the Seance." Through the overhang of the forest's canopy, the clouds were arrayed with hues of orange and purple light. The sky gave them one hour before sunset.

"I'll go gather Brock and Mokes." Moorendo said after gently tucking the mushrooms away in his backpack pocket.

"Endo... the forest is happy here. It loves and respects its guardian spirit, Uka Buka. Flourishing with rampant growth and vibrant life. When we try to steal the forest's guardian tonight we will most likely encounter a motherly fist of natural retribution... As well as whatever magic Uka Buka possesses. Please take care in preparing accordingly." Gem put a hand on Moorendo's thick shoulder, and Adow passed a gray tendril wisp through the shadow of Moorendo's hair on the forest floor.

Moorendo saw this and kissed Gem's hand. "Yes, Priestess. We will be ready."

With the touch of love in their eyes, Moorendo set off SouthEast to gather Brock.

After a good ten minutes walking on cutdown foliage, Moorendo spotted Brock up the steepest incline, machete dangling at his belt and hand pressed to the trunk of a tree. Moorendo continued toward him, thinking Brock would notice his heavy footfalls. However, Brock never budged.

Below him now, on the base of the incline, Moorendo yelled up to Brock, his shirt off and sweat bedding down his skin in the cold shadow of the forest. "Al-librah-Emancipare!" The stout shout shook Brock, and he released his grip on the tree and looked down at Moorendo.

"Endo, I... was..."

"The spirit pulled you in, Mate. Transfixed you into a petrification of ecstasy based on your emotional desires... This must be it." Moorendo gave the eerie tree a moment of study.

"Let's go. We need to get back to camp."

Brock slid down the leafy hill and met with Moorendo's stride back to camp.

"That was exactly what happened, Endo... How did you-" Brock watched the thick druid's back with admiration. Brock never really admired anyone. He's been surrounded by Mr. Zendolini and his wise guys his entire life. They were tough, but there was a reason they were called Goons. Being as big as Moorendo was, his eclipsing kindness was heartwarming. The exceptional mystical knowledge of being was also very inspiring.

"We have all been through this before Brock. There are many natural and unnatural spirits that reside on Earth. However, few humans have a chance to interact with them. Gem believes that this Uka Buka is a rage spirit, crazed with a bloodlust for the humans that deteriorate its Mother… You too must have hatred in your heart, Brock, or you would not be smiling after such an interaction." Moorendo looked back at Brock, and Brock fixed his grin into a level frown.

"This changes things. I think it was a mistake to send someone towards Uka Buka's hovel."

Uncertain and uncomfortable about what was to come next, Brock asked why they needed a trail to the hovel.

"It's simply a clear path of ruin for the spirit to find us. It will be pissed at the destruction of its leafy children and will come straight to us for a haunting. Gem thought if we used you for this… felling, it'd use its power against you first… You were going to be the bait, Brock. However, now that Uka has invited you, I believe you should be the vessel of its spirit."

They reached the encampment, and Moorendo strode straight to Gem. Brock went over to Mokes and helped him stack the rest of the dead wood and kindling in a pile next to Gem's bushes of herbs.

Mokes pushed his dreads over his shoulder, "What's going on Brock? You look whiter than usual."

Brock looked into Moke's eyes with no words, and they both stood up as Gem and Moorendo went over to them.

In the center of the four elemental pits Gem called everyone in.

"Change of plans." Gem's shadow drifted over to the Western pit, marking the Sun's slumbering descent.

"Brock will be dressed in the ritual gown tonight. Crum and Cid, you have your spirit absorption scrolls ready?" They both nodded in affirmation.

"Good, don't stop chanting your incantations, no matter what happens. Once Uka Buka makes it into our ritual circle the incantations will pull it into the unfastened soul."

Brock cracked his knuckles on the side of his head, "Ah, what?"

"Your soul will be open for Uka Buka to settle into Brock. A spirit bind."

"What happens after that? What happens to me?"

Everyone kind of looked around at each other uneasily.

"Well, you become the vessel for Uka Buka. Connected, you'll still be you, and Uka will still be Buka. The best thing you can do from now until then is relax and allow whatever comes to um… come. Mokes, I want you to keep the Northern and Western pits steady with flame. Moorendo will watch over the Eastern and Southern pits. Uka Buka will come through that South East Trail. Be ready, be calm, and try to enjoy yourselves, eh?" Gem gave the group her biggest smile yet, completely contradicting Brock's uneasy frown.

Moorendo held out a long piece of bark in one hand and pointed to one of the six piles of mushrooms for each person he passed. Gem followed behind him, making sure everyone took their dose.

"These are to ground us closer to the natural realm, allowing a stronger connection with the spirits. Signally to them, we come in peace and love, for we are the Druids of their Mother."

Crum, Cid, and Mokes picked them up and chewed without too much hesitation. Once the long piece of bark was in front of Brock, Moorendo picked up the last smaller pile of shrooms and ate them.

Brock's face looked stupefied. "Why do we have double the amount of everyone else? I've never even eaten magical mushrooms before."

Gem positioned herself in front of Brock. "You need that much to open your soul. I'm also taking that much because you need someone here on your level." It was evident as the ritual grew closer Gem's excitement and merriment increased.

"Smile Brock, you are about to become a vessel of Mother Earth's spirit. The world will see you differently tomorrow."

"Feels like being a blood sacrifice to Odin." Brock's cheeks grew red as Gem clapped her fingers around his jaw.

Laughter rang out around the circle, "How did you think the spirit will get inside of you? There will be blood, but you will most likely feel no pain, only warmth."

She pinched, and Brock's dumbfounded mouth opened to a handful of magical mushrooms stuffed inside, with the help of Gem's cute little fingers.

The Dance in the Witch's Cauldron

Moss burned low in the center of the staff's three wooden fingers. Poxer stepped to the trail's edge, pulled some more tree moss off a limb, and padded it on top of the staff's small flame.

Half of their hike they had daylight, the other half, the full moon lit most of the trail pretty well, but after the last fork in the road, the environment changed. Darkness shrouded the trunks of trees, and chills clamped to the back of Baggans' and Poxer's spines.

"You feel that Jack?" Baggans stopped for a moment and looked straight up to the full moon.

"It's like the forest is blocking out the moon's light."

"We must be getting close." And just as Poxer finished, Toko Tuki flew quickly at them and floated behind the fire light of its new spirit bond staff.

"Toko Tuki," He gobbled low and slow. The bone going through his nose masked a lot of his facial features. Poxer thumped her staff twice in the dirt for Tuki clarification. Toko Tuki's eyes rolled ahead of them, and his face morphed and hardened into what may have resembled a Uka Buka face. After watching Poxer's face transform into understanding, Toko Tuki morphed back to itself and then huffed out the staff flame.

For five minutes, they crept along the narrowing path, just able to see the vibrant colors of Tuki's feathers against the darkness. Then Tuki stopped, flew down an embankment, and was lost.

Baggans peered down the mountain and out upon a grand lake holding the reflection of the first full moon of the year. A moon cratered with a mischievous skeletal gaze.

Poxer stepped a little further down the trail and rotated her head as if to pick up a sound with a focused ear.

"Music…"

The chill from the night vanished, a cumulus cloud rolled in from the East behind them, and a heat of excitement ran so hot that Poxer slapped her hood back. Baggans stepped before her.

"That's full moon ritual music, Jack." Unsure of what to do with the information, Baggans watched the humongous cloud roll in over Poxer's head.

"Well…" Poxer licked her lips and squeezed the staff, feeling its grain, smelling its char, its power.

"Let's go check it out." She said while pulling back the hair in her eyes.

At this point they knew Toko Tuki would find them if he wanted to. It was either Poxer or the staff that acted as a tracking beacon for Tuki, and with the oncoming storm and doomy ritual music ahead, she was sure she would never let go of her stick.

While ironically tiptoeing over the off-trail foliage, the music's tempo increased, quick and upbeat, coming from the center of an encampment with four flames and darkened shapes dancing amongst the multifarious shadows cast by the high flames.

There was a dreaded figure hunched over the Northern flame. A mass of fur shaped like a bear twirling around like a slow motion ballerina with two outstretched arms holding two smoking bundles, helixing upwards in his revolutions. Deep hooded, baggy robed monks jigged and strafed side to side around the tallest Southern flame. Their inner arms were around each other's shoulders, and their outer arms held an ancient scroll up in front of them. They were so in sync and constant it made Poxer wish she didn't have Tourettes so she could join them.

Skipping into the monk's frame, a dancing woman flourished her arms above her head, tilting back to the sky. A gritty, gripping, gremlin goblin silhouette of a little witch. Her shadow casting out wide as an elongated wisp, then drowsily flooding back into its master. Her movements entranced by the violin and flute on a fully notched-up speaker. It was like her shadow was dancing with her, though more bombastic and extravagant with its movements.

From their distant perch, a heavy darkness loomed in the center of the four bonfires. An interesting site from where they were; an inner dot of darkness, to a circle of fire, and finally back to the outer circular shadow of the forest. Showing the whole space as a fire ring. Poxer wondered if the four surrounding fires were simply for the shadows to cast themselves throughout the ritual grounds, for the shadows were a movement of vitality, branches blowing and bustling in the regenerative wind. The wind, only identified as such by the look of the now static bear man, standing, arms out to a T, and absorbing the Eastern wind like it was filling his body with outer power, or perhaps cleansing his inner soul.

Bouncing on one leg for a while and then to the other, Poxer watched the gremlin witch transform into a flamingo dancer, who wagged slightly from the briskly breezing wind. The dancer would briefly stop with one leg bent up in an attempt to test her balance or possibly test the strength of the wind. Then she twirled around with an intermediate gust and hopped into the darkened center, where a glorified figure beamed in sacrificial conquest.

From gremlin to seductress, the witch whipped her long, ragged scarf around the thick neck of a man with his shirt off. He stood out from all the rest because this man was bright like a glare, wearing loose white pants and having an upper body of ripped muscle. He stood there looking up at the moon through the forest canopy, while the witch ran a dancing hand over his back, a twirl, and then a tickling hand across his belly. He stood there like an honored warrior, a prized sacrifice.

"Mother flipper… that's Brock." Poxer leaned over to whisper to Baggans.

"I think they are tripping on something, J." He responded under his breath and in awe.

Enough energy was shooting through the trees and pulsating through the soil to make Poxer feel like she was tripping too. It was funny for her to feel so much ecstasy in a moment when she knew she'd have to step in and break up all the fun.

The Witch wove her body around like she was made of a light fabric. An embodiment of a flag to raise elemental morale, to entice the spirit in the nearby hollow. She continued her dance around the encampment until she approached a large boulder near the center of the four flames.

Casting her arms at it like a witch would her cauldron, branches of bush and bits of rocks were tossed onto the stone as somewhat of a lackadaisical merge of ingredients.

Far away, the witches didn't seem too bad, more like drugged-out herbalists, Poxer thought.

After a long moment of ritual entertainment, she suddenly noticed that there was no longer a shadow of fervent dance around the witch. It was difficult to notice as the forest looming over the four fires created shadows amongst shadows, scaling out, warping over and around the lit-up space. Poxer knew the witch had an ambiguous shadow before however, a cast of herself with so many inconsistencies.

When the witch moved away from an area, the shadow would stay rigid, or as the Witch stayed in one space, the shadow would roam. But now… nothing cast itself around the witch.

Amongst the four flames, however, shadows cast themselves from the branches, humans, and elements, which blew, flickered, boiled, and rolled.

Fear ate at her before the chill had even arrived. A curling of Poxer's spine broke the warmth of excitement in her. A tic abruptly craned her neck and her heart pounded against a ghostly iciness that ran over her. She gripped the staff, hoping for another flush of power and Tuki to return.

Baggans looked over his shoulder and gathered an eerie feeling of sleep paralysis. Just a feeling, he first thought, because he was unmoved. A feeling, he gathered a moment later, that became dire reality.

Inches from his face air escaped nostril sized holes from a looming gray shadow. The smell of bonfire smoke gurgled his stomach, and his eyes glazed with tears. He might have even enjoyed the shadows' company if it hadn't been so entirely menacing.

Poxer nudged him and then was encapsulated by the shadow as well. All she could do was give the staff another squeeze. A squeeze that came from the pulse of blood from her beating heart, enough pressure to finally call the largest gale of the night.

The shadow dashed out of sight, leaving gray wisps behind to blow away in the heavy wind. Then suddenly, everything changed. The music seized, and the dancing woman abruptly stopped her mystic mixtures and looked straight at them while the four fires around her roared.

The wind came in like an air tsunami, extinguishing the Eastern pit, descending the Northern flame into its rock barrier, splashing steaming water out of the Western moat to fizzle into the fluttering fire towers, and raged in the Southern end, burning the monk's scroll in an ashen instant and catching one of their hoods on fire. Indifferently, the monk tore the hood from their robe and cast it into the blusterous pit ahead of them.

A smaller breeze blew overhead, and Toko Tuki floated in between Poxer and Baggans, sitting on top of the staff like he was the moss, like he was the sorcerer's orb that would have rested so perfectly in the claw of the shaft of forgotten driftwood.

The monks' incantations were heard clearly, now that the music cut out, and everyone in the encampment faced the SouthEast, where the wind blew in from. The bear form slowly stomped its way to where the howls resinated, blowing his loose garb and coat behind him like a parachute of fur. The mass of bear looked ready for something to come out of the woods. After Toko Tuki's little advent gust, Poxer had an idea of what came with these haunting winds.

Not being the star of the show, Poxer settled in, and just then, as if to jinx her tranquility, the witch called out to the bear, and he looked in the direction she was croning.

"Ah, oh, that beast of a man is coming for us, Bags."

"I'll try to deal with him Jack. Maybe Tuki and you can figure out a way to save our asses." Baggans smiled and rolled up his Grunion Rugby sweatshirt sleeves.

As Baggans stood out of the thicket to meet with the bear. Jacklyn Poxer's eyes moved on their own, used by a force she had never experienced before. She noticed Tuki was looking at the very same thing. High above the witch, above the monks with ram horn tattoos on the side of their heads, above the dreads of Pena Mokalua, *the swag*, was the spirit everyones been looking for. Uka Buka.

Still standing in the same spot as when Poxer first saw him, Brock was looking straight up at Uka floating above him, casually lifting his arms out to his sides in tolerant surrender. A laugh curdled through the monk's chants, like a noisy creaking oak twisting its wood to the side and exuding a groan-like boast, almost like a witches cackle but with much more bass.

The floating spirit flew right into Brock and came out his back, more animated, larger, and more dangerous looking. Brock fell through the air like he turned into water and splashed on the ground unconscious.

Poxer found herself walking forward, staff leading the way, one thunk at a time. Again she was possessed and didn't act on her own. She looked up at stoic Toko Tuki and felt that brotherly security run over her again. She was protected.

As she walked by Baggans and the large man with a heavy fur

coat, their voices lowered, their muscles relaxed, and the prominent swing of a fist turned to a clap of two stone walls that accepted each other for being a wall, for being human and alive.

Tourette's tics tweaked Poxer's neck and shoulders around as she passed the new friends and began to suck up air for a full chest of confidence. One of the monks was a girl who looked right at Poxer as she made her way through the darkness, as if she was an apparition. The crouching witch hopped off her altar boulder and hunched over in a gorilla walk to fallen Brock.

Three fires surrounded them now and all the ground shadows of tree branches and lurking woods twisted together weirdly and independently to face off against one, the shadow sister, Adow.

Poxer entered the light of the Southern flame and stood proud with her staff of Toko Tuki. Uka Buka smiled at Toko Tuki in its doggish way, looking mindlessly crazed and jittering with built-up energy. As soon as the witch blew her crushed-up crystal dust into Brock's sleeping face, he awoke, and Uka Buka reacted by lunging straight into Gem's shadow. All of Uka's forest shadows now separated themselves from normalcy and flew around and around the encampment, reigniting the Eastern pit and heightening the flames of the others. The tree branches themselves stitched together to create a wooden dome overhead, while roots crept closer over the ground and through the vortex of encircling shadows, seemingly enchanted by the howling, hungry winds.

Gem's shadow rapidly vibrated in spasms and suddenly darkened as a greater void of light, thickening defensively and readying itself. Uka Buka flew at Adow, completely embodying her, and moved to the center to face off with Toko Tuki.

Frightened at the shadow of Uka Buka, Poxer looked up at Toko Tuki as she lifted the staff as high as she could and brought it back down with earth-quaking force. A nova of light shot out and ignited the four flames even higher than Uka's shadow winds had, increasing the heat of the encampment.

Poxer could hear the loud footfalls of Baggans and Moorendo. She could also hear the monks speaking another language between each other and preparing themselves in squat fighting stances, whispering their incantations whenever they could. Baggans sounded like he was ripping himself from an entanglement of vines and huffed out two words before the witch's scream.

"Nature's Revolt!"

The pile of firewood in the center of the shadow circle rose into a tornado of spiraling sticks, and Uka Buka's shadow arm pushed it forward in an attempt to tango with Toko Tuki. One piece thunked Mokes in the jaw, knocking him out, and another hefty chunk clipped Poxer in the lip. Blood spit out on the large bear man Moorendo at her side, who was just stepping in front of her and bellowing out a chant, "Alla-Cunda!"

The bellow had clattered the sticks to the ground and back onto the witch's boulder altar. Then the boulder started to shake and move, a stone not tested by Endo's inanimate sound check. The girl monk flipped forward on top of it and put a soothing hand on its face. The boulder jiggled but lost its rocky momentum to escape its earthly indentation.

Holding tight to her staff, Toko Tuki whirled Poxer around to engage with the Uka Buka shadow. Tuki lifted her up off the ground and she lunged for Uka's tiki head, but only caught cold darkness and missed. Uka Buka playfully dashed around her and Tuki, then over the somersaulting male ram horned monk into the speedy circle of shadows still zipping around the encampment.

While Uka Buka looked annoyed at the two acrobatic monks, it still laughed while completely surrounding them, as its head flew around and around, cherishing its moment in the spotlight.

Past the vortex of shadows, a sound of roots ripping out of the earth was heard, and a moment later, two trees that could fit under the taller trees intertwined canopy slid into the encampment, swaggering their branches like coltish thugs.

Finally, Poxer heard the witch's young voice through Uka's laughter and the creaking of awakened woods.

"Put out the flames! Put, out, the, Fire!"

As the monks acrobatically ninja'd around the thuggish unearthed woods, the witch pulled muscle bond Brock closer to her. Toko Tuki, all the while, growled at Brock and the haunting shadows around them.

"Put out the fires if you can! It'll stop the shadows! Please!" The witch yelled like she was in agony. Her shadow getting caught up in the shadow vortex must have felt sickening to her.

Nature's Trents encroached closer and their awakened tree bark began to split open and illuminate with green light. With this renewed vitality a rune-engraved branch rushed through the air and slapped the male ram horned monk ten feet back to where Baggans tried to help him up and away from the ensnaring vines and cyclone of shadows.

Now distraught after watching her brother get pummeled, the girl monk ran up the trunk of the awakened tree and carved three slashes in it that stopped its advance at once. She then guarded herself through the frozen branches against the other awakened tree's rambling brambles.

Heat extinguished from Poxer's back as the bear man dropped the altar boulder on the Eastern pit. The witch, motivated by her warden's instinct, threw a couple of sticks to collapse the base of the Western pit, sending hot embers cascading into the moat of water, causing a disturbed scene of a splash of gooey red water and steam rising out of its kindred smoke.

Baggans caught on, ran around the swinging branches and roots of the wild tree, and kicked in the two dozen stones bordering the Northern pit on top of its flame. The Shadow dance came to an end; the witch embraced her freed wispy sister with anxious arms, and Uka Buka floated in the high flames of the Southern pit, the one designated for fire, and fire alone.

Growing red and enraged, Uka flew toward Tuki with a tail of fire behind him, and Tuki, still at the head of Poxer's staff, flew at Uka. Tiki against Tiki, Uka suddenly dodged Tuki's headbutt and wrapped its fire tail around Poxer's staff. Poxer had to let go, and the staff fumbled to the ground in flames. Instantly, Tuki's feathers dulled, and its head became more transparent, floating lower and lower against a great gravity ascending upon it. Uka Buka turned to the witch and gave a proud face with its eyes closed in triumph.

Thud! And Toko Tuki's bone clunked Uka on the side of the head.

The witch cast a few words with a ringed hand outward and lowered the dazed Uka Buka spirit. She crawled towards it, and quickly blew her crystal dust into its tiki tribal face. Both Uka Buka and Toko Tuki vanished, yet wisps of smoke or spirit flew into Brock.

Cid had eventually frozen the second tree and rushed to Crum's side. Baggans went over to knocked out Mokes and slapped him to wake up, and Moorendo stood between Poxer and Gem.

Both of the girls looked at Brock and then at each other, and both said at the same time.
"What the fuck just happened?"

Greetings & Departures

$\mathbf{A}$ flash lit up the haphazard ceremonial grounds, and Mokes slipped his phone into his pocket while jogging to catch up with the main group.

It had been a full 24 hours without sleep, and he felt like his long dreadlocks had begun to knot around his brain. Now safe behind the group, he looked down at the picture he had just taken and tried to diagnose its true depiction. He gave his phone a disgruntled, twisted stare. The scene was basically a natural mess. The only formidable truth of mystical chaos was the two mostly uprooted trees hovering in the middle of four blackened fire pits and an abundance of uncanny small roots and vines entangled on the forest floor.

Was it the shrooms Gem had given us? If it was, they must have been laced. Was it all a psychedelic trick to get us to believe we had caught some kind of spirit that was now attached to Brock? Just so the Druids could get paid, perhaps? Making us out to look crazy in front of the Illuminati. Those trees were definitely not there before, or were they? Am I still tripping? Mokes uneasily swimming in his mind with indecisive thoughts.

Mokes foraged through every pocket he had, looking for his papers and weed. He smoked so much the night before he'd have to roll another joint as they hiked, yet he couldn't get all three things he needed into one palm. He'd find his weed, then find his lighter, and suddenly lose his weed once he found his papers, with his lighter now lost in a different pocket. He must have still been tripping. The mixture of good and bad feelings had him giggling with uncertainty.

After following Brock's cut out trail for several minutes, the group came to a weird halt, forming a semi-circle around a gnarled ancient oak in the middle of an incline.

"This is- Flower Crack -where Uka Buka *came* from?" Poxer asked. She had already explained her Tourettes syndrome but still attained a few wiry glances.

"I do believe this is where Uka Buka resides, yes. But for now the spirit is in Brock."

Brock held his tired gaze at the gnarled oak and took the other's uneasy stares with no effect.

"Ooo-Kay," Cheek clicks, and a resident bird whistle followed Poxer's long tic that extended her neck out in a strange way and then quickly jerked to the side painfully. She rubbed at her neck and took a breath.

Poxer's voice was prevalent and confident, yet tired and low, as if she were getting ready for another fight.

"We must stay here."

Gem's voice, in contrast, was brisk, loud, and cheerful. "I don't think so little one. You came here with a spirit of your own, and by the spirit-to-spirit interaction, I say you came here to try and stop this Uka Buka."

Gem looked over at Brock again.

Brock drawled out his words as if he were in a dream, "She overheard my conversation. She knows what the Illuminati are after."

Poxer's eyes narrowed, and mouth thinned with glints of snarling teeth.

"I- *fucking ass clown* -know more than you think." A tic shook her blonde curls up and back, only to fall back down into her eyes.

She thought back to what Ki had told her about his dream. He dreamt of everything that happened last night and dreamt of another world cast in lava and bone... This was important, but she desperately didn't want to spaz out at this moment; the struggle within her visibly showed.

"The one *possessed* before by- *whay'ooa* -this *spirit*, sent me. He told me Uka Buka is a guardian to some kind of doorway. And- fucking fuck -this doorway is under this tree... I can feel its energy, its..."

Gem's chest lifted up and her flame tattoo between her small breasts and ragged blouse seemed to kindle.

"It's biz las. I'm guessing your boss wants you to destroy the doorway, but that's not going to happen because my boss wants to keep it open."

Cid and Crum exclaimed the most grievous looks at Gem and then at each other. The others also looked shocked, but still in a disillusionment of unknowing. This Gem had obviously not told her team about their second mission.

"I like ya, and believe it or not, want to work with you, but I can't have you digging up this ancient tree and haphazardly, obliviously try to destroy an Earth portal… Let me be honest; how in the hell are you planning to even do that? You guys don't even have a spade." Another smile lifted on Gem's cute mouth as Poxer flattened.

Gem walked up the incline to Uka's tree and embedded her hand into the foliage. She took a moment. Everyone took a moment.

"We have an eight-hour hike back to the road; this allows us to think and plan." Gem watched Poxer continue the fight within herself. The dilemma of failing, the decision to either surrender or keep fighting, the tensed tourette tics leaving her rubbing the back of her neck in painful frustration.

"Listen Las, things can be a lot worse for you… Let's walk and talk. You can always return later to destroy the portal if you want."

A dual between their eyes wove no absence of time.

Poxer looked at the bone in her hand and tightened her grip, then looked at Baggans for an eye glance of advice, but Baggans only shrugged. She followed Gem's footsteps up the incline.

"My name is Pinky."

Mokes' joint hung limp in his mouth, completely in awe of the portal conversation. He let the group pass him by up the hill and towards the mountain ridge. After an obscured amount of time over two hills and around a mountain bend that looked over the grand lake below, Mokes finished rolling two more joints. He put those in his shirt pocket and finally lit the one in his mouth with shaky fingers. Instantly, his shoulders slouched in relaxation, and his gaze began to steady.

Okay, let's see. Mokes thought to himself as he watched the tail end of his group meander over the hiking trail. He couldn't see the head of the wandering serpent, so he started analyzing the first two in front of him. Cid, a female exorcist, had two bags of scrolls at her back and an arm around her brother Crum, who leaned into her, struggling to put one foot in front of the other. Mokes believed they needed a hit of this joint as much as he did, but hesitated in his approach. It was a seven-hour hike. They all had time. His shroomy mind flipped over itself and made silly little decisions.

Looking past the monkish exorcists was a veteran Grunion, Dave Baggans. He remembered watching him and Jack show up in the middle of the wild and crazy ritual. Actually becoming even more crazy when they showed up, way more crazy. *How did Baggans get wrapped in this? How was Poxer, of all people, a wizard now? And she had a spirit tiki as well?* Mokes asked this to himself, again feeling crazy.

Mokes hadn't seen Baggans for years now, and Poxer, well, she spent most of her time with the Mermaids and at her Refill Store. Seeing her here, with a band of hired Illuminati mercenaries… The questions quickened his step. He could ask them and perhaps get answers, but again, he slowed his roll. There were still other people to wrap his mind around.

Ahead of Baggans was the massive bear of a man, Moorendo. Mokes was envious of his fur coat and loveable size. It seemed that the guy didn't have to worry about anything; however, he held a focused frown on the two in front of him.

Mokes could barely catch a glimpse of Brock past the others that trailed him, especially around Moorendo, who took up the entire width of the path. Brock had taken twice as many mushrooms as Mokes, giving Mokes another urge to rush forward and see how he was doing, hand him the joint as a peace offering, and settle into his thoughts on what happened. Mokes felt uneasy about this as he remembered that spirit funneling into Brock after its shadow-summoning rampage.

What could possibly be going on inside his head now? Mokes wondered and then suddenly jumped at the sight of the monks' shadows steadily trailing their masters.

Gem, Gemini, the witch necromancer, and her shadow sister Adow… She must have been at the front of the line with Poxer, leading them to a safe return. *Or was it a safe return?… She had taken as many shrooms as Brock!*

Mokes finally decided to take the initiative and crawl up the line. *A shroomy boomy witch at the head, leading us to what? Another void in the cosmos where she could collect more ancient herbs?* Mokes wanted to go to sleep.

He reminisced about Gem in the forest with him before yesterday's sunset. So cute and cuddly as she picked up flowers from the forest floor, her dark garb flowing around her. He wanted to hug her and be with her, sleep next to her… but her sister… a shadow, always watching and always making things more creepy than they should be.

He moved up, passed an unburnt joint to the two monks wobbling ahead, and made it right behind Baggans, enough to pop his head a little to Baggans' side, for the trail wasn't wide enough for two ruggers.

"Hello." Mokes expected more from himself, but that's all that came out.

Baggans continued to look ahead, ignoring Mokes' greeting.

Mokes rummaged through his brain on all the possible questions he could ask his old teammate.

"What brought you guys up the mountain?"

"Your deceit." Baggans said matter of factly. This caused Mokes to drift back a bit, trying to stay in the space ahead of the exorcists and behind the big rugger. Four years ago, he had become an informant for the Zendolini Mafia and betrayed the Earth Enforcers Association, betrayed his friends… his family.

"I know I fucked up, but I think what just happened should be enough for us to talk. Crazy right?" The marijuana smell enticed him to flutter back to the exorcists and relieve himself from the heartache of losing his friends.

Baggans looked back at him over his shoulder. Watching for a moment as if to see who he had become.

"You don't deserve our voice. Things could have been different… Fish, Tawa would still be alive if you hadn't joined forces with our enemy… Even now, you are working for the Illuminati." Baggans gave him a disgusted look over his shoulder.

"Now go somewhere else. I don't want you around me." Baggans looked ahead, stoic and proud, yet tired and sad.

Mokes' spirit was filled with regret right then. He regretted his actions before, but to see his old friends again, with the power of loyalty and companionship orbiting around them like bees around a flower. Their auras were too strong for him to penetrate. As he waited for an opportunity to pass Bags on the trail, he rolled another joint with his dreadlocks in his eyes.

Tucking the weed stick away, Mokes passed at the fork in the road where they had stopped to smoke the day before, and caught up with Moorendo.

Moorendo gave Mokes a smile as he waddled up to his side, and Mokes felt relieved everyone didn't hate him.

"Heya Endo… have you experienced anything like that before?"

The silence flipped Mokes' mind back into thinking everyone did hate him, but finally Moorendo answered, obviously just taking his time to think it over.

"Some of it, yes. Some of it, no." He said in a philosophically playful manner, knowing Mokes' mind must already be on a rollercoaster. He laughed at his correct assumption as Mokes looked down at the unlit joint between his fingers.

"A man of riddles can tell no lies, you see." Moorendo enjoys the silence between conversations. Lapping it up like a cat drinking milk.

"I have seen trees move before and become enlightened with ancient engraving. This story is much too deep for me to fully get into now, but what we experienced was called an awakening, Mother's wooden guardians protecting her natural spirits from foes. We had a feeling that might happen, which is why we brought the exorcist monks. They know the ancient language to stop these *Awakened* guardians. Of course, I am on the side of guarding our Mother; however, in this case, we needed to protect ourselves first."

Moorendo inhaled a deep breath, almost seeming like he was stealing the air around Mokes and finally letting it out to send a gale into the back of Brock's head.

"Unseen spirits affecting the elements around them, I have witnessed this as well. Even enchanting natural shadows around them isn't new to us. But... Visually seeing floating tiki-headed spirits, battling against one another, casting shapeshifting spells, and having an extremely powerful influence over the elements... I believe our Mother Gaia has birthed an alternate defense through evolution. Something between a storm and an Awakened tree. Something more covert of which could possibly awaken her greatest enemy, humans, into becoming friends." Moorendo nodded up at Brock.

"We will have to watch over him closely now. Having a spirit of Gaia with that much strength should be carefully studied and cared for."

Mokes hadn't come up to Moorendo to argue, but he got a weird misunderstanding in his stomach that he wanted to remedy. "If you want to protect Mother Earth so much, then why *steal* one of her spirits only to deliver it to the people in charge of bringing Earth to ruin?"

Endo came up with too quick of a response, "Money. And I don't see how giving a tiki spirit to the Illuminati is a bad thing; it might even be good; perhaps this Uka Buka can teach them a thing or two... Why are you working for the Illuminati?" Moorendo smiled at catching Mokes off guard.

"Money…" The word came out as if it actually meant dishonor. What road was Mokes going down? He suddenly didn't care where Gem was leading him, for he was already lost. Dreams and passions forgotten. *Why?*

He could feel Baggans' despising eyes on his back . Mokes nudged his head back to acknowledge the newcomers.

"What about them? Do you know what you'll do with them?"

Moorendo laughed loud enough to make Mokes curl his shoulders even more into his chest. He didn't want the ruggers to think he was talking about them.

"Those two remind me of Gem and I," He laughed again, "Gem is working her magic. She is very wise and knows when to keep important secrets and when to make allies. I wouldn't worry about them Mokes."

Puzzlement sunk into Mokes' shroom flipping mind.

Moorendo clapped a big hand on his Mokes' shoulder, "Two sons of our Mother, rivaling against each other. Someone working symbiotically with one and enhanced by their connection. Absolutely fascinating. Something we definitely want to learn more about. Something, I believe, we need to protect."

Mokes nodded in acknowledgment. "I was going to smoke some reefer with Brock."

"That's a good idea mate, but let me hit it first, eh."

***

The two women at the lead were stark comparisons to each other but marvelously got along quickly based simply on their identical heights. Gem was normally speaking up to Moorendo, and Poxer was normally speaking up to Baggans, but now their conversational plane was level. The little things really did make a difference.

Gem glided with her darkened scarves and ragged clothes swaying side to side. Poxer's light blouse underneath her forest green jacket bobbed up and down as she bounced forward, walking with elaborate and determined hip thrusts that waved her tight-butted breeches back and forth. Curly blond hair seemingly trying to spring into Gem's frizzy black.

"So, Pinky, I want to propose a deal. And I want to be clear with you about what's happening, only if you can also permit yourself to be clear with me." Her soothing, untroubled voice pulled Poxer in even closer. Poxer studied the human bone in her hand and sighed a nod of concession. Lies did not come from a voice like that.

"Good… I'll start by saying, what you did back there amazed me. Working harmoniously with one of these spirits, empowered with magic that has elemental affliction… I thirst for your knowledge." Poxer felt like she should have a response to that, but nothing came.

"I want to move forward with my contract without arrest or delay. Brock and the spirit Uka Buka will be delivered to the One World Order and then informed where Uka's Earth portal is-"

"Ki said it's- *dung rabbit* -a portal to Hell Gem. If you want to begin to understand us, please understand this first. Ki has been right- *ee'oo* -about everything in his vision so far."

Gem walked with her hands folded together at her waist, contemplating.

"If that is so, we may need to use more caution. Perhaps if we wait to see what the Illuminati are planning with this portal, their attempts with it will enlighten us more."

"But then it'll already- … -be too late. They are powerful and evil right? We need to- uhg... -stop this now."

"We are evil hunny. Just because we love the planet and try to save every flower, doesn't mean we don't want to watch the human race burn. Better that than any day in our future becoming a nuclear holocaust, murdering the surface of the planet *and* its people. The Galaxy of the Dead could be a final reckoning for those that burden our planet. A new leadership of ancient afterlifers who want to help the planet succeed over its successor. Wouldn't it be nice to get new leaders who saw Earth for all her magical properties of life, and exiled those who bleed her dry, using her wealth of life for their own wealth of death? If it truly is a gateway to the Galaxy of the Dead, you think you, or even us together, can do anything about it?"

"We can- *m'* -hide it at least." Stammering and ticking even harder now after discovering Gem and her crew's true ideology.

Gem ignored Poxer's plea. "For you, I suggest staying low and watching what happens next."

Poxer gave Gem fierce, abrasive eyes.

"I could deliver you and your spirit to the Illuminati, *Pinky*. That would relieve me of any danger. However, I believe you and this Ki are trying to do the right thing for the planet and *know* secrets that I wish for you to tell me…"

Poxer hated storytime because of her Tourette's. However, she also felt like Gem was the best witch she'd find to tell her about what's been happening to her and Ki. Even though she was working towards a plan of desecration and renewal, she was still the only chance Poxer had at learning more about whatever this Galaxy of the Dead was all about.

***

An orange hue of sunrise melted the darkness out of the sky as the group made it back to the parking lot. Poxer and Gem spent their entire walk telling stories. The Galaxy of the Dead was what it sounded like, Heavenly planets and moons shining on the outer rim's halo, and Hell planets and moons eclipsed near its center, the galactic bulge.

The exorcists, Cid and Crum were a part of an ancient society, The Ram Horned Cultist, who devoted their lives to understanding the Earth and its protectors. Once they learned about the six Sky Sisters who angelically guard the planet from alien misfits, they adjusted their learning towards understanding the Galaxy of the Dead. Becoming exorcists led them toward helping the Sky Sisters protect against nefarious intruders and also pushed them toward discovering the ability to send their souls through these portals. Once they made it to the Galaxy of the Dead, they'd possess a soul of the dead to learn more about the afterlife, somehow preserving their body on Earth to be able to resurrect themselves and tell of their discoveries.

Poxer's story went a lot quicker since most of the magic she's ever witnessed happened within two days before this meeting. Gem seemed stunned and disappointed at assuming she was in the presence of another great witch, but that just strengthened her argument that Poxer needed to stay the hell away from the portal to actual Hell.

Even though Gem said she was evil, Poxer found her quite kind and genuine. Gem even wanted to mentor Poxer and her immense potential. To Gem, Poxer had stitched herself into Earth's destiny, and with the constant thirst for knowledge and clairvoyance, Gem decided their first stop was going to be the Refill Store.

Gem gracefully walked up to Baggans' Cadillac and turned to the group.

"We will look after Brock and this Uka Buka spirit and deliver them to the One World Order. Even as wild and enraged as Uka

Buka was, we don't believe the spirit will ever turn against its Mother.

"Before we do this, however, I need to help Pinky retrieve her Toko Tuki. In doing so, I need to see the ritual space of where he transferred to her. We will all travel together to her Refill Shop, and from there, we will depart."

Kahu

Brock made it through airport security with only a few odd stares. Ever since Uka Buka had attached itself to him, his blood has boiled to the point of leaking out from his facial gestures. He had to keep reminding himself to unclench his jaw and unfurrow his brow so he wouldn't be pulled to the side and marked as a terrorist threat.

He whipped his backpack around his shoulder and set off to pick out some headphones so he could blast his music. He stopped by one of the convenience shops with snacks, drinks, and everything you could possibly want for a long airplane ride. Cheaper than he would have guessed, Brock bought a pair of Bluetooth earplugs and set out to find an isolated seat near his flight gate.

He felt a little bad for knocking Crum and Cid's heads together, but he couldn't be imprisoned and tested on by the Illuminati just yet. He needed to find Ki first and ask him about Uka Buka and how to use the tiki spirit against the Illuminati.

Boarding had just started when Brock checked to see if his earplugs had finished charging. A flashing red light blinked in the reflection of his iris, and his knuckles cracked around his grip. He noticed that nowhere in the earplug booklet did it say the earplug's redlight would flash. It only said it would become a solid red, then green, then blue light for a complete charge. Enraged that he needed to go an extra unnecessary mile, he punched in the technical support number in so hard on his phone screen that the liquid crystal inside the phone permanently created a blue pressure mark in the corner.

Uka Buka smiled over his shoulder, letting Brock boil over into madness. He growled at the customer service representative over the phone, and the rep responded in a calm tone, "This happens all the time, sir. We will issue you a new pair right away. Just destroy the older pair once you have received the new pair."

Right then, a fat Indian man sat directly in front of Brock, facing him head-on with only enough space for one person to walk by them. Brock looked around, amazed, trying to understand why the man had sat right in front of him when the airport was pretty much empty.

"We will just need your proof of purchase, sir. If you can reply to our email with a picture of your receipt, we will be happy to send you the reimbursement cereal code."

"I don't have my receipt." Brock's voice rumbled low, growling more than ever now.

With no time to play games, and only a few people left to board, he became fed up, and Brock threw his new broken earplugs at the fat Indian's face and ripped the man's earplugs out of his ears. He bent down and looked into the man's eyes, drilling holes right through his skull.

With eyes showing nothing but confusion, the Indian man asked, "Hey, why'd you do that?"

Brock set off with Uka Buka sticking its long tongue out at the man. He checked his ticket and stomped down the bridge to board the plane. Hoping along the way he'd snap the bridge in two.

The way things were turning out in today's age, he wouldn't be the least surprised if he could break the bridge. Still astonished at how wasteful their society was in making the cheapest crap, wrapping it in tons of plastic, then putting it on shelves when it either didn't work right out of the box or it'd break after a few uses. He started to feel for Ki, but instantly clenched his fist at the name. Ki may be right about the system of world waste, but he stole his girlfriend Lexi and was the cause of his Father's death.

Lost in his fist clenches, he noticed he'd passed his seat by four rows. As he stopped to turn back, a grumpy teen right on his heels bumped into him and muttered something Brock couldn't hear. He did, however, know whatever she said was annoying. Without words he began to walk back, using his massive body to push the three people behind him stumbling back, the second chick completely falling on her ass with cell phone still clasped in both hands.

What the fuck were they rushing to sit down for? He thought as he stepped on the first teen girl's foot. He released his foothold and looked at the two people sitting down in his row. A fat Amish man was in the aisle seat, and a young man with beautiful eyes sat in the middle.

"Get up." Brock growled, as Uka mean dogged them from above the seats in front of them. They slithered out, and Brock steamrolled in. Finally giving him a chance at being left alone to listen to his metal music.

After about 3 hours in the air, Brock grabbed his complimentary snack and drink from the stewardess. He watched the Amish man pull out a smelly plate of pulled pork and start slapping his lips together as he ate. The middle guy seemed not to care because his headphones were on, and he was speaking into his phone.

"I thought you didn't get service in the air?" Brock asked him.

The guy glared at Brock for breaking his flow. "I'm writing my book." And he slid the headphone over his ear again.

"You're *writing* your book-?" Brock gasped unbelievingly at the guy using his mouth to type the words on his phone...

Uka Buka flushed itself against the porthole window and started to get excited about something. Uncaring and downright angry at everyone around him, Brock whirled around to ask the stewardess for a napkin. In his spasmodic twist, he spun his elbow right into the *book-writing* guy's face.

Brock didn't say anything; he just calmly sat there, waiting for his napkin.

The guy was outraged and asked for the stewardess to help him. However, she saw one man waiting patiently for a napkin and another freaking out from an accidental bump. Brock ignored the humans and tried to look around Uka Buka and see why he was so glued to the port window.

After trying to peek around the back of Uka Buka's blocky head, Brock decided to put his own head into Uka's. As he did this, a river of blood rushed through his body, and he could see the inside of Uka's eyes roll around manically until only the sky's puffy grayish clouds appeared. Finally, to Brock's surprise, he saw what Uka Buka was excited about. It wasn't just gray clouds and rays of sunshine floating in the sky; another Tiki head, the exact one he saw on top of Jacklyn Poxer's staff, was flying against the elemental resistance of high velocity.

Supremely focused on his destination, feathers pinned back and torn from the wind, the tiki spirit outside was quickly receding behind them until they finally passed it up.

Brock sat back and saw Uka Buka happily lounging in the lap of the guy next to him. Obviously pleased, it had a better ride to Japan than its nemesis, Toko Tuki.

***

Tuki felt a negative energy at its current altitude and shot down beneath the clouds, descending through humongous expanses of air and to the heartbeat of the ocean swells. The water spray drizzled over his gangplanked face, running down the canals of indented wood with tribal painted swirls and splattered dots of Ki's blood.

Pelicans soared together in their V formation, dolphins joined in a spiritual escort through the waves, and the salt created a tasty travel treat on Tuki's fat vine lips. Toko Tuki skidded along the surface, following the Pelican glide on top of the water. It was playful and fun for Tuki to enjoy the truly wild beings of the planet. The wild lived every second of their life with its creator. There were no useless materials, no evil schemes created for one gain, no pollution of ignorant crap, only the elements, only family, only life.

Toko Tuki dipped himself further and further into the water, seeming to slow down, until the spirit realized it was just a spirit. Closing its eyes and knowing its destination by its earthly soul, Tuki joined the team of dolphins enjoying their migration through the Pacific. Passing through the world of water just as quickly as passing through the world of air, Toko Tuki gathered a whole new inspiration and felt a pang of excitement over its being.

A broad green mountain was ahead of him, and Toko Tuki decided to go right through its hunk of earth. He really wanted to feel the planetary vibrations around him. To slow down in a meditative trance and understand what his Mother wanted from him. Wanted for all.

Tuki had to keep pressing on to protect his original companion. Uka Buka was coming for Ki, and Poxer's staff had been demolished, severing Tuki's bond between the two of them. The raw emotion of Tuki's love overthrew any other ideas a boundless spirit may have. Tuki just flew, knowing the path ahead was true.

Ahead of him, a plane leaned its wings down to the right and altered its course around another great green mountain, yet Tuki wasted no time in flying right into its heart. He spirited himself in becoming reacquainted with his Mother's sound, and feel the condensed waves of energy rolling through her core.

Pirate's Bay

The sacred rope of Meoto Iwa marriage rocks swung unceremoniously after Ki clipped his arm in his fall. His idea was to slow himself down by grabbing a hold of the rope like Tarzan, but it happened to be more difficult with Bonez in hand. Drained and bloodied from the Toko Tuki ritual spirit transfer, Ki splashed between the big and small Meoto rocks and floated for a while back to shore, every now and then throwing in a backstroke or two.

Like a mermaid out to sing to the full moon, Ki slid his body onto the smooth rocks of the break wall and pulled himself up by the frog sculpture's webbed ankle. He rolled onto his back and looked up to the stars, happy the night was a success and filled with magic, but troubled about an eerie feeling of loss.

Leia appeared upside down in the stars. Ki blinked, grateful to see his mother after all that had happened, and hoped she saw the magic that just occurred. Then his nose picked up a deceiving smell that hit him like a slap by a voluptuous bouquet.

"Elo Zepp, out for a midnight swim?"

Even though butt naked, Ki simply lay there looking up into her blue frosty eyes. Xillian. *Those eyes. He* tried again to remember where he saw those eyes.

She wore a black and white bandana with her hair bun still spiked up above the bandana tie. Her face glinted like the stars with her silver jewelry. She now had a silver mole through her upper lip, a chain going from her nose piercing to her ear, and an ear full of lopped earrings that formed a tiny silver wormhole as she looked down at him.

Her eyes slowly drifted down his chest and to his groin. Ki realized that Xillian must have a twin sister because this was a completely different smile than he was used to. Her hollow cheeks dimpled with silver studs.

A towel dropped on his groin, and a noose slid over his head and tightened around his neck.

"Dry off. You're coming with me."

For some reason Ki didn't mind being taken. He had just completed an epic ritual that opened up a wizard portal for a spirit to pass through. In addition, the bad girl that he had a crazy crush on actually saw him do that and had just finished smiling at his wang. Also, he still had backup. His mom had dropped him off, so she should still be around, probably waiting for the right moment to save his ass.

At Xillian's car, Ki looked at Leia's car and saw no one inside. Xillian gave him one of her baggy sweatshirts and tied more of the noose rope around his body. Towel wrapped around his waist, Ki fell into her whip, feeling nice in the warmth of the contained car air.

"So, where we headed? Back to your Grandma's temple?" Ki asked flirtatiously.

Xillian laughed. This new Xillian seemed older simply by how her chin proudly rose an inch higher than he was used to. The way her body slumped at ease made her seem so freaking cool in Ki's eyes. Xillian was finally herself, and she was more beautiful than ever before.

"There's a whaler that wants to see the son of the infamous Asagaio Dori. He just wants to talk with you before we pull the location of Hattori's land rights out of you."

Ki felt a tingle of pride hearing about how his father still ticked people off. It turned a smile on his tired lips.

Xillian's own smile evaporated quickly, and an angry, malicious tone spirited out of her.

"You won't be smiling later. Anata wa machigatta kazoku to kakwatte shimatta nodesu."

The light bulb finally clicked on that maybe it wasn't going to work out between the two of them. He still liked her. However, fresh, unavoidable trouble definitely reduced the bulge underneath his towel.

They drove for two hours in silence. Ki was super tired and a little worried about Leia. He kept looking in the rearview mirror for following headlights, but there were none. He reassured himself that she was alright. *She was smart as fuck and could heal trees, for Sky Sisters' sake!* His gut twisted up, but he told himself it was good she wasn't captured as well.

They parked at a bay, and Ki carelessly got out of the car and made it onto a dinghy with a metal pole on the stern to hold a lantern. Xillian sat engrossed in the lantern's light close to the engine, and Ki sat tied up at the bow.

The dinghy took off and Ki watched Bonez in between Xillian's legs, trying to think of ways to use his magical staff without Tuki around, and without actually being able to hold it. At least Bonez got to hangout in between her legs, he mused.

His happy sexual thoughts distracted him from the more frightening ones. Ki couldn't escape the feeling that he was on Charon's ferry to the afterlife. A feeling that everything was right in Destiny's eye, but simultaneously holding onto a weird feeling that he had taken on a huge loss. Just another ritual over a gentle swell with a perfect breeze in the air. He turned to face his fate over the bow and watched the moon reflect off the dark, endless water.

Xillian stopped the boat and turned off the engine. The water met the mood onboard; it was calm, dark, and wet. After categorizing things on her person, Xillian took off her pants, spidered over into Ki's lap, and looked him dead in his one good eye. She rubbed her hands over his buzzed head and dipped his nose into her chest. As she pulled back his head, Xillian brought her lips to Ki's and lifted his towel, slowly sliding back and forth on his weenie.

A peck kiss turned to a lick, and a lick turned to a slobbering tongue down his throat. His weenie squeezed inside of her, feeling the pringles of tight skin to tight skin, then a flush of wet warmth and pleasure. He accepted her sudden affection and rolled his tongue around hers, drinking in her saliva. He enjoyed having her cute face pressed to his and the tickle of her nose chain on his cheek. He enjoyed the compassionate lust pouring from her mouth and into his. He began enjoying the thought of her actually falling for him and not turning him into the Yakuza. Maybe she'd even join his side of spiritual, environmental activists trying to save the planet. She moaned out an organism, and right when his arousal met with the butterflies in his stomach, right when everything was going to be E.E.A. okay, her eyes flashed open, and Ki remembered. Instead of puking out of his weenie, he almost puked out of his mouth. The Ghost Ninja returns.

An instant of pain shot through Ki's right hand, and Xillian backed off him and pulled a torch from her jacket pocket. Shock didn't run through Ki, it was a collapse of fear, fear of knowing what was coming. Knowing the bloodline of the crazy ass bitches that were out to fuck him up. Xillian cauterized Ki's freshly cut-off index finger with a flat, red, hot piece of metal and went back to the stern under the lantern light. All was calm except for Ki's mind.

The pieces all clicked into place as Ki opened and closed his eye in pain. Open, smiling Xillian, proud and furious. Closed, ghostly Alisano, scary and horrible.

"That was for my mother, Alisano, Ki La'dori. And for my father… I'm not even close to being finished. I'll getchu to home base before the real fun starts. Yakuza is going to chew you up boy." Xillian looked him over like he was a rancid piece of meat.

***

Ah oh, Ki thought. He didn't even care about his finger pain because he knew how much worse it was about to get. His tough guy thoughts slid away like sand in a cheese grater. Oh, he was going to hurt. A seppuku Japanese suicide was the first thing he'd gladly do in a moment's opportunity.

Ki watched Xillian's face and saw her eyes look slightly above the horizon. The feeling of a bobbing mass loomed behind him, and he turned to relieve his eye of curiosity. A massive whaler ship sat towering over Xillian's little lantern dinghy. Ki guessed it was one of the new slaughterhouse factory ships that had stern slips that could pull a blue whale on deck and harvest it right then and there.

Below the many wenches, ropes, and cables, three men watched their lantern putter toward their bow. More movements ghosted through the mist closer to the stern, and one massive shadow strode out slowly on an elevated catwalk leading to the front harpoon gun. The harpoon looked as large as a shark, and the man seemed as big as a minke whale. He leaned on the handle of the artillery turret, fisherman's apron covered in guts.

Industrialism really made men soft, Ki thought, as he became more courageous, knowing that machines did most of the work for these weaklings now. They were safe on their big boats with wenches to do their heavy lifting and explosive harpoon cannons to do their killing. The International Whaling Committee set a quota for how many whales could be harvested a year; however, ships with a full crew out in the middle of the night had suspecting morals.

Xillian undid Ki's rope bind, and they both climbed up the ladder to the deck, catching a closer look at the man on the bridge. He was the largest muscled Japanese person Ki's seen in his few days on the island. He would have also thought the guy was the meanest he'd uncovered here, but he looked over at Xillian looping up her rope and thought again.

The man made it over to them and spoke with a flat, indifferent stare.

"Xillian… Kare o motto yoku miru koto ga dekiru yo ni, kare o cho n dekki ni oite mimashou."

His deckhands shoved Ki forward, and his towel fell off. He was never good at securing a towel around his waist, and now, with a missing finger, it was going to be that much harder. The boys behind him laughed, continued moving him to the center deck, and shoved him to a chair in the spotlight. Ki would have thought he was on an aircraft carrier if he hadn't seen the ship's totality.

A big hand grabbed Ki's face and moved his skin around, analyzing his scars. He easily pulled off the eye patch and put his thumb in Ki's socket causing him to wince. The man's hand moved to the other eye and spread his brow and cheek so the white ball was fully visible in the pinkish tissue socket.

"Kare no yasashī me wa, ryōshin ga kare kara nokoshita yuītsu no monode, kare o Asagaio. Sōdenakereba, karera wa Yamauba no yō ni mieru yō ni suru tame ni yoi shigoto o shimashita."

"This is Willyomasa, the Midnight Whaler. He's going to soften you up before I bring you to the Yakuza. He said, your one good eye is the only thing my parents left of you that identifies you with Asagaio. Otherwise, they did good work in making you look like a Yamauba, an old witch of the mountains that eats children."

Xillian turned to Willy, "Ga kono fune o saru toki, watashi wa Yamauba ni nari, wa muryokuna kodomo ni naru."

She bent down to Ki's lips, and he flinched, "I told Willy, when you leave this ship, I will be the Yamauba, and you will be the helpless child."

She straightened and kicked him and the chair over, knocking the wind out of him and causing him to wheeze.

"Dō yatte tsukamaeta no? Kataku miemasu."

"Kare wa hentaideari, hahaoya no tame ni naiteiru."

Xillian's raspy, malicious, and evil voice steadily distanced itself from behind him.

"He asked how I caught you, and I told him it was easy to pull a pervert who likes following helpless young women around. I told him you're a coward, and when I captured you and beat you, you cried for your mommy!" Her voice caught wind as she said Mommy, and a skull-cracking thud sound echoed over the deck. Ki's vision went black.

She laughed while looking at Bonez the Cane, its glow slowly fading back into its engravings. "I was trying to break the fucker, but this is really a special stick."

Ki went over in his head. *You're made out of bones Ki. You're just a skeleton. There is no pain. Bonez. How can I use* - A fish-sized fist came hurdling into Ki's head that whipped his neck around.

Great, Ki thought. Xillian left Willy with no grievances to beat the shit out of this loser persona she made up for me.

The harder the hits, the easier it was for Ki to escape. Punches sending him into outer space, into fields of the universe under a rainbow sky. The melting colors of Mother Earth's eye.

Crack! Ki hung over his lap, drolling. He almost thought the droll was seeping out of a new tear in his scarred cheek. Bloody droll was his escape. He created a whole new world inside the stream of saliva bunjee'ing to the ship's deck. *Whales died on this deck,* Ki impressed.

Willyomasa, "...Chichioya wa watashi no nin no kyōdai to chichioya o koroshita. Watashi wa, Xillian no chichioya no Sokuru to kyōryoku shite, anata no chichioya o Hell ni tsureteikimashita."

Xillian just nodded and translated again, but her words passed over Ki. It sounded bad, yet he already knew he was fucked, and words didn't mean shit to him at this point. Pain was what lectured him. Willyomasa's fist spoke his anger.

Even though Ki felt tied up, he wasn't. His whole body was so tired and beaten he might as well have been wrapped with chains. All he needed was one good grasp on Bonez.

Xillian paced around with Bonez as Willy hovered over his prey, his whale massacre scent making Ki want to puke.

He rolled his eye to watch Xillian waltz around. It was like Alisano's ghostly walk mixed with Sokuru's wizardry loose clothes.

Fuck she's their daughter for sure, how could I have missed that.

Knowing her family, her origin, her sex drive, her rage, it had to benefit him in some way, but he was tired, even thinking about thinking back tired him.

Ki blew Xillian a kiss as Willy whispered Japanese curses in his ear between punches. She ran up to Ki about to do something horrible, he guessed, and with as much spirit as he had left in him, he grasped for Bonez.

His good hand held onto Bonez the Cane right above Xillian's, and a weird pause occurred. Willyomasa was surprised Ki, the cowardly pervert, had enough in him to do anything, and Xillian knew Ki and Bonez had a magical connection, so she waited apprehensively for something to happen. Ki also didn't know what would happen without Toko Tuki around.

He gulped, and it felt like the driest gulp of his life, dusty air tearing his throat to shreds, almost strangling him with angst.

Breaking the paralyzing moment in time, Xillian pulled back hard, and Bonez broke from Ki's grip. The worm engraving scrolled along the cane's wood began to imbue brighter and brighter with a dim green light, to mellow yellow-green, and finally a burning orange.

Xillian let go and shook the pain out of her hand. Bonez now stood up straight on its own, radiating with power and heat. Ki thought this was it. Bonez had had enough and was going to save him from these Yakuza pirates. His eye was swollen to a narrow slit to see out of, but he imagined Bonez casting beautiful sun rays out, putting his enemies in bliss. He imagined a healing light from Bonez to give him enough strength to rise out of this chair and get off of this ship, but as he dreamt, time falsified his kind assumptions. The light within Bonez diminished, and Bonez turned back to a regular looking walking stick.

Xillian stepped back up to Bonez, snickering with her chin up high. Back when she was unsure about the cane's magic, her chin was buried in her chest. She grabbed Bonez as it still stood straight up.

"Willyomasa Kaigan ni tsureteittekimasu."

"Aye." Willy grunted while eyeing the cane in Xillian's hand.

The deckhands carried Ki over to the ladder that rung back to the lit-up dinghy. *Back to the romance,* he thought. This time Ki would make sure not to look cute in front of Xillian, just in case she tried to kiss him again. And with a funny sense of relief, Ki watched Willyomasa work his way down the ladder.

Not wanting to deal with the liability of maneuvering Ki down the ladder, full of dead weight and half-conscious, the deckhands threw him overboard to wake him up with a splash. Willyomasa held him under for half a minute, then pulled him up and into the dinghy with his midnight fling, Xillian.

They made it to shore, and Xillian kept Ki under Willy's watch while she made a phone call. At Xillian's hip, Bonez' bottom butt embedded in the sand and flashed with green light, almost as if to wink. The duration of the next flash made it seem more of an S.O.S signal than energy puttering out of its life force. Ki ruggedly thought that if there was a time to make something happen, it was now.

On a far-off forest hill, a line of headlights appeared. Soon the Lincoln Continentals and Toyota Centuries started pulling up on the street. Xillian told Willy to pull Ki out of the dinghy, and then she started straightening him out, tidying up her handy work. They proceeded over the beach and to the back of her car under a small grove of trees with sand mixed in with the grass.

Clean suited Japanese men meandered over to them, talking amongst themselves and laughing while pointing at what Willyomasa caught this time. The older Yakuza men got in close, standing in a lackadaisical way that exuded pride and confidence. Their slouches simply resembling their fearlessness and cool. Staggered behind them were the younger Yakuza, looking like straight-up bosses themselves. All of these men seemed to hold an essence of importance to them. In another time Ki would have wanted to be like them. He imagined his father Asagaio more clearly than ever now, a boss with a hidden agenda of pure goodness in a suit of evil.

Ki blinked as Xillian roughly spun him around and pushed his head down to look inside the trunk of her car.

No...

No, Ki thought again. *No.* And his spirit invisibly shrouded his body. His bare feet were connected to the earth, but the slight breeze wavered his cast-out spirit like a flag on a high mast. A spirit caught on fire with pure red flames. Water leaked out of him. *My Mother.*

Laughter around him made it seem like he was in a different dimension, but Xillian's words rang clear.

"Oh ya, eye for an eye... Ki. You killed my mom, so I killed yours."

Still looking at the blue streak of hair running down the side of Leia's cut-out eyes, Ki took hold of Bonez. With an influx of hot power, Bonez was instantly a part of him, embedded into his body, his flesh, his blood. His spirit now shrouded both him and the worm engraved staff. Thoughts were merely illusionary now; his instincts ate at him like a starving wolf.

Uka Buka's passion electrified through him like he was struck by a lightning bolt.

His focus was Xillian. She tried to pull the cane away but it was no use. Ki blew off her defiant hand with the power coursing through him and calmly turned to the Yakuza. The night turned to day as Bonez blasted out blinding light, which Ki could see right through, turning his vision into bleeding colors of the vivacious shapes around him. He slammed Bonez into the ground and felt like he had become one with the roots of the trees. Instantly, insanely, he popped his new wooden limbs out of the earth and grabbed hold of flesh that he so desperately wanted to crush.

A fist hit his face, and a strong hand tugged at him.

Through his new eyesight, the form was covered in color, but by its size, Ki knew it was Willyomasa. The Midnight Whaler who brought thousands upon thousands of beautiful whales and dolphins to a horrific end. Another piece of shit that laughed at his beautiful mother's dead body.

"TALOONKA!" Ki yelled in a maddened growl, and Willyomasa burst in flames, seemingly like his blood caught fire first and shot right out of every pour in his skin. Ki focused on him burning alive, wanting the moment to last forever. They thought they were demons, so Ki brought them to Hell.

With no pain Ki fell to his knees, darkness blanketing his colored vision.

Old Man

"**Y**ūki o dase…"

It was Ki's forty-sixth hour in his cell. Most of the time he spent lying face down with his arms as a cushion. The other parts were spent gagging, and some parts laughing. Something didn't sit well with being horribly tortured and eventually killed. His gags came from losing his mother, his rock, his angel of love that he had his entire life.

Ki was presently bent and over dry heaving in a corner. The waste drain at the other corner smelt too horrible to even be around, and the other side of the cell, beyond the bars, occupied the voice of another prisoner.

"Yūki o dase." The voice calmly said again. Sounding like years of repetition, sounding like a lost soul, with a hint of advisement.

"What does that mean?" Ki breathed out behind gritted teeth. His teeth bond together with more pain than frustration. Although, he didn't give a fuck about Yūki or this prisoner. He was broken and wanted to be left alone.

Silence, and then the man shuffled closer, his chains clinging on the bars.

"American?"

"Yeah." The two of them have spent the last two days near each other, but between their dungoneous depression, neither of them spoke to one another. Ki didn't even know someone was there until the man took a piss earlier that morning.

"Why are you here?" His voice was still calm and rough but more urgent than before.

"Who cares… they…" Ki perked up enough to stop gagging, but felt more broken than ever trying to talk about what just happened. Still, the thought of this old man being the last kind soul he'd be able to talk to gave him a small dopamine hit, gratefully accepting the buzz of something other than pain throughout his body.

"Are you scared boy?"

Ki searched for the prisoner in the darkness, staring straight at the voice. He gave the air time to shift through breaths and plopped down on his sit bones.

"Who cares if I'm scared? Not worth my time worrying about it, is it? But no, I'm not fucking scared old man." His eyes studied the void form and accepted blindness.

"Tell me who your parents are?"

That question hit harder than Willyomasa. Ki was taken aback; he thought the old man was going to be more pleasantly eager to help, yet he asked a question, which at this time, was the wrong fucking question.

Ki started to feel sick again.

The black shape walked to the two barred vent on the far wall of his cell, silhouetting him from the chest up with the morning sun's light.

"There are many ways to live life. Even behind these bars, I've found gratitude, sanctuary, and hope… I hope to eat a couple of flower petals in the sunshine before I die." He said this as an afterthought, and his silhouetted face turned toward him, making it look more skull-like with no ear on the side of his head.

"You are right. Being scared is a waste. I would have taught my child that if I… could have."

Footsteps clapped outside the catacomb.

The silhouetted man made as if to speak more, but Xillian cut him off with a loud echoing whistle, slamming against the bars in her greeting.

"Elo Lads, you get acquainted yet? We going to cut your boy up pretty good, Asaga, you ready or what?" Her dark eyeliner and pierced dimples through her sunken cheeks gave her a terrifying skull-faced look.

Ki was surrounded by skulls. He was ready for death.

Xillian grabbed Ki's head and opened his good eye. "Did you hear that punk." She pushed the nub of her lost hand in his eye.

"This is your Father you FUCK!"

She let him go and gave Ki another chance to look into the silhouette behind the sunlite bars. Two middle-aged brutes and one Yakuza elder then blocked his view. One of the brutes had a tattoo of a Japanese lady in a skirt from his pinky up his forearm. Ki recognized him instantly as the subway information guy from Narita Airport. They've been waiting for his dumb ass to get to Japan. Ki sagged his head again. His stupidity killed his mother. His stupidity ruined so much. He hated himself. Xillian spilled only lies. His father was dead. He was ready for death.

Xillian lit Ki up with a flashlight. "Look at him! Location or Hell? Which is it Asagaio?"

After no reply she was quick with her scooper and creamed out Ki's last eyeball. He couldn't help but yell. He yelled with a roar, with anger and passion and love, all together. Ki felt like he needed to make his mother proud if he didn't scream like a little bitch, and yet while thinking about her made him want to roar fire out of his body and fry the fuckers around him. He needed to be heard, a primal bellow was all he had left.

One of the brutes tried to slap Ki's outrageous yell out of him.

Ki snarled, "Fuck you! Xillian!!!" A warcry arose again and a towel quickly wrapped itself around Ki's mouth, right before he was about to yell out another Taloonka fire spell.

"Keep his mouth shut! Asagaio… We see you there. You've seen him. You fucking know this is your son… He boils with the same fire you did so long ago."

Strength gurgled on edge from the silhouette.

"That is not my son."

Xillian sighed and turned to whisper to the Yakuza elder. Ki's heavy, painful breath, masking what they were saying.

"Bring her in." Two men looking more like fishermen than well-dressed Yakuza carried a body in, propped her up to standing, and pulled back her hair to reveal her face.

Xillian laughed, "Wow, I couldn't have planned this better. Like mother like son. They look identical, don't they? Even the blind could see their resemblance!"

After finishing her cackle, Xillian spoke again, this time without humor and with an air of inevitability. "We will give you a choice, Asagaio. You can watch us cut up your dead girlfriend and then do the same to your son. Or you can tell us where Honzo's land rights are and we will allow you and your son to come with us to the Property Land Right location. Your whole family is with us now. You. Have. Lost."

Instantly Asagaio spoke to the Yakuza elder. "Kawase, hontōni kore o sonkei surudarō ka?"

The elder nodded without saying a word, and for the moment, the Yakuza gave the prisoner Asagaio time to reflect, leaving only the sounds of Ki's ragged nose breathes and Asagaio's thoughts. So much could change based on one individual's decision in one moment. It's amazing how billions of people worldwide could have the same effect. Of course, some moments are more influential than others. For example, the Yakuza waiting for this decision for thirty years.

Ki gritted his teeth and blew through his nose with as much air power as he could muster, trying to get his father to just let us die! To let go. As a last fuck you to the Yakuza.

"The treasure you seek is protected by the dead... I... and my son, will lead you to the grave it is buried in."

Xillian went to the bars holding Asagaio.

"Where old man?"

"The Koyasan Cemetery in the Wakayama Mystic Mountains."

Portal to Hell

Brock sat on the ground with his knees bent high into his chest, hand clasped to his wrist, and slowly took in the room with no chairs. He supposed sitting on the ground here was normal since everything else was low put. The tea table and the samurai sword stand were next to a little structure with dragon sculptures spitting out water, and candles covering the flat surfaces of the shrine.

Everything was so delicate here, so breakable. The feeling of a great flushing warmth made his butthole pucker with the idea that destruction was made easy. He knew this room had a master artisan's hand in play, but he still wanted to pick shit up and smash it down. Yet he kept his zen, for he was Mr. Zendolini now, and thinking was in order, especially in the dragon's den.

Unexpectedly, the paper-thin sliding doors revealed a silhouette of a girl with a spikey hair bun and a straight as a board posture. A little further behind her, two men stood waiting.

How had they crept up with no notice, no sound? Must have been a ninja thing, he thought. The shadow of the side of her face strayed stagnant for a long moment, as if she were a humongous dragon side-eyeing the city she was about to burn down to the ground. Then the thin sliding door opened with beautiful ease, sounding like a wind sword cutting through leaves. The silhouetted beast turned into a full beauty. The beast still shining within her frozen frost eyes.

"Mr. Zendolini, we see you've come all the way from America with great haste. Our partners are… worried about you." Xillian moved to the low table and stood before Brock, looking down her jewel-chained nose at him. Brock recognized the cane flitting through her hand and the other hand completely missing, freshly bandaged with red soaking through the white wrap.

"You got him?" Brock asked, barely breaking out of his Zen. He wondered how Uka Buka would react with Ki around.

"Our partners are wondering the same thing. Did you retrieve this… Uka Buka?" Xillian's voice was broken up and curdled with anger.

Brock looked over his shoulder at Uka Buka. The magical plank face was actually a lot calmer in this country than in America. He didn't give off that feeling of wanting to rush into devastation. He was more patient, like those fiery eyes of the dragon, waiting, watching.

"Yeah, he's with me."

Xillian threw the worm-engraved staff at Brock. "Prove it."

While catching it, he instantly felt a chill of relaxation, and Uka Buka began softly, blabbering over his shoulder. Brock put the staff across his knees and deeply wanted to snap the mystical stick in two. Uka Buka on the other hand slowly fixated on it. Its light brown oak wood actually matching Uka's planked face.

Xillian nodded at her Yakuza brutes to take Brock away, and then Uka Buka attached himself to Bonez the Cane and stood straight up without Brock's hold. The Yakuza hesitated, but Xillian urged them on while she went for the cane. To her it was still just a cane. She knew how magical it was, her hand got blown off because of it, but she still didn't see Uka Buka. She's never seen Toko Tuki either, only felt the presence of heavy wind and surges of unknown energy.

Acquiring the idea from Toko Tuki during their last summoning ritual, Uka Buka had Bonez for a body now and was ready to try out his calm Japanese physicality. And with the idea of calm Japanese physicality, Uka reminisced back to when he embodied Sokuru, the father ninja of this little brat who needed fatherly punishment. Bonez smacked Xillian hard across her hand and twirled 540 degrees before clocking both brutes across their domes.

"You can't see him, lady, but the spirit is there. Tell the Illuminati Uka Buka is connected with me now, and if you want to kill me, you'll ruin all chances of opening that portal in America."

"Ah, I'm sure the spirit and us will cope with your loss just fine, but if you can help us learn more of the magic within the cane, I guess we'll keep you alive."

Brock was frozen. Xillian smiled, "We leave for the Mystic mountains of Koyasan in an hour. I want you with us to test the cane's power amongst the dead, got it?"

"Got. It." Uka Buka flew to smack Xillian in the face, and Brock didn't stop him; she wanted to threaten the Zen, well, here's some

Dolini to go with it.

"Still working out the kinks. I'm sure you can *handle* the pummeling though, right?" Brock smiled and got up as Uka Buka beat at the three Yakuza, retreating them out the door.

***

Ki tried to use his nose to gather his surroundings, but all he could smell was his sickness, blood and dried puke. Now, even more than the initial scoop, the pain from losing his eye thrummed in his brain like the worst migraine ever. Asagaio and him were bonded by chains, attached to metal bars welded to the car floor under their leather seats. When he took a long inhale, he caught wafts of Xillian's flowery scent that used to send his eyes rolling in the back of his head… Used to. He could sense her trying to unlock the powers inside Bonez the Cane, her fingers caressing its engravings.

On top of his pain, sorrow, and grief, his feeling of anger felt weirdly detached, like something else helped carry his burden. Tuki was gone, yet the presence of another tiki spirit invisibily loomed over his shoulder. Helping him, yet readying him for destruction.

They weren't dealing with some small town mafia anymore. This was the big time. They were in the company of world renowned gangsters, which made Ki complacent in his kidnapping, and pumped that he had already fucked up so many of them.

There was another positive during their car ride on the windy roads up to the Koyasan Cemetery; now that he knew the prisoner next to him was in fact his father, it gave him an excuse to press into him every now and then, distracting him from his pain. A weird form of fate to find his father alive the same day his mother died. Weird emotions running through Ki, like both Toko Tuki and Uka Buka were inside of him. Both love and hate yin yang'ing around in his heart.

Ki pressed the window button with his elbow.

He found Xillian in his lap a second later. "I don't want you getting comfortable… Zzepp." Her voice sounded stuffed with cotton balls. She rolled up the window but stayed on his lap.

"Does your eye hurt bitch?" Ki raised his chin but cringed at her being so intimate and close. A literal monster in his eyes… or in his presence, since his eyes were no more.

"Xillian, Taikyaku!" Ki guessed the quick order came from the elder, his father called Kawase. Xillian removed herself and plopped herself back down across from him. Another moment went by, and Ki's father gave him the greatest joy with his steady story-song voice.

"…Long ago there were six sisters that ruled our skies. Each very different and each magnificently beautiful and special in their own way. Their Mother gave them a duty to watch over her spherical self and every other spirit that roamed her waters and land. In the beginning, the sisters played and grew with their Mother, for there were little to no threats, just nature and harmonious life; however, when their kin, the humans, finally evolved into greater peoples, threatening with destined superiority, the sisters enchanted the most devoted, most ancient of their friends… The trees became their guardians, as did specific humans. The humans to become diplomats between the realm of wood and flesh."

Xillian whispered translation to Kawase as Asagaio spoke and leaned deeper into his son. The Yakuza seemed to revere Asagaio. Ki noticed when his father was speaking they honored what was said. Ki tried to imagine the strength it took to stay sane after being tortured and imprisoned for thirty years, then quickly retracted his focus back to his father's story.

"The sisters would sit and carve great intricate designs in the wood of their branchy concubines, for thousands upon thousands of years creating an army of inert guardians always ready to be Awakened if the sisters needed them. In addition to training the selected human sect of devoted worshippers, the sisters gave them enhanced Earthly abilities. These humans were called, the Totem Clause Sentinels, Tōtemu Ku Banpei."

In Asagaio's voice, Ki found his mother's reverberating over his. He imagined her as one of the angelic Sky Sisters, strengthening the Earth and developing ancient protectors to guard one another. He felt as if Leia and Asagaio were reading him a bedtime story before a deep sleep, and Ki cherished every word.

"The Sentinels drifted around the world solving the Sky Sister's problems, for the sisters themselves needed to stay reserved and secret. Unfortunately, this relationship and way of running their world created a conflicted power transition with one of the sisters. Becoming overwhelmed with too much love for the environment and too much hate for human development, one of the sisters rebelled, wanting to weaken the greedy humans and show them who was truly in control."

Asagaio began to cough, for this was probably the most he had spoken in years.

He continued after wiping blood from his mouth.

"When the rebel sister fell, their world, their Mother, was broken, for she did not know what to do with such a powerful spirit haunting her planes. So Mother Gaia, in her grief for losing one of her beloved, and strife ridden for having to continue to exile her own even after death, created a portal into the Galaxy of the Dead so her daughter's soul could pass over. As the goddess of balance, our spherical Mother then created a portal out of the Galaxy of the Dead in hope for her rebellious daughter to possibly return from her reaping and sin to revisit her sisters and make amends.

"To guard these portals, our Mother created two new guardians that harassed the power to either *allow* spirits to float into the Galaxy of the Dead, relieving the planet of most ghosts, or *block* the dead from floating back into the solar system of the living. Guardians so powerful they could sense your genuine emotions, and even manipulate them in a way; a special ability given to them in order for them to truly know if their rebel sister had changed and fixed her darkened ways.

"One spirit guardian protected the gateway back into The Galaxy of the Dead. This guardian encapsulated the emotions of love and security. The other spirit guardian protected the gateway into our realm of the living. This guardian, always defending its mother from the outer realms, encapsulated emotions of hatred and madness.

"They truly mastered these emotions of Hate and Love, because they either needed to not let alien hate and madness into their world or the spirit of love and kindness needed to know every meaning of love to ease all beings into their transition to the afterlife, for its eternal job was tranquility and peace."

Ki could sense his father staring at him, and Asagaio slowly patted his son on his thigh. His old prison mate, Witch Doctor Irking, spoke of these Sky Sisters before as well; now, his present prison mate preached about them. *How had Irking known about this lore? Had he been a Totem Clause Sentinel?* Ki guessed his father learned about it through his mother… Another great feeling of loss hit him like a ton of angel dung.

"If that story were true, why were the guardians flying around your son? Enchanting him with powers only to get messed up by me." Xillian sounded amused.

Asagaio again directed his information to his son, "Because those spirits must be the true guardian's descendants. Mother gave this duty to her most responsible treants; the treants then made their own children to understand the developing emotions of humanity. And Ki is at the forefront of these transcending emotions."

Silence followed. They were leveling out. It's been a whole hour of inclining up to the mystic mountains. Ki had tried picturing his surroundings before with the feel of the wind, but now he had just imagined a mist-covered mountain with heavy valley dives and a vast forest wilderness extending all the way to the sunset, giving an orange hue behind ridged treetop teeth as twilight began settling in.

"ENOUGH!" Xillian hit Ki in the mouth with something, a foot, an elbow, Bonez possibly. Whatever it was, it laid him back, ready to rest, daydreaming about his dream before where Uka Buka's portal opened up to the Galaxy of the Dead.

In that dream he felt something coming, slowly coalescing into something that was both good and bad. From a skeleton riding on rivers of lava to Unicorns guiding a golden ship of transcendence, here to excavate the world of its waste.

The unicorns morphed into Toko Tuki flying over oceans and through stone, the child of love coming back home. But where was Toko Tuki's parent's home? Where was the tree he came from? Guarding a portal out of the land of the living and into a whole nother galaxy. Ki wouldn't mind seeing something like that. He hoped, when dead, he'd gain his vision back.

The car slowed, and Asagaio nudged Ki with his elbow. "The land is your kin boy, stay love in your heart."

Ki heard another fleshly slam as Xillian punished Asagaio for whispering.

They all got out, and the sound of a dozen doors closed without rhythm. Someone, probably Xillian, unlocked his chains, pulled off his bloodied clothes and towel, and redressed him. Warm bodies surrounded them, quiet and attentive, and a whoosh of hot anger blew by his nose.

"Uka Buka, Uka Buka!"

***

"Mr. Zero, it seems you have had better days bub." Brock observed, looking at Ki's bandage around his eyes and bloodied cheeks.

As the Yakuza formed up into packs and readied their prisoners, Brock studied the eerie lantern path in the grove of redwoods. He felt something here, some kind of attachment that related to Ki. A feeling of peace but underlined with immense power.

Ki bent his head down in deep thought. *If Brock was here with Uka Buka, what had happened to Poxer and Toko Tuki?* His hands were now free, and he scrubbed at his buzzed head, massaging his way down to the bandage around his lost eyes.

"Let's go Asaga, lead us straight to the land rights. Any funny business and we start leaving pieces of your son as gifts to the dead. We will carry him around like a stump until we get what we want."

Asagaio didn't respond, he only grabbed Ki's arm to put his hand on his shoulder and began walking forth through the sacred land of the dead.

Brock followed, being two Yakuza away from Ki and this old man with one of his ears missing and scars all over his head and hands. Behind him a troop of around eleven gangsters followed. Some grieving party.

They walked a good twenty minutes through the lantern paths, surrounded by thousands and thousands of beautiful gray tombstones and elaborate sculptures of angels, spherical masterpieces, and tall five-tiered towers called pagodas. It amazed Brock how clean everything was. Even in the dim orange lantern light, the stones and sculptures looked polished, and the redwood foliage was swept and cleaned around the graves.

The old man finally turned off the main trail established with lantern lights on either side, and into a darkened path, still surrounded by hundreds of graves, even more beautiful and immaculate in the pitch black darkness.

The sound of a sudden approaching wind was weirdly unsteadying. It was rare to witness the initial gust of a storm or gale and even weirder to witness it in the middle of the most mystical cemetery in Japan. With a huge, Whoosh! The headwind spirited through them.

The group halted, and Xillian turned on Asagaio. "What is this? What is happening here? What kind of magic is this?"

Asagaio looked at his son. Ki was slightly smiling in his blind state. "I don't know Xillian. We are approaching the tree where I buried my paperwork. Maybe the spirits here are angry with you for imposing your greed on their land."

"How about I cut Ki's dick off right here, you mangy old fuck…"

Ki ignored Xillian's vulgarity and basked in color as the wind blew by him. His eye pain was gone, and darkness turned into thousands of melting, shifting, flowing colors blending into one another. He couldn't tell why or how the colors were so lively. He was just struck with an uplifting feeling that Toko Tuki was okay, even better than okay, enhanced.

Like Toko Tuki, Ki's vision was also enhanced. Unable to explain how he knew this within the sudden galing winds, he took a step forward to test the pixietry behind these great feelings. Each step introduced a blend of melting, somewhat shape-defining colors, which spilled, slipped, and flowed over surfaces around Ki. Even when he *thought* of stepping forward, the colors moved as if his vision held a connection with the future. He tilted his head in exaltation, and a white and black teardrop chased itself in a slow spiral. *A yin-yang moon.* Seeming incredible in a sea of color.

Luckily, during this time, no one pulled Ki's pants down, and they continued walking forward, through the wind and the unknown, meandering around lines of family grave sites and paths in between hundreds of more graves. Asagaio went along with his son's ambiguous steps ahead and everyone else followed. No one really wanted to see a blind man's dick get chopped off, only Xillian.

"Turn off flashlights. It will be better to adjust our eyes to the darkness, and we don't want to disturb the Kodo." Asagaio grunted and slowed his pace down on top of the darkened stone pressed into the forest floor.

Brock noticed it took a minute for the Yakuza to comply, but they eventually did. They trudged along, now and then passing through thick dark shadows as the waning moonlight broke through gaps in the cemetery canopy. The mass of the wide redwoods was like the dead sprouting from their graves. The contrast of wood and stone, the dark red bark and gray granite, made Brock want to stay here longer, maybe even sleep here. He felt Uka Buka wouldn't mind sleeping amongst the dead and powerful woods. It was even funny how the tiki spirit stayed so quiet now, trailing above and behind the entire group as their overseer. Brock wondered if he could see Uka

Buka, maybe he could see other spirits too. He kept his eyes open and ready for action.

To Brock, this place seemed like one hell of a place to bury land rights to a parcel in the National Forest, but maybe this was just how the Japanese did it; he couldn't protest; it was a grand adventure with his old pal Ki.

Up ahead Xillian became a beacon of light; in fact, it was Ki's cane that slowly began to illuminate the darkness, becoming brighter and brighter with every other step. Xillian halted the group and moved through the two Yakuza guards to step in front of Brock.

"Where is this Uka Buka now?"

Brock became attached to his little spirit friend, and he grew angry at Xillian for being so non-discrete and aggressive about demanding where he was.

Uka Buka flew in to bask in Brock's emotions, and that's when Xillian saw. She slowly rose Bonez the Cane over her shoulder and slobbering Uka shown in its light to everyone around.

With eyes wide in amazement, Xillian put her hand out to Uka, offering the spirit a gift. Uka floated closer and sniffed at her enclosed hand. It seemed a cute image of humans and spirits offering gifts to each other in the redwood forest of the dead, but Ki saw something that the others could not. The color purple pulsed in her hand, shifting and folding onto itself with red sparkly veins of lightning.

Xillian tightened her fingers into a fist and a purple vapor oozed out of the crevices of her fingers. Uka's eyes drifted and tongue slobbed back into his mouth, his hover losing its bob and restless bounce. She quickly opened up her hand and a cloud of purple smoke encapsulated Uka Buka. He widely twirled around in the air with his eyes closed and heavily fell to the ground.

"Hey what the!?"

A knife met Brock's jugular from behind, and he froze.

Ki saw it all, shifting, raging colors pouring in on all of them. It was like matter pushed against a flat eternity of flowing colors, creating embossed shapes in an abstract rainbow curtain. The color-storm tempo changed based on the strength of the elements around them, or it was possibly the energy frequency surrounding the area that made the colors fluctuate in velocity. Whatever the case, the colors of his internal vision now raced in the flood of the moment.

A wild wind arose and blew in every direction, causing the steady gangsters to lose ground and trip over roots. Brock tried waking up Uka Buka with his mind, tried getting angry to stir the little bloodlust devil, but nothing happened. Anger couldn't even come; the purple smoke did something to him as well, and he felt weird, like he wanted to hug everyone around him.

While Xillian bent over Uka, she ordered another Yakuza to slide the spirit tiki head into a specialized bag with purple lining. With Uka's chin halfway in the bag, Bonez the Cane illuminated with extraordinary light in Xillian's only hand, and a nova blast of wind erupted from Bonez' engravings, knocking most of the Yakuza down on the ground.

After the wild gusts of wind, Ki found Toko Tuki nestling its head on his chest.

"Toko Tuki." He said adorably, and color began to rain down in Ki's spirit vision.

Finally, Tuki was there, and Ki relished the feeling of his feathers tickling his chin, having only a few left after the long journey from the West Coast of America to the Eastern Islands of Japan. Ki's heart leapt to be embraced by such a spirit of love and kindness.

Was Toko Tuki trying to save the land his family had been trying to preserve? Was he trying to save his cousin Uka Buka? Or was Tuki merely there for his companion Ki, to guide him into the afterlife, possibly guide him through the portal to the Galaxy of the Dead?

The purple smoke dispersed in the wind, and Tuki left Ki and flew over to Uka Buka. Bonez' light now revealed two Tiki spirit heads. Short swords unsheathed, and men rummaging around, pouring purple ooze on their blades.

Before Xillian tried stuffing the rest of Uka into her spirit containment bag, she covertly squeezed another purple mist bomb near Tuki. Tuki was much too quick, however, and grabbed Uka with his teeth and took off. A moment later, Brock saw Tuki high enough away from the smoke yet distant enough not to be seen by the light of Bonez. His two feathers dangled haphazardly to the side of his ancient headdress. The Kanji characters written in red down his cheek looked menacing from afar. The kindness spirit infused with sinister eyes after messing with his cousin Uka Buka.

As Toko Tuki floated closer and closer, Bonez' light finally revealed Tuki's haunting, bringing most of the Yakuza to look up to the sky. Tuki seemed to be trying to taunt or scare Xillian and her gang, ballooning in size, becoming a sapling redwood amongst its family. The larger he became, the more identical its gangplanked wooden face seemed to relate to the trees surrounding it. Brock stepped around a large redwood, bracing himself for something to happen.

The woods creaked and groaned around the graves, and let out long sighs that turned the heads of the Yakuza. Some of them even pulled their eyes away from the encroaching Toko Tuki to see if the dead were rising or if the woods were pushing out other tiki spirit heads.

Comfortable now, even after the talk about having his penis chopped off. Ki let go of Asagaio's shoulder and felt more attuned to the environment than ever before. It was dark, his spirits were around him, his father was near, and the forest was ready for action. His mother's story must have been true; these trees must have been some of the Awakened and the Sky Sister's chosen ones.

Toko Tuki quickly shrunk for speed and began to zoom around, kicking up leaves and twirling around rigid stances. Puffs of sparkling purple dust hung in the air, and purple oozed-up blades swung at Tuki. The slash of wind and moans of the wood echoed through the hollows they were in. The men were hunched in angst but still hardened Yakuza, quiet and deadly as ever.

"ASAGAIO! WE MOVE NOW!" Xillian yelled out over the zooming air around them. The whole landscape became loud now. The creaking wood leaned in toward the group as if deranged monster trees were scaring away teenybopper hooligans. Asagaio pulled at Ki's shirt and moved forward with his son.

Behind them, a root burst from the ground, popping up a heavy stone, then wrapped itself around one of the Yakuza. Another root began to pull a man down into the dirt, trying to bring the body closer and closer to the heart of its roots. With the flashes of Bonez's light, all were blind in the dark, only able to maneuver by the screams and yelps of their comrades being taken into the depths of the forest tomb.

Brock was waiting for something to happen, but he wasn't expecting this. He pushed away from the tree he was shrouding himself behind and decided the safest place was going to be next to his old buddy Zero. The only blind dude who seemed to know exactly what was happening around them.

The Yakuza now hacked at roots with their short blades and tried creating teams to pull their companions out of the dirt. Xillian, Kawase, Asagaio, and Ki pushed forward, easy enough to find by the line of sun bright light in Xillian's hand.

One tree, different from the rest, stood on its own ahead of them, with one grand grave in front of it and a statue of a woman standing and writing in a journal with wings on her wrists.

Xillian suddenly dropped Bonez the Cane as if it grew extremely hot and barked at Brock. "Do something American, or I will be forced to do something to you like I did, your friend!"

Brock ran over and picked up Bonez. Uka Buka immediately came from around the epic Cherry Blossom tree and rested on top of Bonez the Cane. He had awoken from the purple haze and was pissed the fuck off.

Asagaio cutely and unworriedly plucked a cherry blossom bud from the tree and ate it. The tree shook to life, and rune tribal engravings began to illuminate with a pinkish light. Its bark started to expand and crack open into hollows. With the sound of earth roaring to life, a chest erupted from the ground and slammed into Xillian's nose, knocking her to the ground and leaving a bloody steel chain to her ear.

There was so much chaos, yet Ki felt an essence of security around him and Asagaio. Asagaio ripped the strap which was used to gag Ki speechless.

"Ah thank you Asagaio... is this... the portal?" He was surprised how cool it felt saying his father's name.

Asagaio grabbed Ki's hand and put it on the cherry blossom tree's luminescent light, beaming from its engravings in its wood.

"She welcomes us Ki. For we have the blood of the Totem Clause Sentinels, defenders of this world."

A tear ran down Ki's scarred cheek, and he went to whip it away, but had that ghost appendage syndrome where his index finger should be.

"We need to get out of here. I'll grab the chest and come back for you. Stay here."

Just being Ki and the tree, he began to think about his dream, the afterlife, a weird world, galaxy, universe unknown to him. He felt overwhelmed with honor to be in the position he was in.

A gunshot was heard next to him, and Ki's heart dropped into his stomach.

"Asagaio! Father!... Answer me!"

Blindness hit like the bang of the barrel. In his red-lined anxiety, everything went dark again. A high wind pressed him against Toko Tuki's parent tree and Tuki himself manifested onto his chest. All Ki could do was feel the embroidering power around him and listen to his Mother, Planet Earth, sing.

Through the torrent of wind, Uka Buka roared high above!

"UKA Buka!"

Rising into the air and inflating bigger and bigger until growing into the size of a small building. Brock saw that Uka had even transformed his features, making himself look more like a Japanese demon mask with horns than an ancient forest sasquatch pygmy.

With an inhale Uka filled himself with air, vacuuming up small leaves and twigs from the forest floor and forcing branches of the redwoods to praise his holiness from down under. In sync with another bang! Uka exhaled and began to fall, bringing the sky with him, pulling the wind into his descent and using every bit of his rage to redden his ferocious drop of speed and power. Crazy with blood fury and absorbing some of the power from his Auntie's domain.

***

Xillian laid out and watched Ki and Toko Tuki rest against the epic tree while a storm blew around them. She believed in Asagaio's story right then and felt like the Sky Sisters had finally come for them to reap devastation on the ones against their Mother. Her instincts felt like the absorbing winds were trying to take the treasure chest away from Xillian, trying to take her family's destiny away from her. She felt wrong, she felt evil, but that was just her, and she fought on in her manner. This was not the time to change herself.

Not caring about a bullet ricochet or metal shards in her face, she pointed her pistol at the lock on the chest and pulled the trigger. She clamored off the broken lock and found the paper land rights to Hattori Honzo's parcel in Ise-Shima National Forest. She rolled up the parchment and stuffed it into her cleavage, then gave Kawase a node of completion.

Bonez the Cane pulled out of Brock's hand and stood erect again, emanating with immense power and light, pulsating with the power of the storm around them.

Xillian crab walked away from Asagaio's dead body and situated herself on top of a nearby grave. The sky ceased pulling the land away from her and suddenly pushed all of the sky's air back down, pressing Xillian into the hard gravestone beneath her.

Halfway through the redwoods impaling Uka Buka's gigantic head, she finally realized the culprit of the storm, and with a planetary thud, a quake from Uka Buka's fall cratered the area around them. Xillian collapsed into the grave with the dead, while Ki and Toko Tuki vanished into the earth under the great cherry blossom tree. Two arrows of wispy silver spirit strings flying up toward the stars…

The Maiden, Mother, & Crone

Cid held Crum's bandaged head in her lap while Gem wrapped lavender in Cid's head bandage. Brock was in the backseat of Mokes' van when Gem, Adow, Mooredo, and Poxer went into her Refill Shop to gather more of an understanding of the three new women in Poxer's life. Gem was absorbed in the opportunity of learning more and didn't expect Brock to escape. After she left him alone with the sibling exorcists, and of course, Mokes, his friend, Brock clashed the sibling's heads together so hard it opened up a gash in the side of Cid's head and knocked them both out.

After Mokes was manhandled by Brock, Gem sent Mokes and Moorendo to the airport. They have just now returned empty handed and were presently recollecting themselves at Poxer's shop.

"We will stay at Brock's house and rest. I want you two Ram Horns to relax and breathe with ease. The only thing we can do now is wait. We wait for Brock to come back and we wait for the Illuminati's response."

Gem finished her bandage wrap and kissed Cid on the forehead.

"The essence of the world strokes my soul in a way that tells me this was all destined to happen. I want to spend another hour with you and your Coven Pinky, if that is okay?"

"Yes, of course Gem, your presence is worth a lifetime of knowledge. Please."

Sloan Sullivan, Poxer's girlfriend and mysterious addition to the triunity of women, put a hand on Poxer's cheek. "Jack…"

Poxer accepted the embrace with loving eyes however she tilted her head in perplexity.

"Jack, your tics. They're gone…"

Jacklyn Poxer clasped her hands to her mouth and adjointly moved one over her neck and then her body. With a steady gaze to no where, Poxer felt within, and began to sing.

"There once was a pirate named Jane,
Who was only slightly insane,
Instead of treasures in her chest,
She liked to keep politician's heads there best...
Well, maybe she's not that hard to explain!"

Tears poured down Poxer's emotionally unwrinkled face.

Gem smiled and put a hand on Poxer's chest.

"Indeed, this is where I should be. Destiny brought me to you so you and yours can fulfill something very, very special. Three women popping into your life right after an amazing feat. The prophecy boldens the road ahead of us. These women encompass fate itself."

Gem brought her voice down to a whisper.

"These women have undying fealty to you because fate has made them your destiny. To all be here at the same time, in the same place, and have the same inspiration. This is a tool, Jacklyn. These women have the power to alter destiny to your manifestations. Even as we speak, they are working on your dream without you ever telling them about your ambitions. Fate already knows what you want so they intuitively do as well... I believe you will take a major role in our Mother Gaia's fate, and you will know what that is when it reveals itself... Let me understand you all more so I can help guide you."

Siggy, the older lady with long salt and pepper hair, was dressed in a loose Kimono fitting drab and spoke for Poxer, for Poxer was still taken aback by her overwhelming emotions.

"If we have concluded our analysis of Jack's spirit circle and this magnificent portal tree, perhaps we could all prepare to spend the night here and replenish from the events of the New Year."

Gem nodded and looked around the spirit ring patio at the others.

"Yes, yes this place is all Jack's manifestation. Her business, her lover, her disciples, her magic. Let me do one last test before we all prepare for the night."

Gem shuffled through her backpack and pulled out a large glacier orb. The eyes of the six women reflected in its shine.

"This stone tells me how ancient a soul is. To help decipher this history, an Old One needs to be present." Gem wove a weaving, meandering hand to the grand Willow before them.

"The Old One will hold half of the stone and you the other half.

As I embrace both you and the Willow, I will be able to see your ancestral past."

Gem took out a hatchet and chopped away a flawless crater in the heart of the tree's trunk.

"This tree has witnessed you harnessing so much power during your portal creation. You were even able to pull these women to you. No matter. They are truly the Maiden, Mother, and Crone of your world. They are life, and they are death. I would bring them everywhere with you if you wanted to achieve your ultimate destiny."

As she cleaned up some of the last wood chips, she waved the women over. Gem then undressed herself from the waist up, slowly peeling off her scarves, lightly tattered robe, and loose blouse, leaving only a multitude of pendants and long necklaces to rest on top of her flame tattoo between her perky little boobs.

"It is best that we represent our freest selves… It is not the birth of our past flesh we seek, but our first spiritual awakening that initially identifies our souls."

They all took off their tops, and they all discovered the birth of their souls before comfortably resting amonst the roots of the Willow tree.

Epilogue: The Galaxy of the Dead

Breathing without air was like being in a dream. Ki and Toko Tuki fell into the abyss until the sparklets of silver dots around them slowly became more and more blurred, like they were on a highway through space. A wormhole shooting through the universe with a one-way ticket to Hell.

Ki himself stayed in the void, for his blindness followed him through the Tuki portal. Regardless of being unable to see anything, he enjoyed the feeling of flying. He also felt lucky to have a companion with him in his journey to the dead.

Was that common? If so, where was Asagaio, his father? Maybe the portal worked differently if the living fell into it as opposed to dying and having your soul transported through. He didn't even feel sad about his father dying. He was happy for Asagaio. Afterall he got his last wish of eating a flower from the cherry blossom tree. Asagaio died honorably, and aside from death and dying, there was presently so much unimaginable shit going on around Ki. Exciting things that were causing him to believe dying on Earth wasn't the end. They were on their way to the Galaxy of the Dead, and his dad and mom were probably there already. Conscious and thriving.

Toko Tuki maneuvered around his body. Up on Ki's back, under his chest, on top of his head. A Samurai slice cut his second to last feather at an angle, but Tuki's grin was amazed at his surroundings, excited to see all that sped around them. Toko Tuki and Uka Buka wanted Ki to find help for their Mother Gaia, so they opened the portal to the Galaxy of the Dead.

Tuki watched the beautiful sun flares whip around their worm portal, moons spin around sister moons, making a planet seem guarded by spheres of cratered light, and colorful asteroid dust beautifying near and far galaxies of which they zipped right past. Time was lost, though speed had laid a comforting hand on the two of them. They had passed seven galaxies already and hadn't felt a wink of fatigue.

On top of Ki's head, streamlining through the wormhole, Tuki looked into Ki's face to bond with his companion in the pleasure of intergalactic travel. Tuki's grin slowly flipped as he remember Ki was blind. Toko Tuki pushed ahead of Ki and turned back to look at him, a mass of thoughtful scarred flesh, unworried and at ease. With magic still thriving in Tuki's spirit, he flung himself at Ki, turning at the last moment and fitting onto Ki's face perfectly.

"Hi there brother."

"Tuki? Wait…" Ki pressed his fingers onto his face and felt hardened wood.

"I can see in color again."

"Ye, that is how I see brother. You are my brother. I want you to enjoy this."

Flying through space, colors coming back to Ki, the meaning of no meaning flooding over them. Nothing mattered anywhere. Asagaio's death, his world fluctuating through passages of life. It was all just life. It was all just death. There was no big deal, just the importance of enjoying the present moment.

He could grasp Toko Tuki now, for they had entered an unknown reality for both of them, making them neutral spirits. All was color, all was light with pinpoints of power sparkling like stars amongst the waves of color in the journey through the abyss of the universe.

They were stuck, trapped in a wormhole streamlining through space. Falling through the gateway to the Galaxy of the Dead, now symbiotic with his best spirit friend, Toko Tuki.

If the Ram Horned Cultist could do it. Why couldn't they.